Dr Z

Michael Zaitzow

An MD Zaitzow Publication

ISBN 978-0-9867799-0-9

Library and Archives Canada Cataloguing in Publication

Zaitzow, Michael, 1954-
  Dr Z / Michael Zaitzow.

ISBN 978-0-9867799-0-9

  I. Title.

PS8649.A48D7 2010   C813'.6   C2011-900097-0

Editorial and production support by GF Murray Creative Info Solutions, Coquitlam, BC
Illustrations by Felix Tyndel
Photos courtesy of the author
Printed and bound in the United States of America

Contents

One: Dr Z

Two: Dr Max

Three: Dr Bill

Four: Dr Z and all the ends

Dr Z

For my family and my patients

One:
Dr Z

NOW: GOD IS TOYING WITH DR Z

There is no doubt in my mind that god is toying with me.

Today I ripped the television cable out of the wall. I have often felt the urge, a warm pulse that spreads up from the base of the spine. Today I responded. A bad development, I know. I'm stuck in the midst of bad developments. I have thrown keys at the wall, necessitating reparative plaster, primer and paint once I've sobered up. I have kicked over those same paint cans and hurled useless combinations of half-remembered oaths. In such situations my version of the facts pales against the assertions of others. People who were not there—my children, my wife or strangers—fill in the blanks. They tell me what really happened and slink away from Dr Z.

The first coherent words I spoke today were at the hardware store down the hill.

"Do you have any cable parts?"

My voice sounded hollow.

The clerk smiled when I thanked him and walked stiffly and routinely away from the cash.

As usual, there are two versions to the story. The baby, who is almost eleven, said that I hit her. Those were her words:

"You hit me before I hit you." I remember asking her to close down the television and the resistant stance she took. I edged her away from the screen with my instep, pushing the Off button with an outstretched toe.

"You can't turn a TV off that way, Dad." She grabbed one of the clickers and pointed it right at me.

Zap. Television off, she burst into tears.

"You never," she said.

Never? Never what?

"Never did anything like that before."

And the hit? By now neither of us could remember. She forgave me soon enough but I am not breathing any easier. It will take weeks for the irritability to drain away.

This is the crux of the situation: she lived somewhere else, then I moved her away from that place and brought her here before she was ready. I knew she would not be ready. I knew she didn't want to come.

We were all too busy to ask her much. When we asked her there was no time to listen. And when there was a little time she didn't know what to say. She was too small for us to help her find the right words.

For her and the other children, the new place is not "back." The new place is somewhere else. It is not home.

My children never hit me before we moved. They didn't watch television non-stop. They didn't throw their food at dinner, or spit. They were home on Friday nights and didn't ignore their grandparents. They played in the street: catch, hide-and-seek. They rode their bikes.

I know the way I am supposed to feel, the way I'd like to feel, the way I feel on that rare occasion when I walk along the green space and there are breaks in the clouds and the wind is picking up from the beach. This place is beautiful. The strokes of colour are so powerful that your mind numbs to them: the mountains etched in snow, the everpresent green, the relentless sea. Today there was an ocean-to-sky rainbow in the east as I went down the hill through the ancient forest to the hardware store on the highway. It was so bright and the colours so distinct I thought of animators and illustrators up there making the scene over for production. Thankfully there was no music, and I felt a smile where there was nothing the moment before.

I am back from the hardware store and my middle daughter is teasing the dog with his dental bone in the shape of a stegosaurus. I catch a glimpse of her fast-forwarding *Sleeping Beauty*, looking for choreographed scenes to sketch. My youngest is lying on the floor with her head on her sister's knee. My eldest is strumming a guitar after studying for an exam. I should be grateful for their presence before they are gone. I should love them more.

This is the town on the sea.

The new house has taken its toll on all of its inhabitants. It is a house without a history, or at least a history of transients who have left little mark. It sits on a busy street, turned to the side onto a crescent. Younger children play further down on sunny days and it seems happy enough, but there are reminders of sinister events here and there. Last weekend a police vehicle was smacked broadside at the intersection. The three children watched the aftermath from their bedroom window: flashing lights reflecting off the slick pavement, tow trucks. Once a taxi describing a similar arc plunged through the fence and took out half the backyard shed. You can read the scars in the repaired wood. The beams have been replaced, and the shingled siding on the west face has not yet weathered. I'm told a girl was murdered in the field next to the gas station on the corner.

I attribute everything to a downward drift from the troubled community up the hill and to the availability of money and cars, from the limited architecture to the lack of history.

When things are good I do not know why, and when they are bad I am equally confused. For a while, a friend of my middle daughter's would come by at dusk and pelt crushed noodles, cereal and eggs mixed with a bit of mud at the garage before slinking off down the lane. Sometimes she flung the food mix in the morning before school. I suspect she cut through the yard, over the dog's excrement-laden gravel track, past the hot tub and over the fence. She cut through by pushing down an eight-foot section. When I fixed the fence, she took out a pair of loosened boards. I had to admire her tenacity: the same two boards were removed day after day and placed one on top of the other against the post behind the laurel.

I was thinking of this young woman's perseverance while driving my middle daughter to meet up with another of her friends. I was drivelling on about the recent move, the new house, a book I was reading. Maybe she couldn't say much but at least she could listen. Still, my middle daughter often attends to me in a way that makes me wonder how I manage to tolerate my own voice.

I told her that the book I was reading was less interesting than one or two of our family memoirs. She was startled to find out that there was book about us, written by us, for us. Quite a bit of it was about her, I said. At least it was about the time in our life when the two eldest children were toddling about. It was a wonderful time, then. I faintly recollected that feeling as we shuttled down the main drag, dropped videos off and landed in the shopping mall. It had been a happy time: a time of massive confusion, pain and delight. That story has been lived, written, retold, I told her. It is bound in a folder in a black filing cabinet.

My middle daughter changed the radio station. Turned up the volume. Turned it off.

For now, for myself, I want to know why I would want to destroy these same wonderful children. Where does the viciousness come from? Where will it lead and should I try to explain it?

My father was tempted by something similar. He threatened my eldest child when she was nine months old. Even I could identify the desperation behind the threat. I can package the event with a diagnosis: he was ill; he was drinking; he was confused about the chain of events and the new generation of grandchildren. Hadn't he just left his friends of many decades? Hadn't he begun to drift away without leaving much of a trace? How far could he leave from himself and remain alive? Maybe he was simply more true to his feelings than I. He walked away from us and could not be coaxed back.

Viciousness was rarely far from his lips, something I have inherited and that I have returned to the coast to live with. I was true to my word and kept it out of my father's eulogy. The temptation was there; I ran through many nasty dress rehearsals in my mind. In the end I said, "As everybody knows, my father was a difficult man." Then I said he was famous for the jingly keys that signalled his approach. There was laughter in the chapel, and that was that. A little laughter at the end of a life. He carried his keys on his belt, and in the end generated a wave of laughter. For me there is less to remember. I carry no key chain and will generate less than a laugh when I am gone.

Although gone for a while now, my father is a big player in the family comedy. His death occasioned a blossoming in my middle brother's career. My middle brother has expanded his skills as a video editor and producer to write a script. He calls the script *Planting Dad*. There is a lot of golf in it and a certain amount of reconciliation. In the final scene the father's three sons lob nine-iron shots into his as-yet-unfilled grave with a bucket of balls the script-writing narrator has stolen from the driving range on the river flats.

My middle brother says his friends find it hilarious. I can see it freed him up some. I fear this newfound freedom will be fleeting but I am still glad he is reaching for new things.

As for me, I am going another way. Which brings me back to the new house. It is a house where good moments are progressively more difficult to find. The family room addition slopes off to the side, its tilted spirit reminiscent of pre-foundation days when the area was likely a porch or grass. The library is tucked away in a corner, an embarrassing closet. Life organizes itself around the television in that central nexus between the kitchen and hallway, stairway and common room. The wind screams around the southeast corner above the garage, routinely flapping the shingles. The night spirits are too restless to settle for any length of time. The water pipes crack unexpectedly on cold nights because eight-little-valves-all-in-a-row have been installed back to front. Bulges in the walls and slopes in the floor are not due to character or the settling of age but the poorly-tuned skills of the suburban builders of the time. The ceiling fans remind me of my father in his most banal moments, in his southern condo on the Gulf where he spent the best of his mean-spirited years. As do the brass fixtures and hot tub, the plastic imitation-wood siding and the faintly stained white carpets.

In my weakest moments I blame the deterioration of my family's functioning on the design of the neighbourhood. It was my father's architecture and now it is mine. The comparison is obvious and provocative. When I am like this my wife doesn't bother to answer me. I am an adult, she implies—she will no longer say. I should know better. Ceiling fans and bathroom fixtures mean very little. It doesn't matter that the neighbourhood is ill-conceived and the architecture is all wrong.

The cat, unused to vehicles and coyotes, has confined himself to the house for months. Only now is he heeding the feline perennial itch and climbing out of the industrial basement sink to explore for more than a few minutes at a stretch.

The dog is loping around the place guiltily. He has developed a strategy of calculated evasion in keeping with the teenage noise, incessant drum machines and flying food. In short, he is running with the pack.

And then there is my wife. She is "resting her voice," has gone on medication and put on weight. Three weeks of the month she does not look like herself. Who does she look like? It is hard to tell. She suddenly looks older than our combined memories and I have been speculating that a debt is being repaid somewhere.

This may have something to do with her mother, who retreated into a coma for six months last year before returning to life. There has been a jumbling-about of the accounting of souls, and I'm implicated in some way. It was my idea to put in a feeding tube and keep the old woman alive. Contrary to expectations she bounced back to life, to talk and walk, remember and drive. She had been starving to death and now she is fine. Ever since then I feel I have pushed a heavenly calculation off centre. Intervened when I should not have. Changed fate in some way. Played the hand of god and played it too well.

Now god is toying with me and as usual he is winning.

I did apologize to my daughter. It is not a complete apology; I know I will make the same mistake again. I am too aware of biblical forces, the silence before going forward with unconscious plans for destruction. Do we all somehow suffer from this compulsion to destroy what we love? Are we like god in the flood, sticking to fantasies that are so horrible in their exuberance that, if expressed, could take out the whole world? Do our apologies lack substance, mine to her and hers to me? Can we expect anything else?

THEN AND NOW: PESTO AND PLUM JAM FOR DR Z

For the longest time I practiced somewhere else, on a street with a history in a town with an old soul. Within a two-block walk I could visit a dozen coffee shops, get a haircut or find any book, new or old. I could watch the pimps, hookers and drug dealers across the street or chat with the government workers in the square. I could seek out my favourite pastimes: get my own therapy eating poutine at Jacques' Snack-and-a-Half *patates frites* truck, or seek out a family friend in her father's store where she hid behind a counter barricaded by decades of accumulated paraphernalia.

For years I heard the church bells at noon, real church bells chiming real notes. I heard the biplane do its fly-over a little north, carrying dignitaries and tourists above the skyline. Sometimes I would catch a glimpse of its wings through the leaves out back. Two or three of my patients had been up there as tourists and I came to imagine them looking over the detail of our world—my world—from above. There were so many friendly sounds: the incessant contained blasting of civic development, with its rhythmic warning, wait, and delayed all-clear; the occasional Snowbirds fly-by, so quick you could only hear them in unison ripping up the sky; the click-click-click of footsteps up and down the stairs. Each image, initially clear unto itself, had become a blur lost in repetition.

It is an unusual business, collecting other people's stories to tell back to them. There is a lot of repetition and that, along with the anonymity, takes its toll. In the office I can only say what can be readily understood in the scripted vocabulary of the other person, minimally extended. I can stretch a word here and there if the context is memorable. I am an editor of sorts, editing people's lives. Or the lives they might live. Or I am the rewrite man, paring someone down to essential details.

In getting the narrative there is a lightness that approaches health, or so I like to think. In moments of jealous grandiosity I see these bent and suffering souls flitting about. I watch over them, sitting on their shoulders like a parrot. Commenting. Or I am the copy editor, correcting and cutting and pasting and snipping bits. I have strong views on genetics and predestination. Free choice? I have a say there too.

There is a difficulty in this work, a limitation akin to god's. Like myself, he is very busy and has no one to tell. I transcribe a session, chart a note, write a report, converse with a colleague or complain lazily to my wife, all the while knowing I must conceal as I tell. To tell and not to tell, that is the difficulty. For in telling the detail must be stripped away. Distinctive marks of narrative—tags of personality that make a person what they are—must be deliberately hidden. You cannot identify someone as "a fat Italian man with dyed black hair and loud wide ties..." or "an attractive, childlike fifty-year-old woman with frizzy pigtails, dressed in an expensive suit." Nobody is fat and no hair is dyed and comments on ties are not allowed. You can scribble in the margins of a chart, but you can't tell your wife over dinner or your friends at the pool hall.

But that, it seems to me, is how I remember people. Not by their names. No, not really by their faces. But by a tag, the beginning of a story—a bit of history that will take you sideways. Those tags are rarely confidential. They are the opposite. They take the listener, the watcher, into the person's story directly, right into the middle of it. For anyone to know what I do, what I am, to know my story, I must break their confidence. In other words, to help myself I must harm them. Indeed, I have already done this. They will know who flew in the biplane and who simply dreamed of flying in the biplane. They know from every detail that I am speaking about them. They know how they sound coming up the two flights of stairs, how their shoes echo on the cheap grey tile already sagging in mid-tread. They know how the door creaks open slowly, especially in winter when salted boots are left outside, and the wall sighs in its characteristic way. A moment later the second door will pop open gently, as if by itself. A thin wedge of light will emanate from the inner sanctum of the consulting office occupied by me, sitting there with *somebody else*.

On the surface, everything has changed now. I am in a new place, in a hospital in the west. Hardwood and reclaimed stained glass have been replaced by dirty grey indoor-outdoor carpet, the relentless ticking of keyboards, and tangled limbs in an overcrowded waiting room under the harsh scrutiny of bright temporary walls and fluorescent lights. There is little time here for the unfolding of small dramas, for stories to make themselves up. The task, one could argue, is the same but the scene is harsher, the pace frenetic and uncompromising.

But in the end little has changed. If I suggest there may be important elements to their life worth exploring, they get going with their story. I must be crazy, they think: this is a hospital and there is no time for exploration. But being tipped off balance is a good way to get going. There are stories in hospitals like everywhere else, I might say. I continue to be amused by the umbrellas and purses left in the office, signifying that the patient did not wish to leave or had more to tell or wanted to come back. Already I can sense the new betrayals I am heaping up. Who hasn't left something in my office at some point? Who hasn't wanted to come back to keep things going, to set the record straight?

This is not the first time I have been tempted to speak for myself. Countless times I have launched into a joke or a comment about the day or a complaint about the weather or the revenue department in that beautiful fortress up the street from my old office or the civic betrayals of this recession or that new tax. I have complained about how my income has been slashed because a visit from foreign heads of state closed the roads for their motorcade, how an ice storm landed the clients of my day's work in bed or in hospital, how the ventilation system passed me the pneumococcal scourge, twice. I have complained that my patients are lucky that they get to complain freely (unlike me), that they can rail against the government and lovers and parents (unlike me), that they can have a free uncensored opinion (unlike me). But the word is out now. I have an opinion. A story. And I will break every confidence to provide it.

At first I was drawn to the job because it was so much like reading. I could sit back and listen and watch. I could fantasize, do figures in my head, let my mind wander. I could fashion the story the way I wanted it to go. In one way I could do nothing at all. But, of course, I was doing everything—everything to redesign lives, to get them back on track. I thought it would be easy. I thought it would be fun. And it is all of these things. There is only one thing I did not count on, one which has wagged me like the proverbial tail wagging the dog. If I tell anything I get it back right between the eyes. And if I cannot speak I am not a human telling my own story. And that means—well, you know what that means.

One day recently I came into the new office in the hospital in the new world where I grew up but mistakenly returned to, and I picked up the scent of pesto and plum jam. I knew exactly who sent the pesto and plum jam. I knew what it was, who sent it and I knew it was for me. There, it is done.

By now the seal has been split open and I am about to go straight to hell. That is, the seal on the story as well as the seal on those jars. When have you ever opened a medical journal and read, "A patient, stuffed into a size-fourteen print and intimately attached to the culinary arts, presented to the clinic with panic and a morbid fear of vehicles driven by her younger brother"?

Either I am a liar and a protector of their stories or a violator, presenter and champion.

It turned out that the pesto, after travelling 2,800 miles through the mail, had leaked, little by little, through the lid and a dozen or so paper towels, through the inside plastic, the reinforced cardboard box and the thick, hermetically sealed industrial-strength bag provided by the national mail service. One of my medical colleagues (I shall not confess who) suggested it might be a plot on the part of an angry, dependent past patient to poison me with transmogrified love masquerading as just the right balance of pine nuts, basil and pure olive oil. Fat chance. Sometimes a gift is a gift. And a gift like this is so special and specific and individual that it is precisely designed to keep the sender alive in your mind forever.

Dear Dr Z,

At first I couldn't believe you were going. Now I can't believe you have been gone this long.

The summer was long and humid; the fall a brief burst of colour. As usual. I'm sure you have been following the news of our last winter storm with that special interest of a survivor. Or perhaps you are no longer interested at all. I imagine you smirking as you note the crocus buds pushing their way up through the late January frost. Or grinning from ear to ear about the tulips and daffodils rustling underground just as we settle down to a few more months of real winter.

This week I was shopping and found myself walking by your old consulting office on the way to my favourite boutique. The front light was on and it gave me quite a start. For a moment I believed you were up there looking out. The flower shop has gone, as you may or may not know. There has been a succession of unsuccessful businesses in the storefront and the building has taken on something of the derelict nature of the neighbourhood. It always seemed odd to me that people assumed it was constructed at the end of the previous century. It had all the hallmarks of bad architecture and flimsy construction, a sign of the present time. The foyer was tucked away behind the drive and that odd Japanese garden seemed to appear out of nowhere, planted as an afterthought by aliens. The corners of the building were cut on the hypotenuse, no doubt conforming to some senseless principle of civic regulation and design. And worst of all, the hallway was claustrophobically narrow, with re-markably stale air. On rare occasions I noted the skylight had been lifted on the fourth floor and a quiet breeze stole in behind me on the way up, but that was the exception.

I often thought you were trying to test us agoraphobics, making us traverse places without air and space. The only escape was through and up as opposed to back. And I thought, just as I must go up through this stuffy tunnel, so I must return.

I often sat in your waiting area wondering which church used to house those twin stained glass plates above the moulding. I stared at the pretty glass and reviewed your quiet clinical sadism, repeating my symptoms into my own pounding ears: a squeezing in my chest, a catch in my breath, the faintest tingling around my mouth and in the tips of the fingers of my right hand (my good hand). On occasion my feet went numb. This was in winter, but I did not blame the cold.

I will never forgive your comments about my stomach. Better I come to the session and throw up on your ugly rug than stay at home, you said. I was always punctual and I never threw up, except once on the way out. This is my confession. It was I who deposited the insufficiently light croissant of your neighbour, that spoiled French baker, onto the artificial stone bed of the Japanese garden.

I couldn't believe it had actually happened, and I stared at it. Only then did I notice that your garden was in disarray.

The stones were half covered in mud from the runoff where the ice had pulled the eaves and drain-pipe down. I counted at least three condoms, a French newspaper, an assortment of fliers, plastic utensils and leaves. The wind, it appears, draws the debris around the corner and under the wrought iron gate where it swirls in delight. I took a few steps back and realized the recycled pastry fit in quite nicely with the decor. I was satisfied and returned home. I had intended to tell you before you left, but as usual, I never got around to it. Perhaps I did not wish to worry you before your departure. You seemed preoccupied enough as it was.

The boutique at the beginning of my story is what you would call a parameter: important in real life, a camouflaged decoy in therapy.

In the end, Dr Z, what do I have here? An insight or the excuse for a new dress?

I hope you enjoy the seasonal flowers while we pine in the snow. Believe it or not, we still live in the same country.

THEN: DAD

It is hard to believe some things didn't happen as expected. I forget to look at what did happen, what is going on, what could come of all this. It takes so much work. I have to sit down and think about it without the kids screaming or the dog sticking his nose in my crotch, or Extendamix or *Grease* or Bryan Adams saturating the airwaves. A lot happened before the Spice Girls and screechy boy-bands. Most of it has already gone from my head. I'm bad at detail; I simply forget. My associations follow their own strategy. Most of the time I am wrong but I have nowhere else to start.

The move back west begins with my father's illness. It hit me out of nowhere: my father is dying. Nobody actually said it but somehow I knew. His phone tone had changed, softened, withered. His wife was louder and more overbearing.

We moved east in the spring of '81—a long time ago. I thought it would be a nice place to be if we got stuck there, my wife and I. I got work, that was the main thing, and we were convinced there was little choice but to stay. So we stayed there a long time and now the children are launched. For them it is their only home, the place they think about when they are tired and someone pulls out old picture books from childhood.

When my father started to die, moving west became a bigger possibility. The west is "back home" for us two parents. When I say, "We can visit the Falls on the way home," my wife is ecstatic. Home. She has spent years convincing me that west is where she wants to be. She does not want to be buried in the frozen ground. She does not want to fear the spring, when her coffin will be tilted at an unexpected angle, heaved up and over.

I think of my father as a snowbird gone south to the Gulf, in his ailing retirement with his young wife. With the cancer in his back and leg. In the bone. For a while it was in the liver too, but the bones gave him the most trouble.

I called him for my birthday.

I said, "It's my birthday, Dad. Wish me a happy birthday."

He listened to news of the grandchildren. He was tired; I could hear it in his voice. He had radiation to his leg and back, for the pain. The cancer was there to stay.

His voice said, "They did everything they could," as if he was already dead.

They told him to go home, as if there was such a place.

When I thought my father might be dying, it went around and around in my head for a while. The realization meant there was nothing I could do. He wasn't the kind of guy you could help. You couldn't talk to him. You couldn't ask him questions or give him gifts. He wouldn't say much unless you entertained him. Once in awhile he relaxed but not even the grandchildren had that effect on him now.

I called him to remind him that I am his son, that he is my father.

I sent him little notes, told him his kid cousin was sick, that she also was dying. Then she died and I called him again.

She had had cancer nine years ago and it came back, in her head. Like him, by the time they picked it up it was too late.

Her brother was angry. He told me, "They know it spreads to the brain. Why didn't they look for it there?"

I felt bad for him, my father's other kid cousin, now bereaved. There was a little anger at me—the doctor—as if I were somehow responsible.

My father said he saved her from drugs and she never forgave him. He offered it as an explanation for why he had not attended the funeral, why he wasn't about to waste energy on the past. The logic of this went right by me.

In the old days, the younger cousins would challenge my father at family functions. For our sakes. For the sake of my father's three boys.

We were teenagers then. Sometimes he would bite his tongue and leave his own house through the front door and the rest of us would carry on in the family room, relieved. For a few short moments we would forget that it was his family room, the room he designed and built, where in the recliner, with the sound off, he watched his friends with their two good knees playing in the National Hockey League.

When I realized my father was dying, I made him a tape. I wrote some words and played some songs and sent it all to him. I don't know if he listened to the tape. They were songs we used to do together when I was a kid. He sang and we played—the brothers, his sons.

He sent a message back through my eldest child. "Grandpa got the tape."

When my patients ask me why I am leaving I make up little stories. It was a family decision, I say. Or my wife wanted to return to her roots. I might have said that the politics of the province were getting me down. Or that we had no contract to keep us in this place. Or that the building was falling apart and I had to move shop. If I had to shift the office uptown, I say, I would rather keep on going all the way past the Great Lakes and all that prairie.

The real story is my father: with his illness I could calmly return.

Most of the fun we had as kids with my father was with music. One night before my youngest brother was born our friend Wally and his friend Eddie Peabody came to visit us in the old house down the hill. It was Wally who later discouraged us from a life of music. I suspect he was a drinker and had to throw music and alcohol out in the same flamboyant gesture to get his life in order. The excitement, especially Dad's, went right through to morning. My middle brother was entranced by the buoyancy of that evening. We were up all night singing. My brother and I received green and white plastic banjos from the masters. At least that's what Dad said, although we knew it was Dad who'd bought them for us. After that came the ukuleles and the guitars. He got himself a four-string and learned a few chords to accompany his wayward bass voice. He would play *Mighty Mississippi* and my brother and I would sing, then laugh our guts out. Dad always faltered on the tenth bar. It had a chord in it he couldn't get. We learned to cringe, waiting. It was a scratchy dominant seventh and he had to flatten four fat unyielding fingers on the neck by shifting his wrist into an impossible position.

When Dad was young he lived in a small prairie town and helped his father run a theatre. He and his little brother put together song-and-dance routines to warm up the audience before the feature. Then he would slip into the projector room and run the newsreels. Neither of the boys ever got that excitement out of their blood. Either of them in a piano bar was faintly dangerous and together they were inflammatory. You never knew when they would befriend the piano player and set up their tunes.

Dad loved Jolson, and Duke Ellington. Tanned and under artificial lights he even looked like a black man. His mother, whom we called the Fat Lady, looked like a female version of the Duke. My father came by his eyes and lips honestly, from her.

For my father, those plastic instruments in the hands of his two sons took him back somewhere in himself to a place he had forgotten, to a place he had left behind. He had no sense of time, which was okay for slow songs like *Old Black Joe* and *Ol' Man River*. These were the songs he grew up singing: *Mammy* and *Melancholy Baby* and any number of *I've Got Rhythm* standards. He would sing a phrase and hold a note— any note—until he felt like going on. He sang like a cantor, containing all of time in his hands; it was his note and the congregation would just have to wait. For some reason he liked slow, dirge-like spirituals. He sang these songs with the same voice he used to say *Kaddish* over his father.

My father liked tone more than anything. He liked the sound of the piano too, but his fingers were too fat to fit between the keys, white or black. Inevitably his voice would falter at the bridge and you had to hang up there with lots of quiet sound, supporting him. I don't think he ever knew we held him up like that. There were a lot of things he didn't notice.

These are the selections on the tribute tape. *Take the A-Train*, his official favourite. *Standing on the Corner* running into *Once in Love with Amy*; he never realized they were the same song. *Summertime.* Then *Softly as in a Morning Sunrise*: a real gem. *You Git a Line and I'll Git a Pole*, my uncle Bud's favourite. They used to sing and strum it together to indicate their civility toward each other, demonstrating this attitude to anyone in my mother's family who might be listening. *Mighty Mississippi* routinely brought tears to all of our eyes, filled as it was with the dominant sevenths he couldn't quite master. *Ol' Man River*, played real slow just in case he might want to sing along even now, if he had any voice left. *My Funny Valentine*, with lots of quiet chords played the way he liked. Then *Someday My Prince Will Come*, a tune he liked but never sang, followed by *Darn That Dream*, a tune he knew but never sang because he didn't believe in it, but still one of my favourites. *Happy Days* running into *Smile*: silly songs that triggered memories he might cherish but not recount. *King of the Road* to remind him of us boys on guitars singing in California bars, Christmas '66. *Old Black Joe*, a tune he sang a lot when he couldn't remember much of anything else, running into *Hymn to Freedom*, a tune I love that came from a similar place. And then *Over the Rainbow*, a tune he didn't like much but played the way he might have sung it. Ending with *Standing on the Corner* and *Once in Love with Amy* retaped with an overdub. When I was growing up we knew he loved Amy and all the girls he saw going by while he stood on the corner.

Tunes on the back-up tape include *Begin the Beguine* (more properly my mother's favourite but he had a soft spot for it nonetheless); *Perfidia* and *Smoke Gets in Your Eyes*, favourites of mine that he liked but which were best left out until he remembered he had a son or two. *Ain't Misbehavin'* and *Stardust*: he couldn't sing these tunes, fracturing the time too much. *Thanks for the Memories*, usually sung drunk (a touchy memory). Followed then by *These Foolish Things* and *This Can't Be Love*, next to *With a Song in My Heart*: a set of standards I just happen to like that were on the air a lot when he was growing up. I went on with *Bye Bye Blackbird* and *Button Up Your Overcoat*, tunes he liked but I don't. They fit together nicely in a B-flat medley. They were also tunes he used to dance to with Mom—he was a fabulous dancer before his hockey knees gave out. Next came *You and the Night and the Music*, to remind him of that swing, followed by *It Ain't Necessarily So* and *It Had to Be You*, for completeness' sake. Any Duke tune would have done, or anything composed before 1945. *Mammy* and *Melancholy Baby* are unfortunate omissions. I couldn't bring myself to play them without his voice in the background holding everything up.

The second set is supposed to be more for me than for him, standards I like that he liked. (They are tunes I go on to play later in life, stealing style from Chick Corea and Oscar Peterson like the rest of my friends. Or memorized note for note, like Tommy Flanagan's *Over the Rainbow.*)

I record all the tunes in one long night, the eve of Jewish New Year in the months he started to die. Only the runaway version of *Standing on the Corner* is overdubbed with a bass line. Nothing else is recorded a second time. The list I think up randomly one at a time, the tunes played right off the bat and the tape sent in the mail the next morning before I have time to act on regret.

My wife helps me rig the system. I can't remember where to put the wires. The list of extra tunes came from hope. If he acknowledged the first tape I'd send the second. The first tape was more his history; the second bridged into the history he left us.

The first is for him, the second for me.

I don't send the second tape.

I think a lot about his funeral that fall and winter. Later, I convince the rabbi to let me speak a little. I want my brothers to show up, for there to be something to remember, for there to be a new beginning.

When it's all over we'll throw dirt on his coffin, I say. That somehow appeals to them.

Okay, forget the music. Just come and throw some dirt.

That gets them to come.

We remember other things.

The office keys that jingled on his belt, turning the television off and on from the kitchen.

A vision of his body in motion down the ice, years before he jumped onto Aunt Vera's coffin. (It sprang open halfway down into the grave, and he jumped in to slam it shut just before the heavens opened up and drenched us.)

Dear Dr Z,

I have deliberately not written for these many months to give you a chance to get us all out of your mind. I will resist the opportunity to air a grievance at your untimely departure or to confess one or two of those secrets we all withhold from the likes of you. Indeed, you can never completely know us, which I am sure you understand.

I am writing to relay a remarkable event that occurred one day at your office.

For a while a young woman set up shop in the closet space to the right of the entrance. It was hardly more than a cupboard, with just enough room to sit and read a palm, which was her vocation. That winter, you may remember, was long and cold. When I came around the corner huffing and puffing from the bus, sifting through the thoughts I wished to discuss with you, I noticed the details that eventually added up to this story.

One morning a young man poorly clad, with acne and a disarming sense of artificial intimacy, spoke to me as I came into the foyer. He wished to give me the impression he lived there, I think. I saw him once or twice more and thought nothing of it, until, on a similar morning at the identical time I passed him being led away by two broad-shouldered police. The woman, the palm-reader, who could have been his double only older and thinner, was screaming in a haunting, declamatory voice. In fact, she threw herself on the odd trio at one point and managed to push them off balance on the ice. The younger of the two officers swore in French, but they just picked themselves up, brushed themselves off and mumbled t'en fais pas or some such thing before heading off with the palm-reader's male double in tow.

I'm sure you noticed I was preoccupied for a while. I thought, This woman is more ill than myself; it is she who should be seeing you. Somehow I couldn't come to give up my time for her. I know that is irrational but that is how I felt.

For a while the two were gone and the palm-reader's sandwich board was gone as well, but I paid little attention and attributed these changes to factors beyond my control. I considered coming by the office in the afternoon or evening to check up on her, but I could not bring myself to do so. I was afraid it might be considered a paranoid maneuver. So I kept these thoughts to myself.

Just as the image of these two helpless souls was fading from my mind I arrived one morning to find the young man so utterly transformed that it took my breath away. He was sitting behind the wheel of a brilliantly new white Thunderbird, which was parked outside the bakery on the sidewalk, facing the wrong way up the street. His hair was slicked back and he was wearing a dark suit and, of course, he was smoking. He nodded at me, not as an acknowledgement of times met in the past, but more a suggestion to keep my nose out. My face, as you have said many times, is open and childlike and there are times when I wonder if this courts some of the disasters I have been trying hard to understand.

Seeing him once again worried me sick, but I put it out of my mind and stuck to my therapy. I was starting to fantasize about them: that they were operating a front for drugs and prostitution, that they were lovers and siblings at the same time, that they were on the run from the law and the hospital and immigration.

These imagined stories, truth be known, seemed much more interesting and real to me than my own life. Eventually I came to believe that all of my fantasies were true and there was no good reason to have to choose between them.

The high point in the drama occurred on an extremely cold February morning. It was a morning like any other, only colder. I hadn't seen either of the two wayward souls in months and had assumed the young man was gone for good, to jail or to Mexico, and that the woman had returned to her employment as a palm-reader. As I turned the corner out of the foyer into the bitter cold, I heard men's raised, agitated voices. Then, as if on cue, there was a loud crash. Three men had smashed the palm-reader's window with a large rock and they were making a quick getaway. One of them was the wayward man. As he brushed by me I saw him furtively pushing something into a plastic bag: drugs or money, I assume. Hopefully they bought proper clothes with the proceeds. I could not imagine how they could survive in t-shirts and runners in that kind of weather.

I was reminded of the entire story just last week. I was driving north near the river on the western edge of downtown and I noticed the palm-reader hitchhiking. She was swaying up and down, forward and back, as if carried on a breeze of her own making. I wondered where she was going, given that the road ended at the river in two or three blocks. Her presence suggested a craziness I could never aspire to.

Even now I blame myself for not speaking to her when she lived in that box in your building, for not stopping and taking her off to hospital. She is a kind of symbol to me that I have come into myself, that I am now sane.

Perhaps there is a bit of a confession in this letter.

It is not you that I miss; it is her. I hope you will forgive me.

NOW: WEST

One day recently I went skiing with Dave and his two teenage boys. My kids, all girls, were not keen on getting up that early (before dawn, in fact) on a day when it might rain and might snow, to go to a mountain renowned for its precipitation.

I was amazed at how easy it was to spend time with them. The boys spoke up when they wanted something. They noted the weather and its effects. They had ideas on how to get away from it by going higher up or over a ridge. They paid

attention to their equipment, stopped to examine its operation now and then and didn't tire of identifying the runs or looking for the conditions they wanted. On the way back down the mountain they asked for a pit stop when a gas station appeared on the horizon. And when their dad got on to his current obsession, which happened to be Grey Owl, they listened for the umpteenth time and asked a question or two that he had not previously considered.

If Grey Owl was a conservationist, why did he trap?

How could an Englishman become native?

How did a trapper learn to write?

On the drive back, Dave was like someone who had finally reached that crucial threshold drink. Perhaps it was the fatigue following a day on the hill, the relentless curves in the mountain road or his plummeting blood sugar. I knew he was keen on rivers, recycling and all of medicine, from emergencies to mental health. But I wasn't ready for the full force of his obsession with somebody else's life somehow better lived: Grey Owl, the scholar and writer. Grey Owl the conservationist, Grey Owl the native trapper—the ideal synthesized person who had done what Dave and I only dreamed about.

Of course, there was a down side to the hero's life: drink, women, his showmanship. All of this information required keen analysis, Dave said, laughing. He wasn't serious, of course. Not completely. Dave didn't want me to think his interest was crazy.

Before we crossed the border to our own country, snaking along the road to our seaside community, Dave himself was calling this Grey Owl thing an obsession. He used the word in exactly the same way I use it in the office: as a stand-in or a symbol that brings you up close but keeps you at a distance, a process that doesn't quite cut through to what's really going on. Later, when we were back in the swing of our working lives, Dave passed me Grey Owl literature and for a while I ate it up. He might have thought I was developing the same obsession, which is quite contagious, but I am immune. After reading more than one biography I thought, You can take this crazy man, write a book about him, then wait a few decades and write it all again.

Dave thought I was hooked when I told him about my father-in-law. My wife's father, despite his Jewish origins and be-lated education, grew up in the hinterlands of New Brunswick and Quebec and knew Grey Owl from a series of direct en-counters. It was easy to piece together some of the details from published biographies to check on the accuracy of his memo-ries. My wife's grandfather ran the corner store in town. He was the man who loaned Grey Owl a winter's worth of supplies before the trapper headed into the bush to write. It was my wife's grandfather whose potatoes froze on the trek into the un-forgiving cold, a speck of her inheritance if you will, discarded near Lake Temesquata. It was just like my dad, my father-in-law told me, to loan anything and everything to a man he had not previously met.

When my father-in-law described Grey Owl to me, he could have been describing the dust-jacket of Grey Owl's book: the man, his wife and their pet beaver. It was right even to the way the trapper was with each of them: diffident and contained with his wife, playful and protective with his small companion. The woman was native, my father-in-law said: very small, dark, strong and beautiful. There was nothing new in his account but veracity seemed to pulse through it, bringing it to life.

And what rested beneath Dave's obsession? He had tried to tell me in the vehicle as we approached town, but I couldn't really acknowledge it and he couldn't really say. We needed many more hours for a confession of that magnitude. Given the choice, what would we really do when we finally grew up? Write a book or two? Go into the bush and live the symbolic life as if it were real?

Over the years, more than one of my medical colleagues have cautioned me against reading too many books, a warning echoed in Ecclesiastes. First you dream, then you neglect your life. Finally you are admitted to a psychiatric unit (preferably somewhere where nobody knows you) and after pharmacotherapy, ECT and reconstructive psychotherapy you crawl back to your community on your belly and never, ever, ever open a book again.

Of course I agreed with Dave. If it's in the blood, it's in the blood.

THE DREAM

This is what I told my friend Dave in exchange for the Grey Owl stories.

Some time after the first great war—in the warm-up to the second—my grandfather dictated his account of a pogrom that afflicted the Russian Pale in 1905. He spoke in his comfortable west-side living room while his dutiful wife scratched down the words. He didn't know how to expand the account into a novel. He didn't know what he was trying to write, whether it was a novel or something else. He was too busy smuggling streptomycin into Canada to treat his tuberculous patients.

My grandfather has been dead fifty years but his account is soon to become a major motion picture.

THEN IN THE EAST: THREE GIRLS IN EXILE

They say that bonding begins before the baby is conceived. The process is entirely unpredictable and takes you by surprise. There is nothing you can do to prepare for it.

I remember exactly when I bonded to my first child. Bonded isn't the right word, although it does convey the correct feeling of being cemented in.

The crucial attachment took on a momentum of its own as my wife shifted into the down-slope of the labour curve. Anxious discussions outside the hospital room confirmed my suspicions. My wife was somewhere between six and eight centimetres dilated and screaming for pain relief. This was transition, the dreaded transition: the place in the process that suspends the child between two worlds. Suddenly the pain was different, the contractions different, and my wife was gone. She had forgotten everything she had taught me: the breathing and counting and positioning and talking and listening. The change was evident in her consciousness. Perhaps I lack a charitable edge but it must be said that her consciousness was gone. Nature had taken it over with a vengeance.

At that moment I bonded with the child.

I didn't have to breathe or count. I was superfluous. Quite abruptly the lines were drawn: myself and the baby against my wife's body. She has her story, what she remembers. She is entitled to her version, the version that stems directly from her body. But I have my story, which only I remember, and I insist on its truth.

As soon they wheeled my wife away for the epidural the tension lifted, the noise decreased and she relaxed. The muscular apparatus working its way across her abdomen receded into her gut and she drifted into a languorous, achy trance.

The child, I imagined, was left hanging in the balance between worlds. She wasn't yet a screamer, didn't yet have her voice. Like me she was holding her breath.

I wandered the ward intruding on nursing conversations. I felt my wife's belly with my sweaty palms and tried to decipher the ongoing rhythmic sounds of the monitoring device—they reminded me of a cannibal's dance. My wife hovered in hazy delirium. Delivery was a difficult process, the nurse told me, as if trying to convince herself of something. Difficult? Okay, where was the difficulty? I knew there was trouble in there but I couldn't put my finger on it and neither could the nurse or anyone else.

"But," I said.

But what?

It wasn't my body, only my firstborn not coming out.

The nurse nudged me off the ward to get coffee, buy cigars, anything to get me away. She didn't know that I myself was suspended mid-shift on a ward three floors down. Somewhere in my head I was accountable for the sick: a schizophrenic in restraints who had bitten an orderly in the thigh; a suicidal depressive who had threatened to swim the river rapids off the parkway and had gone missing. Any minute I expected a call from my own territory, from my supervisor or the police.

I wandered back. There was nowhere else to be. My wife lay on her side, mumbling. She had to go, she said. To the delivery room? The bathroom? Home? She drifted away. I had too many questions but language had lost its usual dimensions and changed into something else.

I sat slouched in the corner, lulled by the rhythmic beat of the monitor. The beat became frantic then eased up, quickened and died away. Then it trailed off to nothing as if in a dream muffled by pillows.

The rest of the story was poorly choreographed drama poorly remembered. No doubt I raised a few eyebrows with my agitated behaviour. I was grateful my wife was only sufficiently conscious to stare intently from the heart of her delirium. A few minutes later the obstetrician, a happy-go-lucky francophone with lanky legs, pulled the kid out with forceps. He didn't mind being interrupted and he didn't mind coming to the rescue. The cord was wrapped tightly around the little girl's neck and she fluoresced a murky green in the delivery room light. But when the cold air hit her lungs she released a powerful full-blast scream and the worst headache I have ever experienced exploded in my head. A headache that screeched, This little girl is not dead.

Later my wife and the baby presented a picture of family bliss. No sign of distress, meconium, blood or mess. My wife still says she looked in the nursery that night and misidentified the child as somebody else's, but that is another story.

The second child came with a bang but we all had to wait. Wait while I ran as fast as I could across the Experimental

Farm from the university campus to the delivery room. Wait while the resident was freed up from assisting at a difficult Caesarean next door. Wait while the same lanky-legged obstetrician negotiated a mid-day accident in the highway collector lanes. Wait and wait while my wife got her breathing up and started to turn a frightening bluish-pink. Again wait after the nurse presented her with a paper bag and left the room. Then a medical student took a look, saying, "There is a baby right there ready to come out," and stepped back as if to be out of the way when it happened. I wanted to protest that my wife's breathing was reasonable under the circumstances, but I didn't get a chance. We all breathed and waited and breathed and waited and counted and breathed and waited and eventually the doctor came and the baby came out with a pop as a ton of water splashed onto his rubber boots.

My first daughter has always been loud. She screamed for a year, louder than any child I have ever met. She has a prenatal memory of not being heard.

My second daughter is a great procrastinator. For years she threw up before school or got a finger caught in a door—any door—protesting all the way out.

For the delivery of my third daughter, the staff at the hospital were pleasant and there were no hitches. She came out smoothly, in reasonable time, with no significant delays and no strangulations. Ever since then she has been stable and balanced. She neither screams nor procrastinates. I remember holding her in the delivery room and wondering if she belonged to me, she was so fair.

Dear Dr Z,

It is with great trepidation that I approach the topic of your leaving. It reminds me repeatedly of the time you abandoned me in mid-sentence to sprint to your wife in the delivery room. That must have been your second daughter, who is turning fourteen this spring. I was always good at getting information out of you. From our conversations I was eventually able to piece together where you lived, even the exact house. I knew the man who lived there when you and I were children. He showed me his garden when I walked by in the afternoon after school.

I knew even more than that. There was a scandal years ago, when my mother was still alive and we knew everybody in town. After the scandal that man was never the same. I suspected, as you said, that the house was cursed. The next owner had an affair and his wife reciprocated in kind, so the fourth child born under that roof was not his.

When I first met you I imagined you would repeat that scenario with me and produce a fourth daughter, mine.

It was the house and the street I wanted, nothing else. I can tell you more about that neighbourhood than anything in the world. More than the royal family. More than my lover or my parents. There is a point in life that sits behind the eye like a picture. It is a picture of taking off gently toward where you are going. My picture is of your street. I am in the parking space below the red maple, looking up at the twin silver maples of your neighbour. I should say, your ex-neighbour. I went around asking about you the other day, and the owner, a man in his early fifties, took some time before he remembered who you were. I sensed he did not like you and was so glad to have you disappear that he attempted to deny the linkage altogether.

You will think me obsessed, but I have followed you the length of your working day in my Mazda. The vehicle was easy to camouflage, being an exact replica of one of your other neighbour's three cars. I often sat under your maple, in my screen memory's exact spot, and waited for you to appear. I watched you shovel snow in winter and throw the ball for your dog. A stupid dog, if you ask me: he never did learn to freely drop the ball. I watched you play soccer and hockey in the street with your eldest, who I mistook for a boy. For a while I thought you had lied to me but then I realized my error.

I'd played there too, with the two girls who lived on the corner. They moved away when we were all children and, as far as I know, never came back. That was around the time the city pulled up the railway tracks and built the highway. Once when I was playing with my friend, her older sister, who was swinging in the backyard, caught her lip on the chain link fence. She was an attractive girl and it was horrible to see the blood dripping onto her dress. The man who lived in your house took her to the hospital and the doctor who lived on the corner with poppies from Flanders in his garden stitched her up. It was that kind of neighbourhood back then, a village at the outskirts of town.

I am sure you know where I am going with this letter. You stole into the territory of my childhood. I invoke this as evidence against obsession. (It was not I who smashed in your car window, although I got a glimpse of that person and could provide you with a clue or two if you are interested.) I was simply following you back to the territory of my childhood. You may not believe me, but I was delighted somebody seemed to find the right spot. I would come around the corner and find you exactly where I thought you should be, doing any number of things with a ball and a child. I would like to redefine this for you as an example of transference, and as you know, transference works both ways. You were transferred into my childhood, and through you I was brought back into it as well.

The person who smashed in your car window was a slim man of indeterminate age who looked furtive, vigilant and purposeful. He was driving a vehicle just like my own, only an older model with a dull finish. As you know, I have always preferred exuberant styles, colourful clothes and colourful friends, so I am sure you will believe me when I profess my innocence. It occurred on a day of freezing rain, undoubtedly to make you question whether the two circular holes in the glass were caused by expanding ice or the purposeful work of an irate pedestrian. A nasty touch of class, if you ask me.

THEN: MY HOME IN THE EAST

The consulting room is an odd place. I have been scrutinized countless times by curious visitors wishing to cast a kindly eye on my life. My life has few if any secrets but I have been compelled to behave to the contrary. Often clients will develop odd thoughts—that I have sons instead of daughters, that I was born in Europe, that I have any number of sexual proclivities. They suspect I am a ping-pong champion, that I am a musician and that I have travelled the world speaking many languages. Never have I been accused of scanning the entire works of Freud, which would be closer to the truth.

I am suspected of the most unusual powers, including reading the local papers and knowing the news. Sometimes I consider it part of my job to peruse the headlines but usually this is not necessary. It is suspiciously easy to listen intelligently. A question here and there, properly timed, hints at knowledge that is not really there. In real life I am quite bland, and my most remarkable stories have to do with neighbours and local activities that would never make the local headlines.

Case in point. It is almost May. The ground has frozen again. The paving stones in front have heaved and sheets of white paint are peeling off the exposed southern wall of the house. "Southern wall" reminds me of the old city of Jerusalem, an unnecessary distraction. What I mean is, there is a lot of work to do in the spring and I would rather be in Jerusalem.

The house, admittedly, is a typical new-world barn. My family lived in it for years before this realization hit me. I was listening to an uninspired patient talking about yet another sexual liaison when I became distracted by my options for amortization, my difficulties in paying the monthly arrears, and finally, by a mental snapshot of the house and street, viewed from a slight angle. It was suddenly apparent to me that the house was a modified barn. Indeed, its barn-like elements lent it a rustic connection to a hypothetical past that generated a feeling of home.

Or consider the following. In the late spring I spotted a few ants in the water closet, a reminder of a remote holocaust of shrivelled bodies vacuumed from the poison-white dust in the dismantled mudroom. Recently a neighbour's groundhog waddled down the lane towards the parkway. Last year a family of raccoons lived out back in the lot that had been severed from ours. They ventured out at dusk, four lumbering bodies climbing the apple-blossom-tree. The man who built our barn-house planted that tree before the lot was subdivided. The raccoons (two adults and two children) played around the trunk at dusk. One was often seen washing his hands in a barrel, believe it or not. We stood on the street chatting while the raccoon family waddled in single file beneath our shadows and disappeared up any number of trees.

One of my daughters said, "Look at those fat cats."

I would often be struck by an urge to tell these stories to patients. They would ask, "How are you," or "What's new?" and

I would react spontaneously. It is important to be believable. No one likes to think you are lying to them. But if I told a story it would seem senseless. Eventually I learned to act a little. I found it easier to complain in response. A complaint is more readily appreciated and dispensed with.

Imagine sitting in the consultation seat hearing about bats. Indeed there was once a majestic, injured bat under the front step of my house at street level. That was before I cemented the stones back down. The bat was in there screeching and I lifted the stone and we came face to face. The bat was regal in its own way, staring right at me and standing its ground. It did not move. I thought it might have been a mouse so I brought Max the cat around and lifted the stone back up. The squeaking stopped. Max and the bat stared at each other. At first it appeared to be a standoff but eventually Max backed away. He knew better. Or more accurately, he knew better than I. It was only then that I realized it wasn't a mouse.

I suspect that's what made the event into a story. At first I didn't know, and then I did. What's more, it happened at my house with my cat Max, who taught me something.

My wife called the people who take care of bats. I was too busy telling the story over and over to pay attention to her. They told her what to do but she did nothing and I did nothing and the bat took care of itself. The bat people called back while we were drinking tea and listening to the radio, to make sure that the bat was okay. They weren't worried about rabies or frightened children or octogenarians fainting away. They were worried about the bat.

A friend of mine had a bat in his house around the corner and he did something to it with a tennis racquet reminiscent of a Thurber story he hadn't read. The neighbour-I-do-not-like-who-knows-everything lent the neighbour-I-like a special set of gloves that he, the neighbour-I-do-not-like, uses to remove the wayward bats that find their way into his en-suite through the skylight. This was apparently quite a prevalent phenomenon during his renovations and I hope it has persisted.

In our neighbourhood the bats come out at dusk, especially in the summer. They swoop around the way bats swoop. Sometimes they squeak. It can be quite enchanting to watch them, listening for their sounds and wondering where in fact they bed down for the night. They like one of my neighbours' blue spruces, the tree that will have to come down if the other-neighbour-who-is-likable-enough ever wants to build a legal garage (if he ever wishes to sell and move away). The bats swoop from there to the yard of the neighbour-I-do-not-like-at-all, landing under his eaves.

Am I allowed to speak of my neighbours, or are they subject to the same censorship as my patients? And the animals of the neighbourhood? My pets? My children? Will they challenge my view of events? Accuse me of distorting the truth or worse? Will they put my report down, saying I have made it all up? Will they leave the room if I read it aloud? Will they accuse me of reporting the truth, laughing at my limited fantasies?

Perhaps I can speak openly about squirrels and birds. A neighbour-I-have-not-yet-mentioned found a family of dead baby squirrels in his eaves one year, just below where the birds hang out at yet another neighbour's window. A morning cardinal often sings a predictable minor third, from the top down, usually in tune. What is not predictable is where he will be and when he will wish to sing. My not-so-nice-neighbour has a bird feeder, so he is good for something. The birds were singing on the day of the baby squirrels. It was a day like any other.

Which brings me to cicadas. For some reason, my house collects the late summer cicadas of the neighbourhood. There is a cicada sink near the lilac tree on our property. In mid-summer their pale brown skeletons with the slit down the back can be found under the rhubarb leaves, by the Jerusalem artichokes, or standing upright as if ready to fly away, their sticky legs stuck to the rough concrete of the window well. We found the first one the first summer, on the corner post of the rotten Glen Green mudroom. There was something ominous and beautiful about it. A friend of mine, who helped remove the mudroom and made me so nervous I stepped clumsily on a nail, insisted for years that it was some form of beetle. My middle daughter has collected and traded cicada skeletons for a snakeskin and a beaver skull with one missing tooth.

It is always a bit of a surprise to find those chitinous skins each year, in exactly the same places. I have seen the insects creep out of their carapaces and slowly unfold their wings. This tends to happen in the morning during the dog days of summer. Sometimes we hear the high-pitched buzz and know that a new cicada has shed its skin. Then we go out and find them both, the fat ugly live thing inching lethargically up the stucco somewhere in the sun as it warms up like a lazy gecko, and the skin, looking equally menacing, stuck to the concrete foundation in the shade.

If you do not believe my life is exciting, I would like you to meet Max the cat and his mice. He often tortures them, especially during summer nights, and carcasses are often spontaneously exhumed and flung about by the mower cutting the grass. Max sits in wait, pounces, and pins their tails to the dirt with his paw. Then he lets them go. Eventually they tire out and die. Max tried this once with a chipmunk and the rodent ripped open Max's neck next to his windpipe, which was left to heal by an astonished vet and two astonished parents (my wife and I), by secondary intention.

Max wanders nights, even in winter. In the neighbourhood he is known as "the teenager." He gets into fights and often loses; he has no front claws. He has been cut badly all over: under his eye, on his forehead, across his ear. His cuts scab over, fill up with pus and have to be drained. My wife is an expert lancer. I like to observe the difficulties and she does something about them. I hold the cat and pontificate about anatomy and physiology and anti-microbials while my wife lances the boils and injects medicine-filled syringes into his feline mouth.

Max has outlived his long-time territorial mates. He has crawled under the hoods of cars near the radiator on cold nights and has gone to live in Osgoode or Kemptville or Manotick, abducted by a kind relative of this-or-that-neighbour who was in the area house-sitting. Max has had many near-death experiences, some witnessed. He gets fed in many places and is routinely dressed up like a baby by our middle daughter and the three-year-old neighbourhood twins. He has been lovingly strangled many times by the same Madeleine and Genevieve. (The street picked up a lot of spirit when the twins moved in. There was a rumour that one twin had a freckle somewhere. My wife got fed up trying to identify the imaginary freckle and just called them Mad-e-vieve and Gen-e-leine. Now she couldn't be right, but then again she couldn't be wrong.)

Max is the only cat my wife has ever loved. She hates cats for their aloofness. Now she loves Max for this same quality. She loves how Max sits in the garden like a lion or in the middle of his square of sunshine like a dog. She folds him into a ball on the hardwood and twirls him with a whoop. In the morning the dog sniffs him and chases him around. Max has a hundred sentinel positions on the property. In the semicircular garden. In the lupines brought from Cape Smokey. On the rotted fence beside the honeysuckle. On the green trellis where the allergenic plastic has been peeled back. At the warm south wall where the hydrangeas come up. On my neighbour's purple Mazda. Or on his blue Mazda. Or his white Mazda.

Once in awhile I actually relate one of these events to a patient. My guard is down and I half-realize my error. Images hang in the air like unfinished fables. I catch myself and bail out before it is too late. Who wants to hear, for example, about wasps? By early summer they are out, attracted to the back porch by the intense heat. You can find them in the spring soil if you turn it over.

One year the mud wasps tried to built a nest on the inside of my screen door. They scratched a beautiful brown whorl at the inner top left corner. The day I scraped it off it was back, only bigger. Only then did I realize what it was and what I had done. I had to scrape it away again, disinfect it and scotch tape over the area to keep them away. I did this with the fascination of belated understanding and a touch of shame.

We have paper wasps too. Each year we find a small nest in the yard, discarded from somewhere, washed out of the eaves. For years an impressive nest sat with a half-dozen cicada skins and my wife's collection of storm glass in the kitchen window below the aged scraggly lilac.

Each summer, on a single particular day, the red ants make an angry dash up the southwest corner of the house.

My neighbour Vic, who is deaf in one ear, insists he saw something like a sloth in the tree opposite both of our houses once, years ago.

I heard a skunk moved into the groundhog's home under my neighbour's porch. It is said that this move shifted the groundhog to the house next door and the raccoons across the street. My wife and I like to pull our neighbour's leg about his animals. This is the neighbour-I-don't-quite-mind, who lives two doors down from the neighbour-of-disrepute. The neighbour-I-don't-mind-too-much doesn't take any notice of his property. He used to have a Ford Ltd wagon with two or three flat tires rusting up on his front lawn—that was before the run of red, white and blue Mazdas. He rakes his leaves by mowing them and blowing the remains forcefully into the street. He still thinks that the city comes by each year and picks up the leaves from the gutter, a service I suspect they offered in the '60s or '70s. I have been doing it for him myself for quite a while, picking them up and filling black plastic bags. If I don't the leaves and organic detritus plug up the gutter and the spring runoff goes all over the place, which isn't nice if it freezes. My goofy I-work-for-the-government-and-remember-a-time-when neighbour has been the source of some amusement over the years. His family treats him with benign humour, too. He is a little deaf and plays opera cranked up full blast. He has an enormous classical collection and an unplayed Steinway that his son would like to chainsaw into firewood.

Once his house almost burned down when he was on holiday. My middle daughter noticed the black smoke and called the fire department. Nobody had to break down the doors; we had a key. My daughter was a hero and received a special award. My neighbour-who-is-really-quite-goofy-sometimes has been known to unfreeze our street's co-op snowblower in winter by dragging it into his front hallway and letting it warm up there while it drips all over his wall-to-wall. He doesn't believe anything we tell him about the local animals. He is afraid of all of them, including our dog, and prefers to believe they do not exist.

I will not relate stories about the neighbourhood dogs. Or the spiders. Or the iguana my middle daughter wants to bring home. Or the pink goldfish she won and later buried in the backyard under the honeysuckle.

Years ago my neighbour Vic filmed a great red-headed woodpecker eating carpenter ants out of the hydro pole by the corner garage, in the dead of winter.

Dear Dr Z,

Long ago in therapy I told you about the man with the gun.

I am sure you will remember that I was early for a session and was out in front of the flower shop having a smoke. Someone had removed the rickety hanging boxes there and replaced them with stone pots with globe cedars. The pots were quite comfortable to sit on.

The traffic was picking up; it was late in the day. It dawned on me then and there that your street, so quiet in the morning and midday, is a major inter-provincial artery during the late afternoon rush. The cars come in great waves, and are then held back by the extended red light at the corner, only to rush on again. I was lulled by the ebb and flow of this urban tide, smoking a hasty but enjoyable cigarette, when I happened to look up into the eyes of the man with the gun.

I do not know why I return to this repeatedly. Perhaps it is because the event has something to do with you. Or perhaps because you said something about it I have forgotten. Or perhaps I return to it for reasons I never knew and never will know. Needless to say, my mind goes back there. Sometimes the children are somewhat irritating or I haven't seen my wife in a few days, or the office is getting to me or my mother calls once too often, and click, like some kind of release valve, I am sitting there on the stone pot, inhaling cigarette smoke, about to be aimed at by the man with the gun.

It is always the moment before the man shifts his arm and his gaze. As you will undoubtedly remember from my earlier accounts, the man pointed the gun at me after he noticed me looking at him. He had been waving it back and forth between the two women in the front seat of the compact. The driver, I remember clearly, was dark and the passengers both fair. I do not remember if the women were beautiful or if I would just like to think so. I was astonished at the image of the man in the middle of the back seat moving his hand back and forth as if lazily conducting an orchestra but I was not afraid. I remember you made me call the police right away, although we agreed nothing was likely to come of the call. I am glad you confessed you made me do that for yourself, in order to enable you to think clearly during the session. You got quite confused about Freud and some theory about not acting out during therapy. It seemed to me that you did exactly what you were supposed to not do, lift your hand and act. And what is worse, you were the therapist, not the patient.

But that is not my main concern.

No one can explain why my mind goes back to the moment he begins to swing his right arm in my direction. The image repeats, over and over. Sometimes I try to nudge the camera forward, as it were, to the pointed gun itself, but that never works. I feel that if I can complete the series of images, it will finally end and go away.

Truth be known, I have come to enjoy this obsessional replay. Do not misjudge this sentiment. I do not mean this in the way depressives enjoy the smell of old socks or their predictably recurring pains. It is more like reading an old story or seeing an old film. I will never know those two women or the man behind them. I will never know where they were going or what he was doing behind them even though I have thought through many possibilities. My favourite is that the man meant little to the women and was trying to create an audience with his hand gestures. He wanted them to be concerned about him. (In this version I hallucinated the gun.) In the end I will have to accept this as the best explanation but there will always be others.

So now that you have gone I wanted you to know this truth. Your version of reality is also long gone and there will always be others more compelling. Be satisfied with your limited intervention in my case. I am far from cured, but you have affected me more than you realize. I have become a reluctant Freudian. This was not, you will be quick to point out, the purpose of my initial presentation, but it does have its advantages. What is more, I have recently found it unnecessary to smoke. The pleasure of release, it seems to me, now arrives unannounced from unexpected directions and contrary to my earlier self, I prefer not to explain the transformation.

I have digested many hours of unstructured fantasizing for your benefit in this note. Surprisingly, the process was quite a bit like therapy. The advantage, if you can call it that, is that it happened spontaneously while engaged in activities where little or no creative thought is required. The singular disadvantage to this method has been the absence of company.

Regards to you in your new location. If you have a moment, please write. I would love to hear your thoughts on my thoughts in exchange for my thoughts on your thoughts. I have followed your advice and not told my wife about this aspect of our conversations. I suspect she would in fact know the correct explanation, and where would that leave us?

THEN: TOUCHING UP THE STUCCO BEFORE THE HOUSE SELLS AND WE MOVE AWAY

The day I was touching up the stucco a blue van parked in front of my neighbour-with-all-the-Mazdas' driveway and two women got out. It was a funny place to stop, right under the red maple. They skidded into place like ten-year-olds screeching to a stop on one-speed bikes. It was still early in the afternoon and the formality of their black dresses, each with a white blouse underneath, suggested they were returning home from a grand celebration. The older woman snarled through her lip at her two Mafioso nephews in the back seat. The women were sisters and had grown up in the house that now belonged to the man-with-all-the-Mazdas.

The first sister was perfectly at ease, her short black hair gorgeously pulled back behind her ears, her face unnecessarily rough and plastered with makeup.

The snarly sister scrunched up her already-puckered mouth.

"I need a cigarette," she said.

No hello, no introductions. No eye contact. Hardly a nod.

"Left in '69," the snarly one said. They parked under the tree they hadn't climbed in twenty-five years.

She looked around.

"Never been back," she said.

She looked around again.

"Not 'til now. I need a cigarette."

She breathed deeply, sucking on air.

"I can't take it," she hummed to no one in particular. Something was apparently beyond belief.

Her body was in motion, revving in place. She breathed deeply, scanning the yard, the road, the fence: scanning for memories, for something to come up and smack her back, anything that might match the intensity of her expressed self.

"This is where I got my scar," she said, twitching her lip. "Right here."

She breathed heavily, in-out.

"Believe it or not," she said. As a child she'd fallen off the swing in the-man-with-all-the-Mazdas' back yard, which was really her back yard—and her sister's. This is where she fell off the swing and her face got stuck to all the wires.

She pointed at her two Mafioso nephews.

"I told you guys the story. More than once. My face was stuck right here." She noted the lilacs had been cut back, the garage bricked up as the man-with-all-the-Mazdas' den containing the Steinway-bound-for-firewood. Despite the Mazdas and the renovation, she couldn't help noticing the smallness of everything.

"I climbed this tree, this maple." She hesitated. "I lived in that tree." When all the things happened that she didn't want to talk about, she lived in that tree. Like my eldest child, legs dangling from the lowest branch, back stiff against the trunk. She sat up there, quiet in herself, and watched the world go by. That's when the woman with the scarred lip became who she was and her sister didn't. Her sister became somebody else.

"I don't recognize my own house anymore," she said.

"We shouldn't have come here," said her sister with the pancaked face.

"Nope. That's not my house. I don't remember a thing."

She had played in the grassed-in laneway. She had known the surgeon on the corner, the lady across the street, the people that lived in the bat-house before my not-so-nice neighbour. Two old ladies she remembered had just died within the past year, ladies well into their tenth decade.

"Can't live forever," she said.

When she cut her lip (she flicked her head this way and that, as if realigning the story) the man who built our house took her to the hospital, she said.

Her sister moved toward the car and the nephews took off their ties, one after the other. The younger boy wanted a drink of water. The other said he was hot. They were a single wild mind in the bodies of two beautiful children dressed to kill.

When her face got caught and her lip came out bleeding, the doctor from across the way stitched her up. This was her entry, her performance. She was in that lip.

"My lip," she said. It accentuated her snarl, her thin, hunched posture.

She was born in the same year as I was. It was the first thing she said out of the car and she said it again now.

"When did it all happen?" she said. "Gotta think backwards and forwards at the same time." She held her breath. She was born right here in the year of the four-minute mile. Her sister was born a little later.

Suddenly the woman with the scar seemed old, as if she had lived many unnecessary lives.

Her nephews scuffed their freshly shined shoes through the garden. They pulled out their shirttails for her. They stained their knees with yellow grass, driven to act by her uncensored emotions.

The two boys looked like jewish gangsters. Like pictures of my father and his brother taken in the 1930s. The two boys could have been my father and his brother. In my mind I saw them sitting on the running-board of my grandfather's Packard that was dismantled in Chicago and left outside their hotel on blocks.

The boys brought their smooth, bright faces up to the chain link, as if looking for the remains of their aunt's lip-flesh on the rusted barbs.

"Sam," she said. "Sam, once is enough. Let's leave your beautiful face out of this."

Then, "Jack, Jack, come here. Stick your tongue back in your mouth."

These were names from my own family. Sam, Jack. Names shrunk backward into the bodies of boys too young to be called to the Torah.

The younger woman turned her shoulder to the road. It was hard to tell if she wanted to go or to stay.

She said, "Thanks, thanks a lot; we will leave now," and moved back under the red maple, all the time drifting closer to the house, to my dog, to me. If her sister dragged her into the past she would stare out to the street, to her car and the two jewish Mafiosi, her boys climbing back in.

The woman-with-the-curly-lip was afraid to find out that my neighbour-with-many-Mazdas was normal-nice, that he and his normal-sort-of wife remembered the two women as children. How they looked back then. What their rooms were like.

The gorgeous woman with the scratchy pancake face touched my arm.

"We will stay five, perhaps ten minutes," she said.

Then another neighbour walked over—the man from across the street—and she lifted her fingers from my wrist.

The conversation drifted to the neighbour-across-the-street's house: how it looked the same after all of these years (which was a lie, the kind of white lie that accommodates the passage of time). The lie denied the past; allowed them to pack it away and leave.

In the end the younger sister was the stronger. The latent mobsters were her children and she held the keys to the van. She also held the keys to the future where they would drive off to, directly up the road.

The two women didn't know anything about the previous owners of our house. They remembered them as elderly back then: a nice couple, no children. They hadn't heard about the scandal. The scandal was later, after they left.

"The man in your house walked me across the street," said the curly-lipped woman. "To get stitches. There was a line of red drops from here to there."

She spoke as if she was just filling in detail. Part of her had already filed her disappointment and gone. She had given in to her sister, given up. She was marking time.

"Red drops, right there," she said. Dripping from her lip.

When they drove off I felt bereaved. A ghastly emptiness opened up in my chest. I hardly heard the curly-lipped woman say, "I lived in that tree." The tree was the only thing she saw that was as big as her memory. You could tell by the way she scanned to the top of the canopy and then back to her hands.

Later the man-with-too-many-Mazdas' wife, who is about as blind as her husband is deaf, told me their name and where they had gone. "Pomerantz," she said. My neighbour's wife who-is-just-a-little-too-blind-to-drive-a-Mazda-of-any-colour kept their mezuzah as a talisman to protect the house. It was painted into the back doorpost of the makeshift sunroom (behind the doomed Steinway) where the groundhog lived.

Dear Dr Z,

I still cannot believe someone with a nice house and an office in a chic neighbourhood with hardwood floors and stained-glass windows and everything money can buy (I exempt that ridiculous excuse for a car, that '72 Beamer of yours with the flaking white paint) would up and disappear just like that. Leaving me in the lurch with no psychiatrist. Oh yeah. I'm sure you had your reasons. You said something about coming from out west years ago, Saskatchewan or maybe Alberta. Must have been Alberta. There is a boom in Alberta and everybody is going there to make a million bucks. The country is about to tip into the Pacific Ocean from all the people going there. I never believed any of your excuses.

The real reason you left, I'm sure, is me. I burned you out. Well, I have a confession to make. It was my intention to burn you out. I called you every day between sessions to drive you crazy so you would know how it feels. I know it took ten years, but I am more stubborn than you in the final analysis. I'm sure you admired my energy and persistence. I'm sure you thought to yourself, If she can harness her intrusive energy, she can do just about anything. Five to nine, five to ten, five to eleven I called. I could plot your whole day. I knew when you took your lunches, when you picked up the phone, when you let the phone ring. There were days when I left lengthy messages. Eventually, after the umpteenth conversation, you cut me off. And now you are gone and I have proved that I am unlovable.

I spent most of the first year after you left in the hospital. Every time I got a pass I went down to your old office in the market district and stepped in front of a bus. Or I threw rocks at your window, screaming. The word got out that you were gone and nobody, I mean nobody, was going to put up with me like you did. I would call someone on Monday and they would return my call on Tuesday. Can you believe that? I'm supposed to sit around and wait overnight and all the next day for some idiot shrink to call me back? Just because I'm the patient, does this mean I'm not supposed to have a life? I started doing the rounds. I made a list of psychiatrists as long as your arm. I put everyone from your building on it for starters. Then I went to every hospital and outpatient clinic and got as many referrals as possible and started to check them out. I would ask them questions to put them off guard, to see how far I could push them from the start. I would ask, Should I be in hospital? How could they possibly know? I had just walked in the door without any documentation. Nice thing about this province, you can see a consultant without a referral note. Well, they should know better, accepting a patient like me in consultation without any collateral. I could ruin their lives if they gave me half a chance.

Eventually I freaked out in your ex-neighbour's office. I must apologize to him someday. I was thinking of you, got agitated and started pacing. The nerve of him for being tall, slim and blond. And his language! He spoke so differently from you. He was so, so, so clinical. I didn't like him right from the get-go. But I know I didn't give him a chance. His only fault was, well, he wasn't you. So I smashed up his place that used to be your place, his walls and his leather couch, and I was scuffing up the hardwood that used to be your hardwood and going for those pretty green stained-glass windows you built into your waiting-room when the police came and they took me to three hospitals before anyone would keep me. First the nurses would look me over and not get too worried. Then they would deny me entry. Then I would act up and they would be glad they hadn't dismissed the police. Then they would try to bluff the cops, saying that I didn't have a psychiatric diagnosis, so the cops would take me to the drunk tank or charge me with something. I know my rights. I'm psychiatric and I can do whatever I want.

Eventually I got bored with the bluffing and counterbluffing. Somewhere along the line they gave me some chlorpromazine and I calmed down. Calm, they were ready to admit me. So that's the way it is now: if you are sick, forget it. You can't get a hospital room or a doctor. But if you're calm, well, that's a different story.

I didn't talk much for a month or two after that. I had become used to you understanding me without me making much of an effort. I was exhausted by the thought of trying to explain myself. Couldn't they see where I was coming from? Didn't they know my background? Those awful things my father did? And my brothers? And my mother? Nobody knew anything and I felt like I didn't exist. You left with all of my life written in that thick book of yours that you called the chart. (I looked in it once when you went to the bathroom and I couldn't read a thing and I don't believe you can read a thing either.) Anyway, I guess that big novel of my life I thought you had written down to send to your colleagues to help me out wasn't really the big fat novel I thought it was. The novel was in your head. Or maybe worse, it was only in my head and I thought it was in your head. Anyway, when you left I felt like I didn't exist anymore, that I had floated away in your head while I was stuck not existing back here with my body.

I think you got so tired walking around with that novel that was my life in your head, so tired lifting up the receiver and hearing me yack-yack-yack on and on again and again about the same old things, that you finally decided I would never get better. So, if I was never going to get better, then you—even you—had to admit that you had patients that would never, ever get any better. The best you could do was keep me out of the hospital, which is a ruse and only helps the system save money. Sometimes, you know, I am much better in the hospital where there is constant care and companionship and I don't have to know where my bus pass is or remember my mother's phone number or write down when I have to come see you.

In fact you are probably wondering how I can even put this letter together. I can't. I'm not even writing this. I am sitting here speaking. It's my new psychiatrist's idea. I have been seeing the new psychiatrist for months now and all he ever hears about is you. What you used to do. Or how I used to torture you daily with my phone calls. So he thought it would be good for me to write you a letter.

And when week after week went by and I never gave you a serious thought in between sessions, and never had even an ounce of energy to write anything down for you or anybody else, this new doctor ("the therapist") got fed up waiting for me and decided I was going to talk to you right in a session with him prodding me on like usual. And he would tape it. And then he would edit the session.

We listened to my voice droning on and on, on the tape, and to be honest, I couldn't understand how anybody could listen to that for more than a minute or two. I couldn't even understand the content after a while even though it was me doing all of the talking.

I asked my therapist over and over, What am I trying to say? as if he knew and I didn't. Which is exactly what I used to do with you. I put you on the spot constantly. Sometimes I would ask you questions that even I knew you couldn't know the answer to. Like, is it possible for me to become HIV-positive when I didn't tell you what I had been up to in the last few months? Or did you think that I would get cancer? Or best of all, and this one I pulled every single session, I would ask you what my mom would think or my dad would think or my brothers or my sisters would think if they only knew what was on my mind at exactly that moment. The odd thing was, you always took your time to answer and make an intelligent guess before asking me what I thought. You were often wrong, but by then it didn't matter because I was talking with the person who was on my mind again and I was on to other things.

It started to really piss me off, you coaching me that way. Because now I cannot stand on my own two feet.

Not that I ever could. I went through every psychiatrist in the book, as I mentioned, until I found a patient man. He is blind and a little deaf. He doesn't care that I am on the way to the change of life and am filling out and have lost my allure. Nor has he been frightened off by my many diagnoses. His wife sits in the outer office and helps with the scheduling and phone messages. She calms me down every time I come in and every time I leave. I get more out of seeing her than the psychiatrist. Sometimes he even stammers and I think, This guy is as bad as me. Only I'm the patient who can hardly stay out of hospital longer than two weeks, and this guy is responsible for the likes of me.

As you can probably tell, I am running out of rage, and when I run out of rage I run out of energy. I will leave it up to my psychiatrist to send this to Saskatchewan or Alberta so you can read it. I think he finds me interesting and will put me in one of his books. Not in a chart that can be thrown away, but in a real book. So you can read about me. If you're still in the business and not really burned out. If you are still alive. If you still love me. Seeya.

THEN: VISITING SPECIAL PLACES BEFORE LEAVING

Months before we were to leave for the west, my eldest daughter did something unexpected and spontaneous. After collecting some of her friends from school and the neighbourhood, the group of kids got on their bikes and pedalled up to the apartment on the corner of the hospital compound to re-explore her childhood playground. Under her command they went up and sat on the swing, slid down the diminutive slide and hung out on the deck. They climbed up to the concrete yard above the parking lot where we held her first birthday party. There is a picture of her there, in diapers, resting a beer on her belly. (She has one of those unusual memories that go back to the first year of life. These memories are not reconstructed from photo albums and parental reminiscences but emerge as spontaneous fragments of dreams or fantasies at unexpected moments.)

As she biked around the property, she remembered not being able to jump down from the concrete step onto the grass in her first year of life; it was too high. She remembered the mailroom, with its faintly paranoid lighting and being yelled at "right here" by me for climbing up the fence above the concrete overhang. She remembered the playgroup room, the hallway and the tunnels themselves that burrowed deep underground. Eventually she remembered her wild assortment of early fears (trees and squirrels) and her first friend and playmate, the tireless Mexican who moved away before either of them could walk. She even remembered the playroom where I built the slide I later threw out after her little sister climbed up and over it at eight months. It was the slide that she herself had jumped from. She'd twisted her ankle, drawn in her breath and fainted, twitching and blue.

The hospital was different then. The front steps were where they belonged, leading up to those amazing doors (now locked). In those days a chubby lady sat in the Locating cubicle to the right, exactly where you might imagine her, fielding calls over the phone and directing traffic with her free hand. A set of circular stairs turned away from her right shoulder to the tunnels below. And to the left of that the elevator door would open, revealing the same scrawny doorman year after year managing the collapsible doors you used to see in the Hudson's Bay Company. You had to explore the back of the central corridor to find the Stop Gap retreat with its lopsided pool table and the emergency food supplies for hungry house staff.

Now the entrance sits off to the side behind a wall and past a cafeteria, an afterthought at the end of a modern curve. The bordello-style concourse on the floor below ground persists with its mirrored ceiling that still excites the occasional two-year-old. What my daughter does not remember is the buoyancy of walking that concourse with that other perfect upside-down two-year-old as she looked up, entranced. She watched herself, knowing and not knowing. Thinking, It is me! and wondering, Is it me? She was transfixed by that perfect dangling head that was just like hers, by the pink mittens secured by idiot strings just like hers floating up, by the little girl floating just like her but way up there inside the building's sky, floating just like her but upside down.

Two:
Dr Max

MAX CHAPTER ONE

Max is my other self. He is not Dr Z.

Max is the person I want to be, the person I once was, the person I would become in a perfect world.

This is a different Max, not Max the family cat.

Max is a friend of mine, what the children call a best friend. Max is as close to me as a person could possibly be without being me.

Max is me in camouflage. He can do things that I cannot do. When stressed, Max draws cartoons and finds himself speaking German, things I cannot do. These are things he did as a child and I did not.

Max is bad at sports and I am not. He can still swim a little but that's about it. He has no muscles and I have a few. He has no chest and no legs. He cannot run a single block and I can run a half-marathon in an hour and a half on a bad day in winter, slipping on the ice. At least I could when Max was busy being my other self.

Max the self precedes Max the family cat. The two are unrelated. Later in life when there are three children they named their cat Max. They did not know the Max who is my other self. At least not by name. They had never been introduced.

There is a bit of me in Max and lot of a friend of mine from the next city who used to live here. The friend who speaks German and draws. The children know my friend from the next city. They have known him all their lives. His name is not Max.

If they were to meet Max my children would say, "We know that person," or "That's obvious, we have known him all along. We just didn't have a name for him."

Even now Max has no children and I have three. Eventually he will have two of his own, but that doesn't matter. At the time I began Max's story I had one child with another on the way. I was far more arrogant than Max, because of the children he did not yet have. I thought I was farther ahead.

The person who became Max drew a cartoon of my eldest daughter in my wife's belly. This means that the person who became Max has been with me since the beginning of that life.

In the cartoon my eldest was playing a saxophone.

One night my wife gave the person-who-is-almost-Max her last razor blade to cut off his beard. It was on a night I was certain that she loved me. For this I was grateful to the person-who-could-be-Max. He broke the blades and his face, all in one. There was blood everywhere. As usual, when it was over he drew a picture.

MAX CHAPTER TWO

Max is the guardian of other people's stories. This is his work and he is well suited to it. He sits in his office writing stories for his patients. Perhaps that is not entirely true; maybe their stories are already written. Then what is it that he does? Good question. He is not certain but the time seems to pass all the same. By the end of the day he feels older and emptied out. This process is not entirely bad. Thoughts such as these relax him and he is comforted to know that the process will continue with or without answers. When patients stop talking he says, "This must have happened, or this." He knows and he doesn't know. Usually it doesn't matter because eventually they begin to speak. "No," they say. Or, "This is my story, not that." He doesn't care what they say as long as they talk. Long silences are difficult. He doesn't know what to do with them. He stops writing. He becomes poised, ready. He knows he is waiting by the pain in his own stomach, that visceral gnawing beneath his sternum.

Max thinks that the most important symptoms in the consulting room are his own. He is not in this office to get sick. He is in the office to think and speak. He has a story, too, but his part is concealed; he has to coax it out obliquely. Occasionally he tries to explain this method but the results are disastrous. But he is the doctor so he does not have to make sense. If he is confusing he is at least not being patriarchal. What he does not say is that he routinely manipulates prevailing attitudes to rid himself of the pain in his gut.

He does his job easily. The most difficult parts, he likes to say, are the interruptions. Try and get that one across to Dr Moussakanski, his mentor and teacher, or the ridiculously sensuous Dr Alix Tuttle. Max doesn't bother to explain too much, especially if it interrupts the momentum of the day. He sits in his office and the patients come and go. There is a rhythm to it. The flow is necessary to keep his feeling of balance. His patients wash over him like water. Fifty minutes of talk. Three minutes for a note. A grace note, he thinks. Glissando. His pen glides over the paper.

He puts his feet up briefly, makes a phone call, takes a few breaths. He checks his daybook, files a chart, pulls a chart. He hardly has to move; he does not leave his chair. He can execute these operations in his sleep, even the formulations he must officially transcribe. He detects shifts in weight on the floor, the scuffing of feet up the stairs that elbow around the far right wall, the series of clicks of the doors and the hardly audible swishes as expected visitors enter and leave the waiting room.

Max is slowly becoming a master of small spaces. He is contained by the four walls of his office: new gyprock with spreading orange watermarks. Soon he too will break out, like a bug shedding its carcass and leaving its chitinous shell stuck to the plaster. What little is left of his body will recline, listening.

Understand him well: Max needs his patients. They ensure the walls stay up, that the plaster remains stuck to the gyprock where it belongs. He sets up functional structures and his patients put them into motion. He can do an assessment in half an hour but he lets his patients talk on unless someone is dying on the hospital ward and he has to run.

Off work time reverts to its natural state, more in keeping with the European countryside that produced so many excellent musicians as well as Max. It is not unusual for him to think this way; he is a young man with elderly parents from the old country. This means he is impossibly eligible. He is not threatening and he loves to shop. Shopping fits his voyeuristic inclination, and is his true internship. When he speaks he rarely sticks to the topic. Life is not a journal article, he thinks. His work goes more smoothly if patients think he is a little unstable.

There is a clear connection between Max's work and women. Most of his patients are women and most of the rest of his patients have difficulties with women. Sometimes he cannot tell where the office ends and life begins.

Take Alix, for example. Under sufficient stress she will become sullen and uncommunicative and he is snapped back into languorous, clinical office time. Her irritability betrays a troubled gene. Catholic-soaked. Alcohol-stained. With sufficient stress she will become clinical, and in the end everything comes back to the primitive, to the genes.

Max knows this intuitively. He knows most things this way and he is rarely wrong.

Alix has a skin condition, scaly red flakes on her forearm. Max knows Alix is disturbed by skin (hers and his) but he has never mentioned it to her. She determines what can be said. If he thinks of her skin he ends up conversing with her in his mind. Max does not know how this exchange takes place, yet he regards the substitution as an act of charity.

It is impossible to change a feeling, especially his feelings for her. Alix takes things deep inside so he loses sight of them. He does not understand her deceptions no matter how many times he has seen them. Perhaps she expects him to know more than she does, although it is not clear how Max knows even this and he never acknowledges it. To do so would layer in another level of deception. Alix, he suspects, is what people call normal. Her deceptions are sufficiently disguised. Under pressure she will become labile and sit up nights, waiting. Women, he thinks, are leaving the Earth and becoming more like their irritable fathers. Take Alix and Dr Mendel Moussakanski, for example. They have similar lines around their eyes and patients have been known to mix them up.

Max never takes on a patient he doesn't understand right off the bat. He is a firm believer in diagnosis. In the office he is in perfect balance. He takes holidays so his patients know he is not working too hard. It is necessary to be somewhat burdened by their stories, so every now and then he must disappear under the weight of it all, although in truth he feels little weight. When he returns he is duly punished. He has come to expect the pattern. It is a ritual of the world and no longer surprises him. Very little surprises him, in fact, other than himself. He wonders if this has not always been the case.

Max has committed himself to sitting still in his chair until certain things become clear. Ridiculous thoughts burden him late in the afternoon. He calls the phenomenon "therapist fatigue" and has diagnosed it as a feeling patients put into him. He does not blame the work or its difficulty. Before he leaves the office he chuckles with the realization that within these four walls his feelings are not his own. Yes, if he didn't have to eat or sleep he could sit there forever.

On the rare occasion he is struck by therapist fatigue early in the day he sits in his favourite spot, the patients' chair. He is immediately refreshed, as if he had spent a quick moment listening to himself.

Max privately calls the two seats the in-itself chair and the for-itself chair. The in-itself chair is for the talkers, for real people with feelings and problems. From there you can see the world outside, the drug deals in the lane, passersby in the street and people waiting for the bus. There is a panoramic view of the intersection, the greasy spoon on the corner that used to be a condom shop, the fire escape and the alleys across the lane where cops and hookers vie for spatial control and drug dealers slink behind huge metal garbage bins.

From the for-itself chair you can see the in-itself chair and the wall. Limiting his visual panorama is a conscious tactic. He knows his other senses will expand. It fascinates him that this sensory adaptation renews spontaneously when he comes into the office and disappears when he leaves. He can create it only here, where he is part of the flow of light, heat and air.

The office is small and almost square, with a large bay window facing south. The effect of the weather on his indoor surroundings is profound. All environmental factors are exaggerated: the summer heat, the mid-afternoon cool as the sun dips behind the crumbling brick walls of his neighbours (a secondhand bookstore and a hair stylist). He feels convection currents in the bay window. Cool air from below his feet mixes with the glassy warmth of the sun and street. The cold gloom of the avenue faintly pushes the office light back into its sockets. The room is crisp and cool on the coldest days of winter. He has never had to put on the baseboard heaters; the consultation office holds all the warmth of the brightness outside perfectly.

He sits in the for-itself chair. As the patients talk he half-listens and half-explores their words, listening for parallel structures and lies. These are the tools of the trade. Max is a generalist and a jew but he is not about to climb up on a cross like his predecessor. Indeed, he will never even admit to being anxious. What others call anxiety is, for him, a calibrated electrical impulse. It is a pilot light: a small, hardly noticeable indicator of trouble, a sign that the circuits may overload. He has spent all those years of training to become a professional circuitbreaker.

THEN: THE STEPS ARE BADLY CRUMBLING IN THE SPRING

For now, Max has been put away in a box. There is too much to do.

The steps are crumbling. The mortar is worn away and the ground has heaved a crack across them from side to side. The grass is brown and there is a burned-out patch from the dog. Turf and stone will be repaired, only to relapse the following season once we are gone. It has been warm out back on the deck in the early afternoon, but the canal, drained of its water in the late fall, is still empty. That is a reliable sign, a link between nature and our recognition of nature's patterns. Yesterday there were flurries but the snow didn't stick.

My patients have been sending me notes: sayings scratched on bits and pieces of paper, thoughtful accusations, quick jibes, lengthy recollections and philosophical discourses.

I would like to tell you something, Dr Z.

Put this in my chart, Dr Z.

Dr Z, Dr Z, Dr Z.

I close a box and think, Dr Z is not Max. Not yet. No longer.

Patients that used to belong to Dr Z have been sending me *New Yorker* comics and rewriting the captions. They have been cancelling sessions or not showing up. Some have fired me before I can fire them. Some are hanging on for dear life, grinding me into their despair until my skin flinches with feelings of death and loss. Others have shifted into relative health as if they had just been waiting for an excuse to get on with it.

As for me, I am working on my father's eulogy and, when not too busy, spending some time with Max.

ON THE WARD WITH MAX

Max met Moussakanski when he went to work at the hospital.

The shrunken Hungarian, a sixty-year-old holocaust survivor who became irritable late in the afternoons, exhibited burst malar veins and a coarse tremor. His purpose in life, it seemed to Max, was to map out the computer function of the cerebral cortex. Moussakanski berated patients gently during the day and cut brains in his lab after hours. It was generally recognized that his prognosis was guarded, perhaps more guarded than most of his patients. He would be laid up with a heart attack or would contract septicemia from a scalpel wound. In heaven, the nurses warned, Moussakanski would be assigned the task of conversing with all of the brains he had transected. They called him "Mendele-Mengele," which concealed both their distrust and their affection for him.

The charge nurse, Miss Upton, let Max in on a secret the first time he set foot on her ward.

"Moussakanski spent uncountable hours dangling from a ledge by his fingertips way back when, you know, the Nazis," she said.

Miss Upton was trying to be helpful. She wanted Max to know where he stood. This was allowed, that forbidden. She was full of sensible rules. Castor oil Mondays and Thursdays. Rounds scheduled for nine sharp and "Stay out of the patients' toilets." She had a way of speaking abruptly, farting little blasts from a small mouth that contracted into a wrinkled pit like a sphincter.

"You watch out for Mengele. His hands shake when he picks up a needle."

Mengele, that was Moussakanski.

Moussakanski had been known to break chalk against the board during lectures and throw it across the room *at her*. And his needle was famous, as were his shaky hands.

"You should see it vibrate when he shoves it in the back," Miss Upton loved to say, underscoring her right to exaggerate the truth any way she wanted.

"He'll have you do it if he sees your innocent face. He will show you the hemispheres in the maintenance fridge and invite you to dissect the limbic system on weekends. If he sees you suffering. Only if he sees you suffering."

Miss Upton smoothed her pink uniform skirt. She drew Max's attention to the place above her knees. He saw liver spots on the insides of her thighs: grey, almost purple. Perhaps they were bruises. The spots were clearly visible under thick white pantyhose. He was not in the habit of looking up women's legs.

"Castor oil Mondays and Thursdays," she said as she slid her fingers along the inside of her right thigh. "Tuesdays and Fridays after a long weekend."

Her hair was grey and the wrinkles in her cheeks looped around her mouth and held it there like a droopy scrotum. Moussakanski told Max she was a reformed alcoholic. Twenty years ago she had been beautiful. Then patients enjoyed their enemas and needles in the behind. Her arm was swift and sure, her flesh full and provocative. Miss Upton had been loved. She remembered the cold baths and the white jackets, depressives cowering in sticky masochism, schizophrenics licking her boots. Moussakanski remembered it too. All that was in the days before patients' rights.

Max didn't know a thing about those days, Miss Upton said. When the hospital cut back a thousand beds, a thousand cute psychopaths threw themselves into the river. It was the dead of winter and most of their bodies were never recovered, having found the sea. Tell that to the social reformers.

Miss Upton disagreed with Dr Moussakanski. She cared about her schizophrenics and depressives while Moussakanski remained preoccupied with needles, electrodes and the brains in the maintenance fridge. Moussakanski's medical detective work kept him out of Miss Upton's hair. When it came to ward order she was the boss: rounds, charting, purgatives, rest. Needles at eight sharp, pills at eight-fifteen. When they got to Marjorie Upton's ward, patients knew how to behave.

Max was fascinated by her sense of decorum. He made it a habit of always smiling back at her and resolved to avoid all needles. He was left-handed and had trouble hitting the veins.

"Put on your white coat, Doctor," she liked to say when she wanted to show him something.

What could Max possibly do but accept her at face value? On the ward there was nothing to see. It was a ward like all other wards, only clean: no dirt, dust or blood. Hardly a rumble from the patients. While being investigated the patients were not permitted to display symptoms. They knew they had been transplanted to a place in history beyond clinical signs, to a place where fear was therapeutic and freedom of choice boiled down to good behaviour or the river.

Often when the two of them passed the supply room she looked down at Max's shoes. After she warmed up to him she looked no lower than his knees, averting her eyes only far enough. The supply room door seemed anxiously related to her angle of vision—she looked down for guidance when they passed. Max often looked down as well, at his own blue-striped tennis socks, wondering what there was to see there. He had never seriously considered going into a storeroom. He suspected the nurses kept their coats in there.

Miss Upton often wanted Max to know something. That much even he could figure out. In the office or the consulting room she would be different—relaxed somehow, almost professional—and Max could talk. But on the ward he was hemmed in and protected by the rules. Within her territory he did not have to respond to her needs. He let them float by him, excusing himself with the thought that it must be tough for Marjorie Upton to orient new House Staff every now and again. They fly in and fly out, take over and before you know it, your ward is a mess and the House Staff are on to other duties, leaving you to clean it all up.

The previous House Staff, a landed immigrant from Guatemala, disappeared back to the jungle after his second week at Miss Marjorie Upton's. There were rumours of suicide and revenge, rumours that began with Miss Upton herself.

"House Staff is not cleaning staff," Max said, deflecting her glances. And once he even said, "I suspect brooms and cleansers are kept in that closet, Marjorie."

She frowned, making her scrotal face look much younger. Only later did Max learn that Nursing and Maintenance shared company in the hospital hierarchy. He had seen them on the huge cardboard triangle prominently displayed in the boardroom, slotted between Geriatric and Forensic. Miss Upton sat on committees and spent hours agonizing over that piece of cardboard and its curled edges.

At the time Max had no idea what it was all about and now that he knew, his interest had dissipated. This, he remembered, was their first fight. She set it up masterfully, dragging him right into it. He hadn't even noticed the storeroom until she brought it to his attention. She was very devious. He hated to think about what she really wanted from him.

Behind her back Max called her Miss Uppity like the rest of the House Staff because of the way she shook when you removed a chart from what she thought of as her box, because of the way she got worked up. It didn't matter if you were the head of psychiatry; it was *her* ward.

Rumour had it that Moussakanski had sanctified a connection with Uppity right there in the storeroom sometime after the war. Max was not certain, but he might have started that rumour on its rounds himself. More to the point, he suspected Marjorie had placed the thought into his subconscious when he wasn't paying attention. In the consulting room he had an impeccable memory, which he lost when he shut the door behind himself at the end of the day. But he was not overly troubled. If Marjorie placed a thought into him she would get it back at some point. When the time came it would bounce out of his head all by itself and smack her on the rebound.

When Max took the time to think about it, he had to admit to enjoying rumours. Max was from Vienna and his very own father had known Moussakanski in the Underground. This, he assumed, was true although he did not remember how he knew. Nevertheless, he was certain the two men had smoked a cigarette together in the Warsaw sewer and exchanged guns before the last Passover *seder*. He told many people, including Miss Uppity Upton, that the war accounted for Moussakanski's avoidance of the hospital tunnel system. In the dead of winter Moussakanski could be seen gliding swiftly across the white fields, the tails of his clinic jacket flapping and almost invisible against the snow, his pink ears pointing to heaven. Max's Vienna was near the Transylvania of Moussakanski's childhood, so Max understood bits and pieces of the older man's dialect, especially when Moussakanski swore under his breath at grand rounds or flew across the winter fields shouting orders to a half-frozen and distraught Miss Upton.

Moussakanski, Max was convinced, still fantasized about working for the intelligence service during the war. Then he was never afraid, only numbed, and there was no music in his mind, no music at all. No doubt his memory—grey, bleak and impersonal—was triggered by walking across the Experimental Farm in the fall, or by the sight of a woman pushing a stroller in the distance, or a family on bikes up ahead on the path. Moussakanski carried himself as if his feelings had not shifted since childhood. His view of the world had never wavered and his body had never failed him. He hardly noticed Miss Upton because he thought of her as an extension of himself. This was not a thought, and not, for that matter, a feeling. It represented the lack of awareness of any separation between himself and Marjorie Upton. She was just an electrical dysesthesia, an impulse creeping up and down his legs, a discharge from his own tissue running up and down his spine.

It was a godsend that the truly sick and dying were not admitted to the ward of Mengele, Marjorie and Max.

The environment was too controlled for effective intervention and natural movement resembling life on the outside was duly censored. You never knew how a medical unit worked until someone swallowed his tongue and turned blue. Only then did you find out the nurses were unavailable (charting between two and four), the electrical outlet required a fuse, the chest compression board had splinters and the green-eyed resuscitation cart grinning in a basement closet did not fit in the elevator.

All of Max's life people had been telling him what to do, so he was well seasoned to survive this posting. If Moussakanski told him to stick in a needle it would be part of his job description to stick in a needle, according to Marjorie. If he didn't, Moussakanski would stick the needle in Max.

Max did not relish the thought of blood gushing out. He had, let it be noted, an easier time hitting the unconscious than an inch-wide artery or vein. Each time he punctured a lumen, he doubted his belief in the circulatory system. The heart was the seat of the emotions, not a pump. It was easier to believe in neuronal circuits and transmission along membranes, things you couldn't see. He had educated himself extensively on the heart and his suspicions were well founded. Indeed, the heart was poorly designed. It could ship blood off to the whole body while spluttering and neglecting its own supply. It had to turn back over its own shoulder to get a breath now and then.

Yes, when you came to think of it, the heart was a bit like his own mother in that respect: overextended. She too had met Moussakanski in the Warsaw sewer, cowering in a ball behind the old man's shoulder, up to her knees in free-flowing shit. How they survived, you never asked. They survived and forever after you had to live with it.

Dear Dr Z,

Please pardon my concern, but you are not yourself. Bluntly put, your mind is somewhere else. I have noticed a gradual pulling away on your part. Your response time to my comments has lengthened noticeably and you seem to lose your train of thought, which is quite unusual for you. I can only come to the conclusion that you are not listening. If that were the end of it, I would simply tell you off and move on to a new therapist, if, in fact, I need one. I went looking for a reason to let you off the hook, but your excuses, for the first time in years, sound hollow. I do not believe you are preoccupied because your children are growing up or you are trying to sell your house. I do not believe you are busy with the onerous task of finding follow-up for your patients with your unavailable colleagues. I do not believe you are off somewhere calculating your finances for the move or strategizing your political beefs with the present regressive instalment of our political machine.

I have discussed this with my closest friends, all in therapy. One of them said my observations reminded him of a therapist of his who tried to integrate anaerobic exercises into his therapeutic postures. His body would be in the same position as always, but somehow poised differently. There was a certain distracted tension in the room until he stopped the ridiculous exercises and started going to the gym.

A different friend suggested the astounding possibility you might be ill. That friend had an experience years ago when his therapist became more and more remote, then sullen, then frankly obtuse. The explanation finally presented itself when the therapist was admitted to hospital and a locum took over.

A third friend, who admittedly has a limited flair for intuitive fantasy, thought you were having an affair. I had to laugh. We were getting quite far off track. These suggestions, more numerous and varied than I would like to admit, were farfetched and entertaining, and we had quite a lot of fun at your expense in the market mall while eating cinnamon buns and blowing smoky air back at the government workers.

The most abiding possibility—one I cannot refute—is that you have recently entered the ranks of the unfulfilled and are toiling in a clandestine fashion on a work of art you are uncomfortable to disclose to your friends, family or us. If this is in fact the case, I offer you my most sincere condolences. A close friend, who could not get off shift to join us for our discussion of your peccadilloes, is embroiled in a similar task that has led to his utter dissatisfaction with his tenured position, rebellion in all aspects of his personal life and avoidance of his most prized possession, us. When he does show up he is either preoccupied and remote or bores us with his latest obsessional chapter, each of which, truth be told, sounds very much like the last.

I hope that our form of doctor-bashing does not offend you. It was this final friend who made the most incisive comments and refuted our concerns. Therapy is all smoke and mirrors, he said. You can't make something up out of nothing. I hope he is wrong. He is, I must confess, my only friend who is in therapy when in crisis, is cured this week and ill the next, and who seems to forget what he has said Monday only to repeat it on Tuesday.

FROM COAST TO COAST: THE DEATH OF MY FATHER

The death of my father (anticipated, real or remembered) has the ability to provoke streams of creative energy in all three of us boys.

Case in point: the death of my father brought me home.

Six days before he died I flew west across the country to see him. His wife, a woman of dull countenance and predictable unreliability, made his sudden turn for the worse sound urgent but somehow trivial and inconsequential. I have an innate distrust of all members of my family, whether linked by genes or faulty choices, so I decided to come see for myself.

He was sitting at the kitchen table wearing pale blue pyjamas and sipping a glass of water. He was sipping in a way that I had never seen before, at the lip of the cup, as if learning to negotiate a new surface at the limit of his body.

He looked up and acknowledged me with a surprised kindness reminiscent of a long-forgotten time in his life. It was a kindness that was almost not his. His eyes were the only thing I recognized: vanquished, reconciled. He wasn't broken, just weakened by pain and reconciled to the end.

He stood up to find his glasses, then sat back down to look at pictures of the family: a celebration the previous fall, rites of passage from the last year or two. His reading glasses were on his forehead and he smiled knowingly when he found them there. It was a sneaky, it's-her-fault smile. Somehow she put them there and she was to blame.

Then he wanted to see the pictures and I saw his wife flinch in a gesture of protection, as if the photo album housed a secret weapon about to blow him up.

"Sure," he said. "I recognize these people."

He hardened at the sight of my eldest daughter, remembering how he'd threatened her from the depths of an alcoholic trance thirteen years before. The stiffening in him was very slight and he didn't say anything. He stiffened most at the pictures of her confirmation party. She was crying and he turned away.

How is your mother, he wanted to know. I told him, laughing, how the three of us, now in our thirties and forties, could still get her going.

He expressed no resentment toward anybody, only curious disbelief and protectiveness towards our mother, whom he had failed to shelter from our teenage energy decades before.

Three times he said, "I don't know what to say." Perhaps there was something he thought he should say but he didn't want to say it, an impulse toward something forgotten.

While I was there, an elderly couple from my childhood had driven up the coast for a final visit. The woman reclined in the kitchen and the man stood alone, bent like a crescent moon on the concrete patio, smoking. The woman was protective of my father because she remembered his childhood and his suffering at the hands of his father, my grandfather. What she said could not be heard by her husband, a man too emaciated from his own illnesses to swing a nine iron, but it was understood that he would disagree. Their balanced opinion hung in the air as if witnessing the family disjunction passing between them.

Later, this is how I told the story to my wife.

When I first saw my father from the hallway I couldn't speak. The man before me was very old and thin. His lips were drawn back over his teeth and he already looked like he had joined the dead. He was so thin he didn't look like anyone I knew.

I said that I was glad it was me and not her because she would have burst into tears.

I told her that I'd cried a bit, partly because of not recognizing my father and partly because I had stolen her moment, something she needed and wanted and couldn't have.

There is so little story that I have an impulse to tell it over and over again to drag it out.

Like the musical tribute for my father, one song sung together without accompaniment in his den would have been enough.

One song sung together would have been a sign of a better life.

This is what I told my brothers and mother later that night.

Saturday he slept too much and Sunday he was irritable. The bone pain was catching up to him, I gathered (my mother wanted to know). And he was likely getting ready for another patch of medication (my mother and brothers wanted the medical bits, words like fatigue and fentanyl).

I explained that my father's wife had increased the dosing schedule to make sure he was comfortable. No one else seemed to realize that this would cut down his remaining time, that this was the way he would die.

He was thirsty all of the time, I said, but could not explain what I had seen in the way he held his cup. Nobody could bear hearing about that level of weakness, not being able to hold a plastic cup to your lip.

More than that (I changed the topic) he was natural, himself.

When I said this my brothers looked right at me and my mother retreated to the kitchen to rinse dishes.

You could tell he was irritable with his wife, I said a couple of times, smiling a bit like him. All day his wife was loud and pushy. Check the fentanyl. Only she knew the correct dose and time. Check the drip. Change the IV bag. When she asked my father how to get to unit 121 (I don't know why she wanted to go there but it was "important" and "administrative" and "just couldn't wait"), he muttered a string of unrepeatable things. That was my father: spunky and aggressive, hissing until his last breath.

This is what I told my two brothers and my mother after she returned from the kitchen.

After a few hours sitting there my father and his second wife no longer knew how to keep me out of the conversation. Both their voices were stronger now. You could hear his wife from the next room as she rifled through supplies. He spoke back, expecting her to discern his every sound. My father's wife had concerns about his bed and diet, his diabetes and medication. The list went on and on. She wondered how long he should stay at home and questioned the reasons for his thirst, as if the doctor might have something to say about each and every query.

I could finally see that the details of their death dance had gone on for many months, a dance that clung to its own necessity. His death, their dance. My father didn't say anything. He knew the dance was beside the point, beside him. He sucked back his protein supplement, hissing it between his teeth. He was too weak to rip out the fluid-filled IV bag and throw it across the room.

When his wife went in search of unit 121, my father and I listened to a Sinatra tape.

The next time through the story, I told my youngest brother how my father gave me a watch to return to him. This occurred when my father's wife had gone in search of unit 121. Somehow the story of my father was over, but because none of us really accepted the story's end it had to go on.

The watch had been his or his father's, he wasn't sure. He'd clearly known before but was mixing himself up in his mind with his own father now that life was leaving him. He seemed to have melted into the memory of his father—that was the thing I wanted to say to my brothers. Or maybe the watch was just a watch that had once been his father's and had been handed down, only to be handed down again. Sometime before, my youngest brother hadn't known how to fix the watch so my father did it for him, or so my father said, but that wasn't exactly true either. My brother had returned it like someone rejecting bad love, and my father had contained the enmity, trapping it in a box of discarded objects.

In the same box was a brown lizard watchstrap. Judging from the price it had been sitting there for decades. The strap fit my watch and matched the style so I installed the band absentmindedly right then and there. It was a small thing but it pleased me to walk out with something that had sat in a box in his home for a few decades now scratching my wrist.

I told my brothers that I had said the usual things that felt important to say. I told them because they didn't really know what those things were. That we, especially my three girls, would miss him even though it was probably not true.

My father surprised me by saying he'd love to see my wife. I could tell by the way he said it that he thought she was around the corner somewhere, a distance that could be traversed at the drop of a hat under the right circumstances, a distance that would never be traversed again. I said maybe my wife and I would see his new wife, but not him. I said this slowly and he could see that it wasn't a chance thought.

He took my hand. He said that things hadn't exactly worked out well, but that they had worked out all the same.

I cried once when I first saw him and knew he was dying. And once again when the conversation was coming together, coming to an end. All the losses he had engineered over the years mingled with the possibility of comfort, vaguely remembered. I felt that powerful human urge to pull away from someone you love before the love or the person you love kills you, whichever comes first.

Crying, I suspect, has more to do with that temporary imbalance, of life remembered in more than one way. Crying is about remembering and forgetting, the friction of dissonant memories rubbing up against each other.

My middle brother said he would never have children. He was too much like my father and refused to pass on the trans-generational pain.

This is how I summed things up for them, the story as finally told.

By late afternoon my father had become progressively more irritable and hence completely recognizable—so much so that by the end of the visit I began to wonder if he really was sick and dying.

It was no coincidence that my brothers and I were soon equally irritable. When my middle brother and I bit into my mother's burgers, our methodical bites were broadcasting something my father would have done. By now our mother was avoiding us, puttering in the kitchen. That was one of the legacies of my father, the part of him we carried in us: mourning him by targeting her, mourning him by being him.

Then, six days later, he died. It was on a Saturday toward midnight. Exactly one month after the second Passover *seder*, on the 14th day of Iyar. If you missed the *seder* story first time around, this was the night to make it up.

Okay, my middle brother said. He was sick of the religious allusions. Our father died on Mother's Day and that's what he would remember. Two parents: forever together, forever apart.

In the future the three of us will call Mom up and go out to the cemetery, said my youngest brother.

Or hit some balls, said my middle brother.

For him.

With her.

My wife was very sad, and being far away on the other coast she was at her wit's end. My father loved her and only rejected her when he could see as far as he would ever see, to the end of what he had created.

And what about you, Dr Z? You have been out of the office for over a week. Your replacement is not available and your answering machine is full.

DR Z, BACK IN THE OFFICE AND LOOKING FOR MAX

Now that I am back in the office I am completely the boss.

For example, I have a cabinet full of personal items: light bulbs, bags of tea, cups with scuzz growing along the bottom and up the sides. Articles are piled in, one on top of the other. Packets of sugar. A sign that reads *Please Remove Overshoes* in black lettering on a gold background. Business cards scattered on top of three black coat hangers that used to hang as parallel treble clefs on hooks on the wall until the weight of winter coats ripped them out of the gyprock. I have a place in the cabinet to throw my shoes, next to the Dead Files. I do not like my patients to see my shoes. They are too revealing, too personal.

This morning I stooped to pick up a sunbeam. It was an accidental gesture. I don't know what I thought it was—a prescription slip or a receipt? All in all, it didn't belong there, on the grey all-purpose carpet.

The bright yellow wedge folded itself into the air and disappeared.

My patient, a balding man in his fifties, leaves. It is ten to the hour. I write my note chewing some fruit and a piece of cheese. I am always doing two or three things at once. I write my notes in such a way as to say very little but convey enough information, especially to myself. I am naturally suspicious and well defended. I do this without getting personal.

On the wall opposite my seat is an architectural study of a ball of flame. It is the only art in the room. The reds and yellows of the flame have smeared, losing definition and detail, fading with time. The study shifts progressively toward colour and away from formal structure. I placed each watercolour consecutively on the wall toward a corner, moving from sunlight to shade. This mutes their progressive intensity so no one is distracted or frightened.

Recently a colleague of mine asked me 545 calibrated yes–no questions and pronounced me the perfect psychopath.

It is difficult to explain what I do or why I do it. Even a complete recording with sound and light would be insufficient to convey what happens here. During the first meeting history is being rewritten, achieving a circularity. There is no rush to get it all down, only to keep it properly formed and rolling. Someone might say, "I am sick; heal me," a thousand times in a thousand ways. If the story stops it is my job to trick the teller into keeping it going. Listening becomes part of the story but my patients do not come here to listen to me. For that I have to resort to Max.

What would Max have to say about all this?

Max's father, the intellectual physician from the old country, has always stuck to the limits of consultation reports. This is both a conscious decision and a point of honour. For Max medicine is a family tradition, especially the part where one human being tries to influence another. Max's father is not a patient man. He believes in knowledge more than friendship or character. He does not know it, but this means he has given up on treatment. Once he has seen a pattern he hands the case over and is not interested in seeing it again.

Max's mentor Moussakanski, his father's friend, has solved the same dilemma with knives and formalin. When patients rewrite their stories for Moussakanski he calls them liars. He is disappointed by the inconsistencies in their lives. But you said! he often thinks, processing a contradiction and rubbing the weaker statement out. He has a recurring nightmare that his limbic pathways will derail, that his thoughts will shift to the wrong cerebral destination. Like a train shifting tracks, dismantling his inner grammar. He never thinks of the meaning of trains or who might have been on them.

In contrast to Moussakanski and Max's father, Max himself does not have a history. History is something that happened to his parents, not to him. History is what they have spent their lives protecting him from.

Max's body is part of this deception. He has always looked like an adult. In a snapshot taken beneath the Eiffel Tower at the age of six, he stands in shorts between his parents, holding them up. He has a face that can be trusted. At six it is already the face of a responsible professional. His parents stand firmly to his left and right, held together by the frozen love of their shared history.

A rhythmic series of clicks interrupts my thinking about Max. Someone is trying to get me on the phone.

I can tell the rhythm when they hang up and when they call right back.

I turn up the volume and jot down the name and number.

It is five to the hour so I know you are free. Please pick up.

I note the red happy-face on the receiver and the series of apple stickers, vernal green on white, trimmed in red, climbing up the black bookshelf frame.

Dr Z, where are you?

When my patients use the phone they see the stickers and look at me in a way that confirms their suspicions. I place responsibility for the stickers on a patient or I lie and blame a fictitious two-year-old child of mine, or my wife.

In the office I would like to be Max: unmarried with no children, unable to think of the hurdles to be jumped in that daredevil act that will make a prospective woman acceptable to patients and parents alike. I already have a wife from somewhere else and a mother who supports everything I do. Unlike Max, my parents are from here. Unlike Max, I have a poor ear for all those other languages, from up the river or down. Because I know so little it seems to me that regional allegiances have long since disappeared. Accents are unreliable and histories are no longer etched where they used to belong. When I throw up my hands my mind returns to the city. Indeed, the city remains sane when the weather intrudes. In broken trails and ploughed ice there is life of a sort. People get out in the air. Couples can be seen skating in unison at two in the morning, their faces covered by wool masks, their arms linked as snow removal machines whisk by with their blue lights rotating in the night air. Young men impress young women by skating backward in circles at incredible speeds, peeking behind themselves at provocative angles.

Patients complain to me about their sleeplessness. (My patients complain to Dr Z and Max's patients complain to him.) It astounds me that they complain, that they wish to blot out the imageries of their lives. They look at me puzzled and appalled when I show interest, that dreams might represent a link to the unknown world, that anxiety may guide the human body, that psychosis marks a distinctly human territory. All this censorship and restriction comes from the culture of the street, which is a place foreign to me. I would line up for therapy myself if I thought it would make me anxious, keep me up nights dreaming and push my bodily synchronicity off balance.

I am jealous of my patients' illnesses and it is part of my retribution that I should cure them of these ills.

I will try to explain the risks of my job. You may want to know if I have been mugged or beaten or if my patients follow me around and firebomb my house. I have heard of such events on the news and a friend of mine was assaulted at her hospital duties almost monthly, but rest assured, for me there is little risk. If patients have something nasty in mind they usually put the feeling into me in advance and I am forewarned. This way I remain safe while I rest comfortably on my backside.

And the real risk of staying put in this way? Blood stops moving in both your legs. You remain in place, glued to a chair, and your body turns to stone.

Late one afternoon I started to spin. For once this was not a transference feeling. I was spinning and time was doing something funny, speeding up and slowing down like in the cartoons. I can't possibly drive out of here, I thought, shaking violently. I had to ask a patient to call the hospital and transport me to Emergency. "Please," I said. "I am spinning. I am ill. It is not you. *It is not you.*"

It was twenty below outside but I rolled down the window and opened the neck of my shirt, and by the time the car pulled up to the hospital my temperature had dropped to a hundred and four. I sat and looked at the clock and it stayed five o'clock for quite some time. The hands of the clock—even the second hand—seemed to be steadily moving but maintaining an identical position over time.

In the emergency department I could feel the area of consolidation in my chest. I could put my finger on it, exactly. "It's right here," I said to the emergency physician, pointing. And there it was on the x-ray: white like packed snow, surrounded by fluff. "I've been breathing bad air," I said with a conspiratorial look, as if providing classified information.

I had been carrying the bug for months, waking in the middle of the night after discussions with the family dead. I was holding on to the appearance of the fatigued near-well when the venom poured into my blood and suddenly I was sick.

After the pneumonia came and went I knocked a bigger hole in the wall of my office and installed a fan. I started leaving the window open half the day.

What kind of doctor am I, my mother often wants to know. And the answer is, a doctor who, once well, feels bereaved of his symptoms.

Dear Dr Z,

I was sitting around reminiscing with my partner and we both remembered the time you told me you were "spinning around." At the time I thought you were making one of your important, incisive comments into my behaviour before I realized that for once you were talking about yourself. You may remember that I didn't quite believe you, even after you tried to punch in the phone number of your doctor. Your hands were shaking so badly that your fingers flapped unsuccessfully and arbitrarily against the plastic keyboard with a series of harsh clicks. You had a funny look on your face, as if you were too happy or stoned and I suspect that is what delirium is all about. You said, "Don't be frightened. I cannot do our session because I am delirious. Do you mind driving me to the hospital?" There was a curious release to your behaviour that seemed to sever you from your usual responsibilities, which turned out to be true.

The following week, when your colour had returned and you were back at work, I ran into another patient of yours who had seen you at that vulnerable moment in the emergency department. She reported that your hair had been awash with sweat, your white shirt was open to the navel and your tie, still around your neck, was flipped over your shoulder. Like a fool, she told me, she had commented on how normal you looked, undoubtedly to soothe your embarrassment and deny your obvious disarray. It is a great threat to see your therapist in public behaving in a manner reserved for the back wards or the movies. She finally realized (you may have forgotten) that you were trying to magically check into the hospital by inputting the correct PIN number at the bank machine. She removed your card from the Interac slot, ensured it was replaced safely in your wallet, and walked you to the triage desk in the department. I was told you thanked her like a polite demented fool.

This event has been repeated around town and has become embellished to the extent that if it gets back to you, you will not recognize anything of yourself and will take it to be an urban myth.

Please accept this gift for your departure: a picture of your febrile unimpeded self that has been making the rounds.

Best wishes in your new locale.

Dear Dr Z,

Now that I have settled down I can respond to the events of the last few weeks. I am sure you can believe what I have been through because you have been through it with others in the past. The most amazing thing to me is how my feelings about you have been transformed as the events unfolded. In the past you were both demon and saviour all wrapped up into one. Now you are taking on the qualities of a normal human being by simply moving away so I am ready to tell you this story.

When I was in the emergency department without any clothes, despite what the police and my father said, I was not causing anyone any harm. I know I must have looked more than a little odd, peeking into all those houses and discussing topics even I cannot remember with that housewife in the pink nightdress. Her door was open and in my state I took that as an invitation. To conversation, that is. I went in and sat down on her sofa and we began to speak. I was certain I knew her from somewhere. Perhaps she was the mother of one of my friends or a teacher's assistant from a college tutorial. She had a protective air about her, a bit aloof but caring, and initially I felt betrayed when the police arrived, especially when she did not bother to attend in the ambulance. Had she come with me to the hospital I don't think I would have struck out quite so violently. Those straps I put on (willingly for the most part) reminded me of period movies—Mozart's tormentor in an asylum, and the piano player on stage with the nasty father watching him fragment at the keyboard.

There was a nurse in the emergency department, Gail I think her name was, or Gloria perhaps, that I smacked on the leg. I saw her limp off during one of the codes. I thought at the time she was the rebellious daughter of the woman in the pink nightdress who had come to take me away. When you are in the state I was in, thoughts transform so quickly they have no time to solidify. Before you know it they have shifted into something else. At first I thought the nurse knew my sister. Then I thought she was an agent of the police. Then I had a flash that her smile was like that frightened woman in pink's, only different. And then, as quickly as I had kicked her in the leg, I felt guilty. The entire hospital experience was surprisingly like reliving my life in a jumble all at once. For that, and for imposing some sort of safety, I thank you.

Even as I resisted I thought an inside demon was acting against me with superhuman strength while my real self tried as best it could to hang on to a shred of decorum and reality. You said something repeatedly, and the words, I must admit, were meaningless. But your tone won me over: that sonorous voice where you erase yourself until nothing but the directive is left. More than anything it was that self-less tone that convinced me to put on the straps, to take the medicine and to stay in hospital until I got better. I was grateful to be in restraints with the broad leather digging into the skin of my wrists and ankles.

I thought you exorcized that demon, but truth be told the demon was back before you even left the room and went to the nursing station to write your infamous orders. My thoughts were racing so quickly there was a wonderful energy to them, and it felt like being at the Olympics as a contender in some speedy event like the giant slalom or the skeleton where you tumble head first and freely as fast as humanly possible and all of the worlds you know zip by you like pure wind.

It is an amazing state to be in, that haze of energy, and it draws you in like the vortex of a whirlpool. I gave it up only reluctantly this time. Despite what the experts say, there is always a choice to be made whether to come back or not. A woman in the next room made the opposite decision ten or fifteen years ago. When you are ill like me you understand these things. She became ill when she was my age and tried to kill her baby boy. The child, which she only ever mentioned elliptically in her quiet raving, went on to live a new life in a safe environment somewhere else and his mother knew nothing about it. This woman did not require the doses of medication I required or the level of concern or the protective comfort of those restraining straps. She had stabilized in that horrible place and decided never to return. She will wander forever because she cannot speak of what happened, because she no longer knows that once she was back there, alive.

As for me, I'm sure you can tell I remain somewhat ill. There are moments when I still think I am Houdini, John Lennon and the Prime Minister wrapped up in one. Thankfully these moments do not last and I have come to see them as thoughts splintered off from my feelings. There is a laziness to psychosis, a soft spot where you don't have to explain how you feel: whether you are trapped in little boxes and angry at medical staff or haunted by your own image wielding a gun, or plagued by ideas that could enable you to shake up the country from the top down.

So for now I will take my lithium and my epival and my haldol and my cogentin and my lorazepam (did you know that the average bipolar worth his salt is on four and a half different medicines at any given time?) and I will get my blood drawn without delaying too long. I will go to that group for the medicated restless who need to learn how to sit still and plan their lives or else no one will ever really fall in love with them. And I will show up to my appointments and try to make my physicians happy with me along with my mother and my brother and my sister who have been heartbroken but are coming around slowly as I improve.

Please understand that it is difficult to resist the flight to a land where thoughts themselves are whirring about restlessly and generating more of the same. It is a wonderful place and I have no trouble understanding why god stuck that predisposition into some of our little genes, as you like to say. I only wish you could have taped the entire month, especially the things I thought but didn't say. I am sure it would fill a thousand pages and make as much sense to me sane and sober as it did to me then.

P.S. My counsellor is totally freaked out by what happened. She has never heard of anything like it before, has no clear ideas about medicines and thinks it is best that I put the whole event behind me. I tried to set her straight and intend to write about my experiences in Intro to Creative Writing.

P.P.S. I met your successor in the OPD or the POD or whatever that place you used to have your office is called, and I am entranced. She may not be as smart as you, but she is young, cute, less defended, watches more television, follows hockey, and best of all, is forgiving when it comes to her medical expectations so I will be able to negotiate the freedom of my doses as I please.

THEN: SAYING GOODBYE TO VIC, WHO WHISTLES OUT OF HIS GOOD EAR

The house is emptying out. Blank walls everywhere. Bits of blistered white paint on the navy blue of my youngest daughter's starless sky. Scrapes and gouges in the hall from the couch that would not fit onto the landing.

The person my patients call Dr Z wonders, How did we get the couch in here in the first place? How did we negotiate that impossible corner? I must have taken it apart somehow but it seems impossible to transform it into smaller bits.

The flagstones are cracking away from the foundation again. Benches and shelves, walls and floors are empty, returned to their flat potential. The Jerusalem artichokes are running wild, their runners penetrating the grass. The dogwood obscures the front window. Even the peonies are dead, their exuberant heads bent over in wet clumps, lying neglected and rotting. The whitewash on the south face is peeling in great winged arcs onto the pavement. Bags of garbage extend around corners, blocking doorways. Sprawling leftovers cover all available surfaces with the penetrating grease of Chinese food and pizza.

The children are loose-minded and distracted. The eldest is flippant; she is buzzing inside and does not seem to notice much of the world. My middle daughter is pulling away, hanging out with her neighbourhood friends "one last time, Dad," and talking on the phone late into the night. My youngest daughter is procrastinating more. She cannot seem to get started.

All three admit they will miss their friends but the urgency has gone out of their voices. They argue light-heartedly about our new address and ridicule me when I cannot remember the street number. There is an A at the end which I tend to forget but they remind me, "A, Dad, don't forget the A. Without the A, Dad, all the mail goes to the wrong place. Our friends will never find us." The A makes the new destination a little special.

I find the postal code tricky. I cannot recite the address without hesitating and the children laugh again. It has helped them adapt in advance, knowing they have a location in the new place, a place they have never seen. They have discussed bedroom choices, decorating, how to get to the shopping malls. They are way ahead of me.

When I go to say good-bye to my neighbour Vic he tells me about his ear.

Vic had been playing on his computer and suddenly realized that he could whistle out of the *good* one.

"It is a long story," he tells me, sighing.

It was not a long story, I could tell. It was just a story he wanted me to remember forever.

Apparently those who know Vic know that he has one good ear and one bad one. He had just come back from the emergency department, where he convinced them that his good ear's drum was perforated. How did he know? When he cocked his head to the side he could hear the wind zipping through, from one side of his head to the other.

Now I can whistle out of my good ear, he says.

Good-bye, whistling Vic.

THEN: THE SUICIDE AND THE GUN

One of the first things that evolved when I arrived out east was the insidious process of becoming Dr Z. I myself am innocent. The name was initiated by all those government workers looking for a quick pension.

I'm anxious, Dr Z. I can't possibly go into the office. Ever again.

It took months before I noticed the patterns in people's movements, years before I understood the word "catholic."

I, the Dr Z they didn't know, come from out west. That is the way I have come to think of it: "out west," a place cut off by mountains and political extremes, where the horizon draws your vision higher and your own judgment about the weather is more accurate than what you hear in the daily news.

It took me years to develop a respect for the local environment here. I need the radio to keep me informed; the morning sun's deceptive warmth brilliantly reflecting from the snow is not to be trusted. Someone told me the outdoor ice will soon be ready and I should prepare to dust off my skates. To welcome these thoughts may imply I am no longer a tourist but I am not so sure. I register the signs unconsciously—the shifting water level below the locks in late fall, the shacks on the forming ice—but I am not reassured.

The monotony is similar in the office: the predictable patterns of the traffic below the window, the hookers across the street, the repetitive beep-beep-beep of furniture trucks moving backward, the flow of garbage, drugs and cops through the laneway opposite. People move in and out of the alley furtively, glancing back but feigning nonchalance. I have seen sofas dumped over the wobbly second-storey railings, women slugged behind the huge blue waste bins, needles thrown casually over shoulders and scuffed into the dust.

With my patients I look and am not seen. I am an excellent mirror, lacking in substance. When my patients ask me about my role I speak vaguely in the second person. "The most useful tool in the business is your own personality," I say. They do not know if I am speaking of myself or them, whether I am serious or not.

The discrepancy in their awareness is what they call Dr Z.

Dr Z is a person attenuated down to a procedure. This they know and accept. It is what they want and provides them with a certain immunity. Eventually they come to own my space. Dr Z gets one letter, not a full name. He is an afterthought at the end of the alphabet, a partial person; his space does not belong to him. My patients are disturbed when I move the furniture or adjust the blinds, threatening to be more than just Dr Z. They are insulted if they notice my art or my computer for the first time, as if I have snuck into the office in the middle of the night with a whole bundle of letters and let them loose to disturb their dreams. They are concerned when articles vanish and they are protective when the dust piles up or the paint peels away. They watch me as if I am a windup toy or a barely tolerated pet in their living rooms. This is a place for them and they want it to remain intact and particular, as intact as the womb. My every act is observed: my clothes, my books, the pattern of dust on the shades and lights, the angle of the tissue box and the digital clock on the black end table.

I have been known to say, "If you see me in the street you may be surprised." They recognize me well enough but my height is wrong—I am too tall or too short and the angle of my back is incorrect. In the street I will look off to the side and they will turn away.

I twist the key in the lock, flip on the lights and the electric baseboard heaters (it is twenty-four below outside) and open my daybook. At these moments I yearn for the old image of the doctor, for the power of godly healing that leaves the practitioner intact. I think of quitting my job and going into practice in the north. I imagine that in the north there is less calibrated time and I would have to keep moving to stay warm, to remain myself. This thought is a gesture of false modesty and hopeful escape. I know the north is something to read and dream about, not a real place.

Perhaps if it is twenty-four below outside, I am already in the north.

I took this office because of the bay window and the neighbouring brick wall that draws attention to the street. The line of bricks points to the lane where the cops park and the prostitutes stand and the cook at the corner restaurant leans against the wall and smokes on break five or six times a day. I sit there and feel the building shift its weight. I recognize patients coming up the stairs by the way they hesitate in the outer hall. I have become a part of the building; I hear things they do not hear and know things they do not know.

I turn on my answering machine and retrieve messages: *Dr Z this, Dr Z that.* My voice on the outgoing message is calm and deliberate. The tone is so surprising and unnatural on playback that I have stopped calling in for messages on the weekends. I have been known to swear into my own tape machine from coffee shops and cell phones, breathing in a hostile parental tone, "This is yours truly Friday night at six-fifteen and I am hanging from the inter-provincial bridge by my fingertips. By the time you hear this I will be pure ice." When retrieved, such self-directed messages wake me out of my routine morning stupor and remind me of what is generally missing here—myself.

Now that I am leaving, I look around the office at the small signs of neglect: dust on the vines, a screw loosening on the chair, newspapers piled semi-neatly in a corner, a half-dead violet with withered leaves that no longer knows how to sway gracefully toward the sun. There is something too artificial in the balance of continuity and change that suggests I may leave but will return, I may cut my hair but it will re-grow, I might read new books and shift my terminology but not significantly, I might be different but I will remain the same.

A wonderful pattern of light and shadow penetrates the slats in the blinds and spreads across the chairs and books and plants onto the faintly orange-freckled plaster. I have achieved a state of perfect arrogance. The goal is to be like god: to change only enough to remain camouflaged.

There is danger in this room. A suicide once occurred here on a weekend, sometime between Friday afternoon at five and Monday morning at five to nine. In fact, many patients warned me. They sensed the danger but I shrugged it off. My plants were making them crazy. That's what they said but I didn't believe them. "Your plants are making me crazy, Doc. That one in particular." It was my *Dieffenbachia*, with its wild, vine-like stems clawing their way over the edge of the pot and across the floor in a wide circular arc, toward the sun. "Those leaves are reaching out, Doc. You had better listen. I can hardly stand it. If you don't pay attention someone is going to get hurt."

I opened the door at five to nine and immediately noted that something was seriously amiss. The patient's chair had been toppled into the middle of the room and the light was too harsh. The blinds had been pulled off their hooks and lay in a bundled mess on the floor. The main trunk of the *Dieffenbachia* had been broken at the base, where it crossed the edge of the pot. The long, thick stem lay rotting on the floor, the leaves already withered and yellow and the sick smell of decay in the air.

When I am asked about suicide I tell the story of the plant. The tip of the branch, placed in water for a month, eventually grew new roots. As it grew into its new life, I learned to listen a little better.

When I am asked about violence I tell the story of the gun.

I have told this story many times and cannot trace its lineage. More than one patient has appropriated it as their own, as if it had happened to them and not to Dr Z, as if my thoughts were theirs.

The story begins with me standing outside my office building across the street from the cook who is leaning into the wall, smoking. He is on one side of the traffic and I am on the other. His head is always visible to me but his body moves in and out of focus as the vehicles swish by.

I am at a slight angle, my left foot crossed over my right, and my right shoulder leans back into the bricks. I sip

my instant coffee and register the flow of late afternoon traffic.
I know this is my story and nobody else's because I have done
this a thousand times over the years, stood here in exactly this
posture for a few minutes between patients. I usually go down
the back stairs after somebody leaves and climb back up a
minute or two before the next patient arrives. All in all, this is a
personal event and I do not appreciate intrusions.

    The traffic is different at street level: immediate and
noisy and full of waves of salty dirt. Late in the afternoon,
colours are deeper and lines lengthen as the sun disappears.
The transformation to night is delayed at street level because of
the brick wall behind me, which fails to block the setting sun.
The air is cool and breezy and the light is harsh.

    Looking down, I see that my shoelaces are frayed. I
notice them, knowing it will be months before I buy a new pair.
I will buy a pair precisely when I expect my patients intend to
comment on them, long after they have noticed.

    The traffic congests and frees up, congests and frees up.
The cook has flicked his cigarette into the gutter and gone back
to work. On the third set of lights I find myself watching two
nervous women in the front seat of a grey compact. The driver
has her eyes riveted on the car in front of her. The passenger
is turning to her anxiously, but her hands are held in her lap,
perfectly still. The man in the back is dark and attractive, and is
gently moving a gun back and forth between the two women. I
know it is a gun more by the posture of the women than by the
form of the black metal. The movement of his arm is precisely
sexual, with a slow rhythm that I can readily see. His posture is
natural and relaxed.

    When he sees me watching he swings the gun and
points it at my face. To be exact, he points the gun at my eyes,

waving it gently. For a moment my eyes have become the two women—right and left, back and forth. There is only a thin pane of glass and a small stretch of space between us.

Nothing changes for three seconds. I do not feel anger or fear. This I know: it is the women he wants, not me. I am only a witness, a part of him watching. When the light changes, the car shifts into gear and the gun returns to its original mark.

I have achieved a level of being that is safe and balanced. Despite this I am irritated by the episode. The few moments between sessions have been turned into therapy with a stranger.

MAX AND ALIX

Miss Upton clears her throat.

"You weren't listening." Her voice has gone soft. "I was telling you about the orders."

The day nurses are coming out of Report and a group of patients is coagulating at the desk. An elderly man with a psychiatric shuffle wants his wife. The woman has been dead for twenty years, Miss Upton whispers. (That is her favourite number, twenty, meaning forever or before Max was a grownup. Or worse, before he was born.)

Miss Upton says her patient is demented. She does not know why Moussakanski accepts people like him—too old to hit the toilet, no home to go to. She will have to organize papers for placement.

"Can't keep him on the floor forever," she says in a reverie, oblivious to her surroundings. She is certainly not running a babysitting service, she lets Max know.

Dementing patients provide her with great pleasure. "Go smell the old guy's room," she taunts. "Can't keep him around here stinking things up at the taxpayers' expense."

Max gets the message: Uppity Upton wants to discharge the guy into the river, more or less. Then fumigate his room and start all over again.

"You write the order and I'll sign it," says Max.

He does not know this man, has never met him, has never seen the chart. Every day is his first day on the job, it seems.

Miss Upton continues to inspire a calculated belligerence in him. She takes him by the wrist to get a good whiff of the old man's room, as if he doubted her clinical judgment. She casts him a look of complicity, then catches the inside of her thigh on the edge of the nursing station counter. The wood corner scratches her thigh, tearing cloth. Max's estimation of her inflates when she hisses under her breath, "Suck a duck." Her scrotal face pulls back smoothly, as if ready to spit out all of its teeth and collapse into a black hole.

The fat lady in the locating box at Switchboard is the first to figure out that Dr Alix Tuttle loves Dr Max Kuhn.

In motion, Alix's face is hardly recognizable from the mug shot in the dean's office. There, her face is plain with small northern craters. Up close one notices holes and pits from the cold. It is a face best kept in motion and Alix knows how to do this. She knows how to highlight her looks with dark dresses and her expertise in depression. Her clothes suggest Moscow, Budapest and Max's black-and-white Vienna.

How Max arrived in Vienna after the war she's never found out, but his accent—a trace of the old country—can somehow put Alix in situ, with her three-quarter-length dresses, her right sleeve ending just above a patch of discoloured skin. The skin is thick, raised and scaly, the splotch more discrete than eczema and more sinister than psoriasis.

Max speaks of her on those long nights at nursing stations, his beeper always about to go off. There are attentive nurses nearby. The beeper presses him against time and into their orbit. He speaks of lupus, immune deficiency, death. One of his patients, an old Italian man, is bleeding again. Painlessly the stinking black stuff oozes out. Years ago Max loved a girl with that colour hair: black, faintly purple. He is no longer interested in blood. He has seen it in too many places and it has become impersonal.

To the nurses he says it is difficult to watch old guys bleed out without conversation.

"Expect a stinking end," Max whispers. "A *myeskeite-sof.*"

Without warning it has come to this. Let your patients bleed out pale into a bucket. Let them empty themselves into the bedsheets despite someone else's blood dripping into a limp arm so slow you have to imagine the thick red globules breaking and reforming. Conversation with the nurses takes him well into the night.

Alix has given him a book of stories to read. Stories from what she suspects is his background. His hands rummage deep in his white pockets.

If Alix wants to marry him why doesn't she just spit it out?

When Alix leaves to attend the Vienna conference he accompanies her in fantasy. They meet in an open market and go for coffee. This is their final parting. The maneuver has been rehearsed in three languages and can be executed only here. It is not correct for the downtown mall or while eating hot *frites* on your haunches over concrete, salty vinegar stinging your fingers and tongue.

She remains seated. A fullness in her eyes keeps him looking at them, a fullness he is familiar with. Her eyes fill up while his peel away her layers through dark silk to those amphibious scales, to the wet flesh fashioned from lonely nights waiting for people to die. She crosses her black-stockinged legs. A thick novel sits flat beside her right hip and her lips tremble purposefully. She has learned to wait, how to speak with her body. "You must push through this thick, sludgy novel before you can push through me," she seems to say. The procedure requires study of all of Volume One. She luxuriates in it, moving black silk up and down her arm. Shades of grey in the street reflect her mood. Here they do with clothes and the street what she does with her emotions. She knows this from shopkeepers in Budapest and Prague.

Max remains inert, standing straight up on his stubby legs. "Things haven't changed much," he says, looking around. They are alone in the restaurant. His legs are too short for his body but they get him safely about. The city is in his blood, right down to his feet and toes. As far as Alix is concerned, Max can trundle off to dinner with his parents and whatever vestiges of the Austro-Hungarian Empire they can drum up. She wants to lose herself in old Vienna with all those burnt books and black memories. She wants to be the famous doctor's spurned woman, the woman of his very last days. She knows about this kind of violence from her studies at the institute. She wants to set that noose around her neck, to fire the metal slug into her own head. She half-loathes, half-reveres Max, having caught him reading a novel by Zweig in the first week of his clerkship. It was a piece of old Vienna tucked deep into his white coat with his hammers, forks and lights; his elastics, tongue depressors and lists of telephone locals; his neurological gadgetry and the numbers of nurses he never called. (If the nurses thought he might call, they were more likely to process his orders. In the name of science and patient care Max wrote Mabel, Melinda and Muriel in his little black book.) For two weeks Mabel, Melinda and Muriel nuzzled up to Stefan Zweig. It is no surprise that Alix has fallen for him, stubby legs and all. She wants impossible things, starting with the bones of Freud and the sombre childhood of more than one of the master's female admirers.

Max imagines this encounter halfway around the world. He is on call, pilfering pages of prose, trying to avoid the wedding proposal. He steals paragraphs between schizophrenics, depressives, phone orders and taxi slips. The night nurse has turfed the final derelict of the evening back to the gutter. To this Max turns a deaf ear. The night nurse, a burly man with an impossible slur to his speech, has been shot at in his day. He has frisked knives away from aggressive women and derived no pleasure from it. Max knows who the boss is and it is not *him*.

At five in the morning Max goes to sleep. The clear prose of the book he is reading, the book she has given him, marches on. Here Max is safe. He knows these market people with their faith and foreign languages. A mother laughs with her lower-town cronies, all established west-enders now. A *zeydeh* cajoles his nag, sells rags, rages at god.

In sleep he returns from Vienna sporting gifts and anecdotes. He has developed new insights into the jaw jerk. On the plane he sees his own homecoming: the hills, the town, the loons of the nearby lakes. He sees snow and dead sumac and finally the pathetic tulips: spiny in block colours before their heads are chopped off.

He wakes up in a sweat, trying to bring her picture into focus. He is always trying to bring something of hers into focus. He thinks of returning the book she has given him. He suspects her skin condition represents the onset of a disease, something nasty and emotional. He cannot discount the usual clues, beginning with her personality, followed by her rash and obsessive avoidance of the sun. Max pulls his reflex hammer out of his pocket and swings it in the dark. He is sleeping upright, fully dressed, ready to pounce into clinical action. One day at the beach and she is corrugated like an iguana, he thinks, and goes back to sleep.

The next morning Moussakanski can be seen smoking inside his office. Max stands outside and twists his tools like a full-fledged specialist. Moussakanski understands this and displays a father's pride. If you carry a reflex hammer on to Moussakanski's ward, you are sure to receive a warm welcome. If you mention the words "tumour" and "thyroid," the heavens open their mighty arms and welcome you in. A quote from Harrison's *Textbook of Medicine* is a ticket to the throne of glory.

Max removes the hammer from his pocket and says, "That mean Alix Tuttle," out of the side of his mouth. "She is a prickly one," he says, meaning her skin. "Like an artichoke," he says, as if he has touched her. Max thinks he is the first person in the world to compare a woman to this particular vegetable. He likes to joke that there is no time for love even though he knows that love requires no time at all.

Whenever he thinks of graduating he is reminded of his perpetually adolescent state and banishes the thought from his mind. Being from Vienna, a single specialty is not enough. His mother hardly turns her head at his achievements. She is the real reason he will not touch the likes of Dr Alix Tuttle.

He couldn't bring Dr Tuttle home without Mama whispering (in two or three foreign languages) into her soup and

Dr Kuhn the elder engaging in an erudite pre-war diagnosis of her skin condition. "Neurodermatitis," he would say, meaning sexual feelings squished out the pores of the skin. There is no point in arguing with any of this. It is impossible to turn the clocks forward from the war. Mrs. Kuhn makes the soup and everybody else must eat. She is what is now called a survivor and because survivors once starved everybody else must eat on command. When her legs become swollen each spring from the heat, she dreams about sewers, tunnels and mouldy bread. When she is ill, doctors are suddenly *naars* and "full of *drek*, may they lie in the earth and shit in the sea." The curse includes her son Max, a blight on his lazy intellectual head. There was a great uncle Fred (Friedrich) who worked in von Jauregg's clinic and an aunt who had suffered a brief analysis with Freud himself, for all the good it did her.

Max and Moussakanski spend the day getting on splendidly. The alliance is ratified during rounds when Miss Upton says, "Castor oil, three tablespoons," for the third time and Max replies, "Stop that, Nurse." Moussakanski thinks the young stubby-legged doctor has said *"shtup"* and experiences a pleasurable flashback to a young-skinned Uppity amid the rags and brooms.

ALIX AND MAX

In the spring they sit out front and share clinical vignettes like war veterans. Max lives here in the medical residence; Alix has moved on to a two-bedroom suite in town with hardwood floors and stained-glass windows. She takes short walks around the corner to outdoor restaurants and secondhand bookstores, and dreams of New York.

Max stays put. There is security here. It is as if he has never left home and never intends to leave.

Alix is giving up on him. Her last boyfriend swallowed pills after she pushed him into a heavy discussion. She is wary. For her it is happening again.

Max loves to talk senselessly. He shifts the story this way and that. He does not know how to slip in the commas, paragraphs and page breaks. He speaks with his body and his hands. He remembers useless detail. He never stops.

Listening to Max, Alix becomes unsure of her own voice, when it is hers and when she has stolen it from him.

They sit on the concrete steps in the spring sun. The glare is in their eyes. Women with great round bellies perambulate by on their way to the clinic. They waddle tipped back on their heels like enormous ducks. Behind them an old man with no lower jaw drags his left leg down the sidewalk.

Alix sees the big things: the buses and cars, the flock of schoolchildren, the slabs of concrete buildings before them. How can Max live this way, at the hospital? How can he see his patients playing outside *his* window, sitting in *his* picnic area, sliding down *his* play-structure?

She cannot ruffle him. She cannot cast him down and pull him up. Despite this, she covets his powers of observation. She knows that she sees straight while Max, believing in the interchangeability of light and space, can see around corners.

The sun disappears behind a cloud and Alix begins to complain. The House Staff do not like her call schedule. The boss, Dr Moussakanski, had placed his hand on her thigh. Moussakanski said something she couldn't remember but it wasn't good, she emphasized to Max. Even the thigh might have been a trick of memory, an extension of her feeling small. Moussakanski, himself slim and of average height, had peered down her body at her pencil scratches outlining next month's work. There are too many restrictions and limits, she told him, but she did not know how to put down her foot. One of the jews would not work Saturdays. The catholics were boycotting Sundays in return. When she gets into these binds she counts on Max to bail her out.

Max has nothing to say. He cannot help her. A mnemonic from Hebrew school enters his mind unbidden: "*Who* is the word for he and *he* is the word for she and *Doug*, well, *Doug* is the word for fish." The rhyme runs through his mind again, *Who is he and he is she and Doug is fish*. He knows that he knows nothing and she knows even less. He bites his tongue.

Alix shifts the conversation to safer ground. One of their lost classmates has curled her hair, bought a van and found a man (a likable man at that), all within a month of receiving her medical license. "Is this security," Alix asks rhetorically, "Or the result of instantaneous wealth?" There were stories of bank managers falling to their knees before interns, advancing them huge lines of credit secured against their education and good characters.

Max sits and thinks medicine. He always thinks medicine. He wants medicine to expand and include the entire world. He can walk into any hospital anywhere and take control on the spot but that is not enough for him. He tells Alix that the nurses who drink coffee with him are remote, servile, even critical before they drag him off to abandoned closets in the middle of the night. Or try to. Does Alix understand the loneliness in that, how he is drawn close to them by a similar dread and their collective inability to master it?

"Stop it," Alix says. "It's our day off. Let's talk about something else. Booze. Money. The movies. Anything."

"Shopping," he says.

Max does not continue. In his opinion there is no such thing as a day off. He is tuning up his bicycle while she looks on. This is his answer to her: spanners, vise-grips and penetrating oil. She can hear it if she wants.

The snow is finally gone and he is off to see the canal sludge pumped to its summer level. When he thinks of the city he thinks of a lump of earth. Lifeless. Flat. The ripples in the terrain are too gentle; there is no tide and little wind. But the weather seems to require a ritual celebration. For this reason he takes out his bicycle in summer and skis in winter, something he would never do in his own city.

Alix is not pleased with the bicycle, *his* bicycle. The tires are bald and the back wheel is short on spokes. The derailleur cable is wrapped around the central bar with clear corrugated half-inch tape he has lifted from the intensive care unit. It is the kind of tape used to attach limp intravenous lines to paper-thin skin. Alix is amazed that Max returns from his outings unscathed and that his patients do not die.

Max rides the bike path. An edge of irritation trails behind his left ear. Alix sits there at rounds, doubting his clinical skill. Behind his left ear. She chews the ends of her pencils and riffles the upper right corners of her charts. He has come to view these nervous gestures as intended for him.

Max crosses the canal at the locks—where he has seen the bloated bodies of dead students pulled up in the spring and fall, where joggers whiz by at the end of their runs, where grey-bearded professors hold in their bellies as their pink faces rise up into their eyes—and realizes that Alix is not there.

Below the falls the air is suddenly cold. Swaths of granular snow block his way. The fender rattles; the frame creaks. The bike jumps out from under him at odd angles. Red-winged blackbirds swoop down on his head. They flap aggressively at his moving mop of hair. Furry rodents trained by human garbage duck out of sight in the rocky slope. The swans are back from their winter sleep under protective cover.

He cannot discern the sounds of the train within the rush of white water but he knows it is there, can feel the rumble up through the tires.

He sees a couple crossing the train overpass, two specks on the horizon between the trees. The ice is breaking up. Huge slabs drift and crash between the bridge pylons.

Max says to himself, "Tell me, Doc. How can I do what those lovers are doing? How can I bring all this dreaded observation to a halt?"

His thoughts are submerged beneath the sound of the rushing water and the train looping the university car-park. He stops and leans the bicycle against a pylon. The couple on the overpass has disappeared. He hears their voices above him and tries not to think of them but is compelled to ask, Where was he at their age? Composing, drawing, memorizing one-act plays? Eavesdropping behind the doors of famous musicians? Practicing scales on three instruments? Busy proving the impossibility of a divided life? Something in him has not learned a thing. Even now, rotations in different medical disciplines echo those incomplete efforts: reading x-ray films, working Emerg, consulting the specialty floors and operating room, managing the Arrest Team.

He tests the icy water with one hand. This is what he wants from Moussakanski: the ability to move forward with fanciful audacity, the clarity of cutting through brain.

Max is jealous of his patients' illnesses and their explosions of flamboyant symptomatology. He remembers a woman he calls the Romanian flute player. She had more symptoms than Harrison's *Textbook of Medicine*. She was healthy, slim and tanned, perhaps twenty-six or twenty-seven years old, and flipped complaints at him randomly, implicating every system in her body. She was one step ahead of him at all times. If he seemed to catch up she moved ahead to the next incomprehensibility. Max could only observe the litany of biological breakdown between her curved nose and slender fingers. He was forced despite himself and at her urging to explore her body, from her long smooth neck to the nodes in her thighs. But even this was not real to him. He was a puppet to her unstated need to be examined, to be touched by cold metal. "Warm up your instrument, Doctor," she had said, not unkindly, marking her own pleasure. She extracted her due and Max wrote the words of diagnosis and treatment in her chart. Thus the woman could leave, alive in her body, unaware within her cycle of deceit.

Yes, the woman was alive, Max thinks. He removes his hand from the icy water again. The tips of his fingers are a hazy blue. His hand is unyielding and limp. The heat has been drawn from its dorsal surface. It is a lifeless, clinical hand. Wherever he looks his mind comes into focus and his body betrays him. He likes to remember the Romanian flautist fully dressed, when her power shrank back into her slim stature and he could not take his eyes off her hands.

Max closes and opens his fist to bring the blood back into his palm. He notices a shoe has fallen into the foam and is bopping furiously against slippery stone just beyond his grasp. He knows who has thrown it in the water and why. He can conjure a story anywhere but he also knows that his interest in the couple overhead (Will she strike him? Will he push her into the foam after making love?) would irritate Alix. "You never leave the clinic," she would say. "It's not up to you to diagnose the whole world. Well, I've got news for you. The world doesn't give a damn." He doesn't realize he is conversing with her in his head. Not even Max knows if these thoughts originate with him, her or the young couple balancing on the tracks over his head.

Max is doomed. He has always been like this and will never change. Case in point: Alix and her skin condition. He sees himself peeling her silk blouse away to reveal the limits of her scales and red flakes. He feels for lumps in her broad neck with his cold hands. He says, "Excuse me, my hands do not retain the heat well." Alix glares right into the eyes of Dr Max Kuhn but Dr Kuhn does not speak her language. He will not do the thing she most desires. Max has mastered a type of deception. He moves his imaginary stethoscope under her left breast. He holds it there with his right hand as the left, uncomfortably bent over her head, pulls the breast up with just enough force to be considered professional but not sufficient force to be considered crass. A slight jerk in the motion diffuses any sexual longing. A cough or a twitch thrown in for distraction seals his professionalism. "I'm as much interested in scratching my nose as your nipple," he seems to say. He nevertheless occasionally brushes a breast with the sleeve of his left arm as he adjusts his position to listen to the heart. Listening to the heart, he often forgets, is the reason for being there in the first place.

Max gets back on his bike and pedals through bush that is pretty and muddy and green yet somehow manicured. The air is calmer, cooler, protected. He is drawn to the library and river and paths and university grounds. It is a pull to an earlier time now gone, when he and his friends believed ideas created and destroyed worlds. With the ascendancy of his clinical skill the world is turning into a series of unexplained vignettes, disconnected fragments, unrelated stories. Somehow the bits of gravel ticking in his spokes bring him closer to Moussakanski— the Moussakanski who lives in a semi-detached bungalow on a curved dead-end street filled with children he does not know amid neighbourhood rituals he has never noticed.

Dear Dr Z,

I was listening to my favourite radio show the other night (the sex show that the cable network has decided to beam east over the mountains) and there you were, talking with the hostess and the public. I recognized your mumbled voice right away. The hostess with the counselling monotone asked you a question or two as if you were an expert and I thought you handled it pretty well, even though you weren't prepared and didn't have an answer. I must admit, you are pretty good at managing the public and can talk your way out of just about anything. Your views on medication were quite complimentary even though you don't know much, and that could get you hired on with any number of drug companies, if you ask me.

The weird thing about the broadcast was that you were explaining intimate things in a public forum. I thought about that for a while, especially when you were arguing your way out of a sticky corner. Then, in something of an epiphany, I realized an amazing thing: when you are rambling on about this stuff, you're not allowed to talk about us. There you were, being reamed out by some stranger who lives in a different city who sees a doctor you don't know for a condition you have not diagnosed. There she was, berating you on public radio and not only do you have to take it as if she were your very own patient within the privacy of your office, you're not allowed to talk about your biggest asset: us.

So, for the record, when it comes to me you can say anything you want. I won't hold it against you. You can betray my panics and traumas, my mom, my dad and all of my girlfriends. You can talk about my penis and what I do with it, followed by what, in your professional opinion, I should or shouldn't do with it. If you talk about someone else's penis and they don't like it, I'll come to your rescue. I can always say you were talking about me. I would get my lawyers to draft a formal release of information or responsibility or whatever it's called in your new jurisdiction out west, and sign it with witnesses and a notary seal, but I know that even that wouldn't be enough if the College or some detractor threatened to take you to task. Or even me, if I changed my mind and decided to run you in.

But I won't change my mind, believe me. I want you to betray my secrets.

I was listening attentively to the party noises in the background of the broadcast, waiting for a summary comment that might indicate you were getting ready to finally talk about me. You could have your own radio show and talk about me every day of the week as far as I'm concerned, and all of my friends and relatives would be listening.

So, with your leaving, I send you what's left of my empathy and a few heartfelt regrets. I can't imagine how you do it, censoring our lives. If it were up to me, I would confess all of the secrets in the world at once—yours and ours—and get it over with.

Good luck in your radio career.

THE DEATH OF DR Z'S FATHER IS FOLLOWED BY THE EXPECTED PAIN AND A VERY LONG DRIVE

In the west there is nothing more for my father to say; he is dead. We were alone at the dedication of his headstone, the three boys and the rabbi. None of us had seen the stone or the cemetery inscription. We found my father in his usual place on the aisle, so he could make a quick getaway for a smoke. Nobody wanted to admit the truth, how his suffering stemmed from his self-imposed separation from us.

Back in the east I am running every night, reluctant to say good-bye to the familiar routes of the past fifteen years. From the university to the hospital. Along the toboggan hill where the wind blew the blood out of my youngest daughter's cheeks, where we all learned to cross-country ski. Past the locks where they dredged for the body of a student on the first day of classes, where the frost bit our toes. Past the stumps of all of those poplars-in-a-line, cut down years ago, once-tall spindly trees that had provided the perfect up-draught for kites. Where the dog chased hares and groundhogs, and the children climbed the bright green-and-red tractor. I run past cow bums and little pigs behind glass and sheep huddled together. I run where my eldest fell on the gravel and skinned her knee, leaving telltale corrugated scars. I run where we tested all of their bike skills, where I went over on my ankle and couldn't walk for a month. Where my wife found refuge in the snow with her first infant. Where the kids went to bug and swamp camp with the enormous paper wasp nest over the entrance. I run past the spot where I came across a single-gear bicycle leaning against a lonely pole in February, white drifts up to the seat. Where the wind is so bitter in winter that it is impossible to walk forward, even in a balaclava. Where the urban cornfields turn into tundra and the roads become a frigid desert of shifting white dunes.

The mist is thick by the arboretum. I am conscious of the countdown to zero, time slipping away. We are being invited out to visit for what may be the last time. The children are sleeping over. At the good-bye party there will be nowhere to sit. Pretty soon it will be time to put gas in the car. The house will be empty. Sound will bounce hollowly off the walls. At the crack of dawn we will pull out, heading west.

NOW: REMEMBERING GOING WEST

The trip out was an odd mix of going somewhere new and going home. There was no mention of Dr Z from the beginning to the end.

We followed the setting sun from territory to territory. Travelling across unfamiliar space protected us from the hard emotional reality of leaving. There were new details to be seen everywhere: the pockmarked moonscape of the Canadian Shield, stands of stunted birch melting into bogs, the ever-present mist on the lakes tracking us for days like old friends.

On the prairie we followed a lightning storm north up the river valley into the night. The next day a mayfly as big as a sparrow got caught in the windshield wipers. Miles later, at a gas station, it flapped its wings and catapulted onto the gravel, astounding us with its renewed life.

When driving I like to watch where I am going and I can be quiet for days on end. My mind finds a way to survive within the rhythm of movement and the sound of the vehicle on the road. My middle daughter took off her shoes in the prairie heat and stunned us with their smell across two provinces. The three children sang songs from their childhood camps and schools, the sounds of their voices creating a competing weather system.

The prairie was a set of surprises: undulating hills, a contracting sky and a patchwork of fields of similar colour stretching forever. I thought of places my father had lived, the places where both of my grandfathers began their lives in this country, but there was no time to stop. The prairie was a place you joked about, a place your forefathers came to and left as soon as they could. There was nothing to do there and no one to visit because they had all moved away.

The city on the river was oppressed by heat and bugs. Faraway flashes and quiet thunder lasted throughout the day and the rain brought no relief. After a while the children refused to stay outside. We hid in a mall near the river that let in the light and kept out the air. There were children in strollers about and I wondered how their parents kept the bugs away.

Over the years I had met more than one individual who insisted I had family in that town, but the phone books yielded no clues and we left as we had come. Everybody I had known or heard about had moved west over forty years before.

It didn't take long to develop an attachment to the prairie river. Its muddy brown surface drew our attention back to its banks. We wandered away and we wandered back. The river set a fickle, meandering tone. Even its banks were variously defined, where the current had changed direction and moved its bed. On the highway west of town the river was still there. We crossed it and crossed it again as it gradually thinned out to a serpentine swamp and finally disappeared.

Soon the prairie dissipated into barren tundra dotted with geometrical devices bopping up and down. At the next hotel I screamed at my middle daughter for walking close to danger. The swimming pool was located on the roof and she sauntered right over to the building's edge and lost her balance against the flimsy rail. A stranger in cowboy hat and swim trunks bawled me out. "You're crazy," he said. I had no right to have children and they had no responsibility to listen to me. I didn't feel reasonable again until the next day when we found the next river and began following it into the mountains. And what would the children remember? The mantle of my father on my shoulder? *His* thunderous voice out of *my* little chest?

Then the children heard stories of their parents' honeymoon all those years before. We looked way up at the slopes and peaks and were astounded; all of our eyes, accustomed to the ridges of the Shield, had to readjust upward and that was enough for me. It was then that I felt I had arrived, that geography was on my side. The rest of the journey was downhill, more or less. The car rolled on and the children wondered, "Where will we sleep?" and "Who will be our friends?" and "How will we know where to go?" They had all been born somewhere else.

MAX AT WORK

Max catches up to Alix in the cafeteria. Moussakanski, a white-haired count, has sprinted up the back stairs to join them. The cafeteria is a dingy, astro-turfed hall with small painted-shut windows that look out on mouldy red stone. Outside, a green mushroom-shaped water tower with rusty stairs goes straight up fifteen stories into the clouds. When the last tuberculosis victim died they fenced in the spiral staircase. Now patients can look at the sky and safely wonder what it would be like to fly before plunging to their deaths. It is a special luxury here, to tempt fate from a position of safety in a hospital bed.

Moussakanski speaks into his collar. He has shifted his clinical interest from hearts to necks. Alix, stockinged legs tucked beneath her, gestures to Max with her one smooth arm. Her unadorned fingers come to rest semi-purposefully on her coffee mug. Max sits down warily. He pulls in the chair, scratching up the green turf. He must watch himself closely so as not to become suddenly garrulous. When anxious his feet go right up into his mouth.

Moussakanski is quick to cut him short. "Check the man's thyroid," he says out of nowhere. It is not at all clear if he is referring to a patient of his or to the dirty-faced man sitting alone at the next table. The human neck has captured Moussakanski's fascination: the thyroid is his organ of the month. He is busy memorizing the thyroid chapter in Harrison's new edition, which has just tipped the scales at a hundred dollars. Max has been memorizing the same chapter nightly from an older, neglected library copy. He wants to be ready to strike Moussakanski thyroid for thyroid. He finds it difficult to examine most thyroids without going pink and dizzy. It is safer to diagnose from the foot of the bed or while cuddling the text after lights out.

Alix herself has a smooth little lump in front of her voice box. Moussakanski has been observed to eye this aspect of her neck as it goes up and down.

Alix chews her salad.

"You ought to have that checked out," says Dr Moussakanski.

The agitated schizophrene at the next table is speaking gibberish, drawing a crowd of lunchers behind Moussakanski's head.

"Send the guy to Emergency," grumbles a scruffy male nurse.

"He's already from there," replies somebody else.

Alix speaks in a lilting voice that is not unattractive.

"Around here the patients have a habit of turning up in your lunch," she says.

"Vas?" says Moussakanski.

His coattails are stuck under his chair and he tears the lining standing up. Psychotic noise throws him into action. He flaps his white tails, getting ready to retreat.

Alix sips her coffee. Her neck bobs up and down like a water lily ruffled by rowers. Moussakanski has reminded Max of his own mother: her bony neck. Her knobby cartilaginous appendage sticks out like a bunch of cherry pits.

As Moussakanski stands and speaks Max daydreams of Alix, her iguana skin half-concealed by the three-quarter-length lab coat.

Moussakanski explains a complex lab interpretation before he gets fed up with the psychotic noise. Two orderlies with salad between their teeth are wrestling the angry man onto a stretcher.

"If it's elevated, there's a deficit," says Moussakanski. Thyroids are reliable. Everybody has one beneath the chin. If it has been excised, there is an identifiable horizontal scar that slides under your finger like a piece of fishing twine.

Calculating hormonal relations reinforces Moussakanski's insomnia. Over- and under-function throw his mind into curious states. "There is a direct relationship between malfunction and the symptoms of a diseased mind," he says. The curiosity of inverse relationships jars him into action. Life is predictable and linear, he often thinks at night, alone in bed. He drags his thick nails across the bedsheets, rehearsing the next day's lecture material. If life is linear, then god is alive doing predictable things. Indeed, the war (where else was the potency of the deity so actively challenged?) is being fought, re-fought and won daily between Moussakanski's pointy ears. This inner conversation attests to god's post-war sense of humour. On the other hand, curvilinear notions deal Him an ugly blow. Moussakanski refuses to discuss anything beyond simple inverse relationships that tip Him on his head and dangle Him from his toes. Each night he thinks these thoughts and each night he takes a deep breath, turns off his reading lamp and rolls over, asleep.

Moussakanski leaves the lunchroom, hard on the heels of the angry man who has pounded an orderly in the chest.

"Restraint," shouts the angry man.

"Restraint," shouts Moussakanski.

"Restraint," echoes the orderly who has received the blow to the chest.

Alix does not move. Business has penetrated lunch and she will not acknowledge it. She assumes this posture daily between twelve and one. Max sips his coffee. Alix's plate is full of hospital food but she cannot eat in his presence. Nor can she eat and talk medicine at the same time. Max does not understand this. Even her chewing motions seem to invite conversation. When he opens his mouth, Alix slips back into her pumps, a sure sign she is about to fly away on a pressing errand.

"Today is cold," she says. "Although thirty below is not as cold as Moussakanski's memory."

Alix says this looking into the emptiness of Moussakanski's chair. Moussakanski's memory is a story the old man has told her often, a story she and Max know well. It is a lie, Max thinks, with a bit of truth thrown in. Moussakanski says that the likes of Alix and Max do not know about real cold—where your piss freezes in an arc before it hits the ground, glistening yellow in the winter sun. Moussakanski has never seen anyone piss ice in this country. It is clear that Moussakanski has been tortured and he wants Alix to know it without being told. He wants her to console him without calling it that. When he gets close to saying this his heart races. Then he gets up abruptly, flaps his white tails and retreats to the wards.

"In all of my reading of Tolstoi and Turgenev," Alix says, uncovering pie beneath clotted plastic wrap. Her plate is full of hospital food: cottage cheese and gloppy potatoes with tiny brown balls of gravy, limp broccoli with rose-coloured tartar sauce, plasticated apple pie and lukewarm coffee with three creamers. She does not complete her sentence. She prefers Max to be elsewhere, far away and not listening. Max knows that at times like this she has thought of throwing her body in front of a train. He also knows she would never do this; people would not understand that she is quoting, that she has taken somebody else's story, that she is too tired to make up a story of her own.

Alix sighs. Her fork touches this and that. She moves the food around with the flexible white plastic. Perhaps her neediness can be filled up with some of this glop and goo. She stops eating. Gravy is there to be pushed into creamy white cottage cheese and gelatinized cutlets.

Max watches with his mother's critical eyes. *"Trefeh, neveleh."* His mother's disapproval roars in his ears.

Max's mother is like a grandmother to Alix. She gives Alix hardcover novels in translation and in return Alix eats her coffee cake. Eating cake while she touches the family library may help seal her place among them. She threatens to break in and steal a shelf or two but only if Max's mother dusts them off properly first. Alix laughs falsely every time she brings this up. It is easy to imagine her reading in bed, holding the cold leather bindings opposite her heart.

This is the way illness works in Max's family. When he is sick with the flu he spends the afternoon chasing the throat swab from lab to lab. "Strep?" he says into the receiver, then

"Staph?" Covering the mouthpiece with his palm he has been known to say, "I am my own jewish mother."

When Max is sick at home his mother often tells him war stories. "There were times when a soggy black loaf had to last a week," she says. The loaf grew mould and was shared with mice. When they burnt her city she spent days with her friend Frieda under a stairwell. After that, Frieda was carried away by a blond soldier and Max's mother remained invisible, left for dead. Once she told him this as she teetered over the drain sump, pulling up clogged muck, leaves and dirt that had crept back in from the fall runoff. "I never saw her again." Max knows not to ask about Frieda because that is the end of the story.

"Eat, eat," his mother often says. It is her way of defying the past.

"You're not eating much of your lunch," Max says to Alix.

He often accuses her of something before she gets her teeth into him.

She has touched the crust of her pie and drunk down half a cup of coffee. A creamer has drained into the gravy. Its oil slick glistens the entire spectrum of the rainbow.

Dear Dr Z,

Here is my question to you. Have you ever heard about the Dr Z Book Club? Many of your old patients show up and even speak of you on occasion. For months I assumed you knew about the activity and maybe even set it up. When I realized my error I developed a strong itch to tell you about it, so here goes.

As you probably suspect, the Dr Z Book Club is not a normal sort of book club and may have little or nothing to do with the real Dr Z. I had been in book clubs before I got sick, and beyond the usual problems about whether to bake or not and the perennial absence of men, I was a seasoned participant in this sort of activity.

At first I was reassured in a sort of rehabilitative way to be participating in an activity I knew well. Then I began to experience the oddest feeling that the books being discussed had not been read, that the books did not even exist. For a fleeting moment I thought you had written some of them, but I could tell that was a trick my mind was trying to play on me and I banished it from my consciousness.

The suspicions began with a particular man named John whose truncal obesity is the type often attributed to the effect of psychotropic medication. He carried himself with an intellectual bearing and spoke in a punchy, articulate style I am familiar with from the university. It was soon apparent that his thoughts on neurochemicals and receptor proteins did not hang together and that he dropped difficult scientific terms here and there in conversation like rare unadorned gems. He assigned you authorship of a work entitled Brain Chemistry in the Service of Mental Health, although perhaps he was simply stretching his thoughts toward credibility. The book was eventually re-titled Brain Chemistry in Sickness and Health and went through further revisions and emendations before his time on the floor was up.

Heaven knows I have heard a lot of chatter about brain chemistry and none of it makes coherent sense to me. As John said in one of his moments of jocular lucidity, "As if brain chemistry could explain why you might want to kill your father and sleep with your mother." John is not the sort of guy who would contemplate either of these prototypical behaviours and it was clear he was quoting. Of course there are those who would support and defend the imbalance-in-the-brain position but thankfully no one in the group had read their books. John, having attributed that obtuse Oedipal comment to you, could say little more beyond the standard mantra: serotonin, serotonin, serotonin. I suppose that any mantra can be civilizing, especially if it helps one actualize a relationship to a higher power, which hopefully in this case is not you.

This brings me to the point of my present letter. A young woman joined the Book Club, which I have renamed The Reading Group for Books Existent and Nonexistent, Variously Titled, Interpreted and Attributed. This title is nicer than any of the other options anybody else came up with and is a reminder of the less-than-serious purpose of the club. I suspect the chapters of the young woman's book proceed according to the story of her life but I will leave that determination to you. This is the story that she told us.

In her book, a woman with a single leg (the real storyteller, of course, has two like the rest of us) hops her way from man to man, job to job and epiphany to epiphany. It is a story of delighted promiscuity. Eventually she uses her trusty good leg to seduce her therapist, a woman of extraordinary beauty who loves her as a mother would a child. I waited expectantly month after month anticipating each subsequent instalment, and I must say I was beginning to pine for the woman with one leg.

As they say, "time passed," and the young woman disappeared along with her character with the pliable leg. Our members are erratic at best and it is common for them to disappear. The participants, being somewhat transient, have a habit of shifting like unpredictable waves. So it took a while for us to realize that she was in fact gone. We had moved on to the history of Hollywood and psycho-biographies of those nasty tyrants Hitler, Stalin and Freud. However, as soon as we had successfully banished her from our collective consciousness, the lady with the one-legged heroine was suddenly back. Her reappearance in the group was fresh and she had spruced up her own gait, as if all vestigial connections to her stumpy heroine were emphatically erased. I wasn't the only one to note her bipedal sturdiness and wonder about the now-gone heroine sporting the shapely stump.

There was general disappointment all around when it became evident that the woman we called One-Leg (to remind us of that lingering sexual danger) had a new book

on the go. It was called Crime and Punishment *but bore
no resemblance to the original. A well-thumbed Penguin
paperback (the version we all read in high school) thwacked
on the coffee table dispelled all anticipated challenges in
that direction.*

Crime and Punishment *is a series of stories about a
woman with various disabilities. The crimes are not known
until the end of each instalment but the punishments I'm
sure you can guess: a severed limb, an enucleated eye, a
tumour, consumption. As always, it is the crimes that hold
our attention. We are already too familiar with the inevitable
punishments hanging over our heads and ready to fall.*

*We are now waiting for the final chapter, the story which
no doubt will represent the ultimate inner deformity. But
we also know that this is a literary tactic and the woman
previously called One-Leg will likely disappear again before
she reaches the end of the telling.*

*So that is that. The Book Club is wonderful therapy. I
heartily recommend it to all patients. It is amazing what can
be said when the doctor is not there.*

DR Z AND EVERYBODY ELSE
IN THE NEW PLACE

The first couple of months after the move to the new place weren't so bad. The trees were green and the sky was gorgeous, especially in the evenings. Children played in the street and people came out of the woodwork to help us settle in. A young couple, new neighbours, took the three children on bicycle rides along the trails and my wife and I let them roam. I was smiling and people smiled back and I thought I had moved to New England.

The sea was forever present in the freshness of the air, but after the summer I found a dreariness overtaking me. I noticed something lacking in local architecture. Corners cut too close. Lawn ornaments. The streetscape, I gradually became aware, was too low; the houses had been plunked down on grade. Despite pockets of old growth preserved here and there, I became distrustful of the forest and its perennial sameness. Blackberries ripened and stained the gravel but I saw no women with buckets along the edges of the fields.

Before long a friend of my middle daughter starting pelting the garage with foodstuffs most evenings at dusk. Another friend of hers left school without any warning. We speculated it was a case of parental neglect or maybe pregnancy but nobody knew for sure. A child had been murdered the previous year around the corner. In broad daylight. On the main street. In the heart of town. The details were gruesome and people were reluctant to talk about them. When the train took another young life and another memorial was established at the scene of the loss, I began to rant against the streetscape.

Then an acquaintance from my remote past moved in around the corner and I began to yearn for the heart of the city he had recently fled.

The mail piled up. *Dr Z this, Dr Z that*. My patients wrote and wrote but I left their letters unanswered. Someone else would have to take care of them. As for me, I had to take care of myself.

My boss accused me of sporting a Kleinian conscience. He gave me a book of Ellenberger essays, trying to get me on his side.

"It is obvious what you are all about," he said. "Anyone can see you walking around in a daze."

Here, nobody called me Dr Z. This was a new place. If anyone was going to call me Dr Z it would have to be me.

My boss said I would only recognize the daze in a year or two when it would suddenly lift. Some things I could accept, but what was a Kleinian conscience? And when it lifted, would it be replaced by something else? A Freudian limp? A Jungian squint?

I read and reread my *New Yorkers*.

I went to the doctor and asked for drugs.

I went to synagogue to pray and to my mother's for dinner.

I read thick novels and neglected my work.

And I wrote about Max. At times I could not tell myself from Dr Z, or Dr Z from Max.

At times I yelled at my kids.

When I yelled at my kids I thought, This is not me doing the yelling, it is Dr Z, or it is the character I call Max later in his fictional life when his children are grown.

A ridiculous thought, I know. Dr Z's children are much younger than mine and Max is currently single and alone.

What is more (I had to remind myself) *I am Dr Z.*

Day after day the three children skewered me with plaintive yearnings. "My homework would be easier if... " said my youngest. "My friends would like me if... " said my middle child. "Nobody ever threw things at the garage before we moved here," she added. "I would know how to get around on the bus if... " said my eldest. That was their collective opinion, relentless, uncompromising, spontaneous. The only possible salvation was moving back to the land of their birth.

My wife could hardly tolerate my presence and bonded progressively with the dog. I knew I was in trouble when my sentences started falling apart. I could not sustain introductory clauses, expecting to be interrupted. I developed a nominal aphasia and a tic under my left eye. My speech was at best a sustained complaint and my thoughts were directed at people I could not speak to. I began reading the dictionary out loud, trying to simplify and clarify my inner voice, to ground myself.

My children laughed in my face. They spit out their food and denied it brazenly, as if I couldn't see the particles flying through the air. They wanted their reality, not mine, and I couldn't blame them.

My wife said, "You are in the business. You know what to do."

"What is that? Drugs?"

"Get a support system."

What she meant was, take care of yourself and leave me out of it.

The bulk of my support system was in the studio. My friend Dave was busy with his Grey Owl production, my brother with the screenplay. My wife's father had become a historical consultant and fact checker. My youngest brother was scouting for locations, carrying camera gear, setting up the shots. My middle brother was director of production.

As I see it, in this kind of situation there are limited options. You can go see someone like Dr Z to get a diagnosis and a clinical recommendation. If you are lucky, the treatment will hit enough variables to tip the balance and you will get through. Good enough. But that's not what I decided to do.

As usual, I wrote in my journal and went to bed. In the morning I tucked away the embarrassing lines and went to work.

MEDICAL HISTORY

1. Mental Status
I am not suicidal,
I have not killed.
You know these are not my own giggles.

2. Personal History
I have not washed
in fifty poems.
I am lucky
there is a mother to tolerate the smell.

3. Systems Review
My false teeth
are inappropriate.
They talk at night in the jar.

4. Physical Illness
I told her
I put my balls there
nightly for safekeeping.

5. Disposition
Pen fifty poems,
become a millionaire.

MOUSSAKANSKI AND MAX

Max is not surprised when Moussakanski coughs up pink spit and stares intently at his shoes. Moussakanski is living on borrowed time. This is something Max often says and everybody knows. Moussakanski has survived the worst of wars and has no children. You can't call his hundred-plus journal articles his children no matter how well they map out the limbic system. It is a clinical observation everyone shares: that if Moussakanski stops twitching and stubs out his Export A before the dull flame eats the inside of the filter he will himself flicker and die. First impressions often sustain the clinical arts despite a profusion of computerized diagnostic aids. It cannot be proved that Moussakanski is dying; it is just known. No one takes the issue up with Moussakanski himself. No one even whispers this to his secretary to pass on to a concerned relative or his stately wife Bella. It is assumed that everybody knows.

Moussakanski drops to his knees and wipes his brow. Sanguineous streaks have found their way into his palm. No doubt his mind kicks into its usual gear at this point. Pink sputum: what is the differential diagnosis for that? Tuberculosis? Perhaps in the old days when he lived underground and the walls wept every secretion imaginable for their suffering. Contemporary consumptions were of a different sort. Cancer? He had always defied the warning on the package. Pneumonia? Heart failure? Even he knows he is coughing up life's blood. What else is there to say? Death is on his face and blood is in his open palms. He doesn't need pathophysiology to see his soul circling his head.

It is a Friday in February. Snow moves about in swirls, never seeming to settle. By now even Moussakanski uses the tunnels to move from building to building. Beards and curls freeze daily on the walk in from the street, melting into charts and reorders. White coats stiffen to cardboard. An intern crashes into a semi on his way up to work from the Seaway, fracturing the smooth tissues of his lower gut. Black ice. Moussakanski cancels rounds. He has too much on his mind.

"Why do they have to send us down the Seaway for an education?" Max says to Alix. "Aren't there enough crazy-sickos in the area to poke, prod and stick needles into?"

Alix chain smokes, leafing through some notes. Moussakanski's secretary protects the inner office with her body. Moussakanski is in there, spitting up, preparing a report.

Alix rubs her thigh. Her head is suspended in smoke. She wants to be seen but Max is not ready to look. They play out this drama silently. In his presence Alix shifts inward. They do not speak openly to each other. They seem to prefer a quiet public tension. They hear things spoken behind their backs. "His mother keeps her away from him," or "His father is malignantly stern. Dr Max will never break away." Alix hears these things and reports them to Max. She gets worked up and he agrees with her; what else is he to do? It is impossible to disagree with a woman when her eyes overflow with the tears of prior need. But agreeing with her pushes her away. He doesn't want her getting too close, where she will tamper with his connections to the past. What does she know about old country sewer systems before the ghetto went up in smoke?

Moussakanski, exhausted in his swivel chair, gathers his strength. The family of the student who has been in the crash does not want a thing from him. Yes, their son has been in a serious accident. He is in the hospital, in stable condition. The father is cordial and respectful on the phone. The couple is grateful their son is alive. They want to ensure his continued education under the pressing circumstances. The relief leaves Moussakanski drained of tension. He sits with his unspoken memories. The son he never had is trapped behind the wheel, his pelvis crushed, his guts splayed on the dash.

Moussakanski spits pink into his own palm. "Damn," he says, lighting a cigarette. Soon it will be his turn to puff and stagger breathlessly up the green water tower and tumble to the earth.

In the outer office Max rubs his knees and Alix flicks her bangs. It is a habit she remembers from her teenage years. They wait. Alix throws open the window. When February comes blasting in Moussakanski's secretary says, "Please, Dr Tuttle," despite her age, her pure white hair and her grandchildren older than Alix.

Moussakanski is going to die. The window flies open and Max knows. Moussakanski stares out at pure white, not seeing a thing. His window is glazed opaque with snow. To move requires breaking into that mass of light, getting beyond the glass and snow and winter sun. Max wonders what the pain of a broken body is like. What is it like to lie flat on a hospital bed and piss red through a tube, over a silver rail, into a bag?

Moussakanski replaces the receiver. The line has long ago gone dead. Voices argue in the outer office and beyond, his secretary keeping attackers at bay. He cannot see through the glass frosted over with his sickly breath. He has seen a lot of senseless death in the war. Someone raises his arm to say hello and you gun him down—try and make sense out of that. Might as well run headlong into the rear of a skidding sixteen-wheeler. For once Moussakanski blames the vacant face of god. He tailgates god in the dead of winter and flies straight to heaven over black ice.

Moussakanski laughs. He is not that far gone. Heaven knows, if a patient of his ever said a thing like that even once, Moussakanski would order bimonthly shots in the ass and be done with it. On the ward god was a symptom. What better way to regulate His power, negotiate His sanctity, kick Him in the ass? Moussakanski thanks his lucky stars god is mainly catholic in these parts, stuck to wood and bleeding through the palms. The real god, he knows, does not own a mortal pump and has never bled in his life.

Moussakanski can see shadows outside through the glass, a body swaying on a winter swing, kicking up snow.

Max and Alix leave the office arm in arm. She is a half-inch taller than he, teetering on heels, her back bent. "We must tell the others," she says. Perhaps Max will tell the others and she can go on to morning coffee. She loves to play with the creamers, throwing them into the air in the middle of a conversation. Max can tell the others and she will get on with her paperwork: dictating, reviewing her case notes. But Max, she knows, will never tell the others. He will get sidetracked. He will fiddle with his reflex hammer the way she fiddles with her coffee creamers. Men are funny that way, loving their tools. They walk around with their instruments dangling from white buttonholes for all the world to see. Or they wrap themselves in white coats, protecting themselves and erecting a barrier. With all the men running around the hospital she gets stuck with a pair of stubby legs in a white clinic jacket.

She cannot deny the envy in her attraction to him. Her reflex hammer angles under her breast and falls to the floor when her belly bunches up. Her pencils catch her chin and poke her when she stands. Every few weeks she throws away her white coat and piles her medical gadgetry into an old shoebox. She makes a point of talking to patients. That is her role. Patients are clients. They deserve to keep their clothes on and their orifices closed to the outside world.

Moussakanski stares at the white glass. He knows they are waiting for him but his feet are lead and he cannot fix his soul to his body. He has begun to think in a disconnected way. Upsurges from the past appear in the fine print of the *New England Journal of Medicine*. They are waiting for him, but who are they?

Just that morning he'd berated his secretary. Then he'd grasped a chart in his trembling hands, ready to whack Miss Upton. "This is my ward and I am in control," she seethed, right back at Moussakanski. He could see what they were doing—conspiring to take it all away from him. Moussakanski raised his voice and the whole ward looked at him, even the ancient demented man who pissed in the corners of his room. (Moussakanski's nose was as trained as Miss Upton's. One whiff and he could tell what the old guy had eaten the day before: garlic toast, carrots.) A wave of smells and emotions filled all of his senses, the stench of fifty-five years behind a government desk. He stormed out of the geriatric consultation room, Miss Upton smiling into his back. Miss Upton could afford to smile, standing behind his retreating frame, while Moussakanski's white wings flapped all the available air up into the ventilation ducts. She knew what it was all about. Long ago Dr M had lost control with her: spittle at the corner of his mouth, wet drops tracking down his pants.

Moussakanski sits forward in his swivel chair. His feet are lead and the window glassy white. He finds the receiver in his hand, a severed limb. He has been speaking. He has been sliding through white. He thinks of Bella, his Bella, slimmer by forty years. Once again he is carrying her on his back over Russia and China. That was before she straightened to her full height in the New World. By then, looking so hearty, it was hard to believe she could not bear children.

Despite his own arrogance he had himself checked out. He deposited his seed in the white paper cone for the American doctors and received his diagnosis. Deposition was a clinical act and diagnosis always pleased him. But what of his wife, tall and hearty? "The Nazis sewed a cat in my belly," she joked as they crossed the sea to the New World. The sewed-in cat was the baby that fell bloody to her knees as they retreated east ahead of the war. For months Bella trickled blood, the terror of flight worming its way through her body. Then the worm fell in a blue clump to the ground followed by a spurt of black blood, and they were free.

He sees the world in motion through hospital white. The smell of formalin floods his brain with years of stored memories. He lifted the knife above the spongy tan tissue then cut down, transecting material with the consistency of wet cork: fornix, cingulae. Those words had a power over him he did not understand, the power to make him lift and cut, the power to stop the emotions resonating along his inner circuits.

He held a grenade under the earth. The air was black. Bella pressed her bones into him from behind. If he could carry a hundred pounds of wood or coal, he could carry wild Bella. She dressed like a boy and went down with him into the sewers. There whispering voices vibrated faintly in their ears, like men at prayer, or doves. The ghetto burned above him and he exhaled in relief. Pieces of cork crumbled in his scientific hand: his mother's bowels, his father's torn side-locks. To survive he cut into brain. He had to imagine the structures, to shade them in with the mind's eye. Formalin was the stench of rats burning in the sewer. His foot caught fire and he felt no pain. It was the same smell, the smell of no-pain, of sitting secure on a ledge waiting for the soldiers above to leave with their dead.

The boy's face was white and he had no shoes. He had spent the winter underground, his only heat the bodies of his sisters. And now it was spring and the earth was on fire. There was no *matzah* for Passover; he would eat bread, he would eat mouldy potatoes. The boy's face tilted toward the sky, as if there still was an earth and a sky. He watched from behind the barricade. His feet were on fire. He would watch. He would eat human flesh.

"We lived in the sewers under fire," he told Marj Upton, wiping the corner of his mouth.

She leaned up against the supply room door. Her back was cold between broom handles, tendrils of mop against her right leg. He saw into the black hole of her mouth and pinned her to the wall.

Dear Dr Z,

I am writing to inform you that I have made the adjustment to your leaving.

At first I was very concerned to be left high and dry without a psychiatrist. Then I decided to contact an old friend of the family, Dr Moses Kanski. Dr Kanski, as you will undoubtedly remember, is an old and respected member of the medical establishment. He has been in semi-retirement for quite a few years now, working out of the study in his home. It is a very simple house, a bungalow a few blocks from the greenbelt.

Every morning he and his wife walk their standard poodle along the bike path and back. I have a regular appointment, at ten to ten on Tuesdays. He is an active and punctual man with many social interests that run according to schedule and I am required to protect my spot as one would a biblical lineage. He had a bit of a heart attack years ago, but he has recuperated and if anything the brush with illness has softened him up. I am reassured by the occasional interruption from one of his children visiting, intruding with a question about the coffeemaker or when he will be able to take over his grandfatherly duties for the day. There was a time when these intrusions would have been unthinkable. A gentle familial tendency to obsession is still evident in all he does and says, but I must report that he is now a man whose restful countenance has softened from those harsh angles where tradition has nevertheless left its mark.

Dr Kanski does not remember working with you but sends you his regards all the same. He suspects you know his present wife, Alexandra, a contemporary of yours in the program years ago. Around the time of your training his first wife, Bella, died and he suffered his own little panicky depression until he and Alexandra linked up in marriage. In contrast to yourself, Dr Kanski has the old-school attitude to psychiatric impartiality. In theory boundaries are important to him, but in reality he doesn't mind letting you in on his private life and making you a part of the family.

So rest assured I am well taken care of. My illness is in full remission and my explorations of the past have taken on a light-heartedness I would not have thought possible. Dr Kanski is not a particularly attentive listener, which has unexpectedly freed me from the intensity of my treacherous expectations.

Dear Dr Z,

How are you doing in the land of the free?

In your absence my clinical situation is being managed by my family physician, who has proven remarkably competent in psychiatric matters. I only have to see him once a month for ten minutes and the schedule suits me fine.

My wife has been following the story of Dr Max Kuhn avidly in the Medical Inquirer. As you know, she is a family physician and often leaves copies of her less-than-reputable medical rags in her waiting room or around the house. They make wonderful bathroom literature. The jokes are sufficiently scatological to be entertaining, the articles lend themselves to considerations of physical function and they are, how shall I say, perfectly brief.

Now, some things must be noted and perhaps challenged. In this case it is the meandering style of Dr Max K. As my wife says, Dr Max never seems to be in a hurry. She is quite intrigued that a single individual can be a physician yet hang around thinking as much as Max does. At this rate it is not at all clear how he makes a living.

My wife has made this observation off and on— commented here and there—and I somewhere, somehow, processed her observation. Eventually the internal ramblings of Dr Max began to remind me of something more personal and, I should say, closer to my heart: my rambling therapy of interminable duration. One night close to morning I sat bolt upright in my sleep and said, "The man with the gun," with the utmost conviction, and then faded back into my topography of the unconscious.

My wife brought the topic up at the breakfast table and referred to the Inquirer *series. We had quite an animated discussion about being seen, being seen seeing and whether having a gun pointed at you tipped the balance of awareness toward the Watching Other or not. I was somewhat awake and thinking about opening my camera store within the hour, firmly entrenched in a perfect state of philosophical vagueness, when I found myself back in bed with a more enjoyable purpose in mind.*

Later, as I was pulling up my left sock, my wife became seriously focused and said she hadn't yet brought the Inquirer *article about a gun being pointed at Max home from the office. As usual, her clinical instinct was accurate. There is something to medical experience after all. In other words and simply put, how had I known what she was talking about if I had not read the article? Her voice was too soft to ignore and I wondered if someone had died.*

I admitted that the style of the Dr Max articles reminded me of a voice already internalized, a familiar quiet drone. Here was the brick wall I looked out at week after week, the Kleenex box that always returned to its acute angle at the corner of the end table and the black Timex clock that moved relentlessly toward ten to the hour.

Max Kuhn, I guffawed.

I didn't see any reason to explain my expostulation and took the stairs to the street two at a time. I carried on laughing. My wife (as usual) thought I was a little crazy but I believe I maintained your cover.

I look forward to the next instalment of Dr Max K. I hope the feeling of being watched doesn't put you off. I wonder if knowing this will affect the content of your semi-autobiographical ramblings. I often think of you when I sit on the potty; no doubt this is good for my health. Every once in awhile I find little bits of transformed remnants of myself floating around, whether I am actively sifting for them or not.

Dear Dr Z,

Once upon a time I wrote you and told you all about my new therapist and the tape recorder and how I have to come in here and get prodded to talk to him even though I don't really want to talk to him and I only want to talk to you.

I told you this already but I am telling you again now. As the weeks and months fly by and it becomes clear that you are never ever coming back I am still dreaming about you and my therapist (just like before) wants it all recorded.

"We are going to need this," he says.

"It is better I get this down on paper," he says, "Or tape."

I don't know what he's talking about.

I have been to the Disciplines Committee and the Review Committee and the Slap on the Wrists Committee and they don't care what I have on paper or tape of what I remember or anything because I am crazy. That's what they say. Anything I tell them they ignore especially if I am all over the place and can't remember the time of day or whether Thursday last week comes before Wednesday or vice versa.

Well, I've been talking about all of those nasty topics with my new doctor and it has become clear that you are right in the middle of what you call my sexual associations. I always told you that I loved you like a brother, but it seems that that statement protects me from a more serious connection.

My new psychiatrist is too interested for his own good, if you ask me. He has been exploring and prodding and nudging me to talk about it and you know me. When pushed I rise to the challenge. I'm like a trapped animal except with a good sense of humour and there is nothing I can do about it.

Here is my confession. My dreams have betrayed you to the authorities and my new therapist is writing it all down. When my therapist asks me quietly if these dreams are real or associations, if they happened or are coloured by transference, I am quiet and say nothing and he waits. You know me better than anyone.

"Where are you?" he asks me.

"Dissociating."

"Is that your word?"

"What do you mean?"

"Is that your word or Dr Z's?"

I say nothing.

"What are you doing there?" he tries again.

"Hearing voices."

Silence.

"What are they saying?"

"'Take me on the carpet.'"

"'Take me on the carpet?'"

"'Yes, put your hand on my shoulder.'"

"A voice is telling you to tell me to put a hand on your shoulder?"

"Not you," I say. "My other doctor."

"What other doctor?"

"The one I had before."

"Dr Z?"

I say nothing.

"The doctor wants his hand on your shoulder?"

"On my waist."

"On your waist, too?"

"Yes, no. All over."

"Is it a voice?"

"Yes. No."

"Is it a memory?"

"Yes. No."

"Tell me more about this person."

"It is more than one person," I say. I wait. I give him a chance to process what I have said. It is difficult for me to describe all these feelings, these states of mind, these people. It is difficult for him to put it all together.

I tell my new therapist as little as possible. It could be my father, but it isn't. Thanks to you, my father's nasty voice has long since disappeared.

"Okay," I say out of nowhere, "I know the person."

"And who is it?"

"It is my brother."

"You have been touched by your brother?"

"No," I say. "That was other stuff, in the crib when I was one and he was three and he wanted to kill me. After that he was a good brother. He never tried to get his hands on me, although I wouldn't have minded. He is a cute guy and gets into trouble for things he doesn't do."

By now my new doctor is getting edgy.

"Do you know this person?"

"Yes."

"And what does he do?"

This is a difficult question for me. Voices rise and fall, come and go. They change before I can put my finger on them. Eventually I answer.

"He touches me all over."

"The voice is a he?"

"More or less."

"And he touches you all over?"

"Yes."

Thank goodness, I think. Thank goodness for Dr Z.

By now I have rattled my therapist's reality testing. He is feeling dizzy. I may have to name this fantasy so he doesn't pass out. Or worse, put me in hospital.

"The voice," I say, "is the voice of my doctor. The voice is caressing my shoulder. The snakes in the corner of the room disappear when he does that."

I hear my name being called. The voice is no longer in my head. I am touched all over. The rug is dirty but I don't mind.

When I wake up I feel much better. It is only fifteen past the hour. I think I have been asleep. When I wake up I force my new therapist to play a game of Hearts. He has a pack of cards just for me. I gave them to him to keep in a special place. They are the same deck we used to play with, you and I.

The snakes threaten to return to the corner of the room above the computer, but they are a blur and disappear with a sigh. They are no longer needed. At least not today.

I think my new doctor is going to contact you in Alberta or wherever you are. He thinks you have run away as far as you can get. From me. If he does not find you there he will likely chase you all the way to the coast or up north, if you haven't slipped away to China or Australia.

He can't imagine a doctor who plays Hearts in therapy.

Now he has become a doctor who plays Hearts in therapy.

At the end of the session he is still writing. He doesn't say anything when I get ready to leave. I have another appointment right after the weekend. At the end of the session he is still writing and it reminds me of my mother forgetting to kiss me good night when I was a little girl. She was not rejecting me. She was just too busy with other things—the wash, the dishes, my father, all of those children. I didn't mind. I feel her presence all over me, touching. That's how I put myself to sleep.

We are almost out of tape. I will turn off the machine. I had better go now. My new doctor does not look up. I clear my throat and he says good-bye. I wonder what he will say about this on Monday.

ME, MYSELF and MAX

I sit in my office and mark time. I watch the shifts in light and heat, dirt and Kleenex, paper clips, paper and boxes of tea. I scratch at my nose between sessions, waiting for the sensation of the crusty membrane pulling away from its base. Sometimes I cannot work if this has not been achieved properly along the plane of cleavage.

I bite my nails. I quit once, at thirteen, waiting for my piano lesson. I used to be like that—decisive and irritable. The irritability has persisted, but not the decisiveness. I have learned not to resist certain natural rhythms. Nail-biting returned soon after I opened my own office. It was not difficult to sit on my behind and listen. One natural rhythm led to the next. It means I have something of my own in this room, my own little compulsion.

I do not remember my own dreams, only that I wake in panic with the sensory knowledge that I have been speaking with the dead. At the end of the day I never take the office home. I know the limits of what I can do.

I know I am not Max but I am forgetting how to make the important distinctions.

This is the way patients give me a headache.

I scratch my nose the wrong way or I repeat a comment that should not be repeated and suddenly the patient is gone. He has muttered something confusing and bolted. If this happens in the morning, by late afternoon I have the beginnings of an itch in my head. I can tell it is a migraine because the blinds do not close adequately. I turn the blind mechanism but this does not shut out the light. The thought flickers in my brain that the blinds are broken again (they have never been broken when I come to think of it) so I tinker with the mechanism, flipping it back and forth aggressively.

Then I remember: the patient has put his feelings into me. That is what I am experiencing as a headache. These feelings have taken root and pulsate behind my sinuses, refusing to leave. There is nothing I can do about it. Sometimes these feelings will remain until I get the patient to take them back. I do not need patients to agree with what they are taking back. The transfer process is not very specific but it must occur or I cannot go on.

My patients are an amorphous clinical mass. On bad days they conspire to get under my skin, to get me to react, to drive me crazy. If I am pushed too far I pull out remnants of my medical school days: the silver-coloured tuning fork that plays C 256, the blood pressure cuff. I swing the double-barrelled stethoscope that dangles limp and black. I take out the reflex hammer and twist the rubbery round knob from its white plastic stick.

I am hemmed in on all sides. Soon patients will be able to read their own charts. They will want to read their stories there, with all the grammar and punctuation correct. They will tremble as if peeking into the book of good and evil on the Day of Atonement just as the gates of repentance begin to close and the sun disappears below the horizon. I write notes in my charts to forestall this process. I write down the process that cannot be described: fragments of life distorted and explored. I write down the future that might be, the part of the patient that might get into heaven.

As for Max, he feels the migrainous tension in his left eye on cloudy days. The clouds do not filter the intense light. A patient sits unconsciously rubbing his right eye and suddenly Max's left eye twitches as if sparked by sympathetic mirror magic.

He complains to Alix.

"Nerves," she says, chortling. The chortle is for the physician who should know better.

Max calls Moussakanski and complains like any old patient, even though he knows vaguely that this is inappropriate. It would be appropriate sixty years before on the other side of the sea but here it is a stretch.

"Nerves," Moussakanski says.

"A conspiracy," says Max.

"It is the light," Moussakanski explains. "Man was not created to sit in front of a bay window day in, day out and have his left eye track the arc of the sun across the sky."

"And why not?"

"That's god's job, Max. Not yours."

Max sits in the chair and waits. If the patient is not ready, he takes on a disguise. The disguise throws itself over him gently, like a sheet. The patients know yet don't know. Max speaks with the voices of their parents and future lovers. Healing begins this way. When they leave they take the sheet with them. What Max does remains hardly visible.

Max explains this process to his father. He hems and haws and all of his words come out in a jumble. Dr Kuhn the elder says that he (as a parent and member of the health insurance plan) is compelled to throw his hands up in dismay. Max considers his father to be a crotchety Old World type who could climb into Moussakanski's body and nobody would notice. Nevertheless he wishes he could get his words straight. Dr Kuhn the elder is admittedly an anachronism, with his pipe and his study, his articles and his untempered intellectual bitterness. With the wave of a hand he dismisses the Western world, the world that has not followed the path of his own mind into old age.

Max looks like his father. He cannot deny it. He may be broader, fuller in the face, two inches shorter and dark. He is a Semitic version of the slim, fair body bending into old age. He is all his father has to work with.

Like his father, he is alternately "ignorant" and a "genius." Like him, he loves to read and to talk. Like him, he has an enormous respect for the past and cannot imagine anything worse than the present. His father's respect for the early masters of letters and science is not intellectual. It stems from the leisure of smoking and thinking, and from the enjoyable exercise of writing things down at two or three in the morning while his wife sleeps in the next room.

Like the early masters, his father is a failed translator. Max and his father argue over words, their origins and how they are best rendered in English. Max has a habit of avoiding such conversations when his mother is in the room. Undoubtedly she will soon need him to carry a pile of dishes from one counter to the next. She bashes about the house in two or three foreign languages: Polish and Russian, Yiddish or German. These are languages that lack clear definition, languages people used to speak across hostile fluctuating borders. They are the languages of the kitchens and markets and pogroms of Eastern Europe decades before. Her kitchen movements are a prayer for the collective dead, a memorial to cultures smashed to bits, their sounds and letters dissolved into the soil.

Only Max knows his father needs his mother. His father enters the kitchen balancing a spoon and cup on a saucer. He lifts cake crumbs meticulously to his lips with his wet thumb. Max's father does not wish to diminish the world of Max's mother. He needs to remember but does not know why. The confusion brings out an edge of bitterness in Max's father's voice. After fifty years of marriage she still mistakes his forays into her territory. She thinks he has repeated a word she used to know in the gymnasium when he has been merely clearing his throat, anticipating her arrival.

The Kuhn family lives in an area of the city where the homes were built between the wars, when one world was crumbling and the transfer to a new world was set in motion. According to Max's father, the world collapsed with the fall of the empire and the first great war. Millions went blindly into gas and bayonets to fight the unseen danger. They went to fight other men dressed surprisingly like them, men stirred up by similar thoughts on the other side of the trenches. These were men without history, men with the spirit of the modern age in their blood, men who had thrown the books of Dr Kuhn's childhood into the consuming flames.

Dr Kuhn the elder can never determine which side he is really on.

Contrary to expectation it is Mrs Kuhn who still reads. She devours novels in English from cover to cover. She can no

longer read in her native tongues even though when she is ill
or febrile she babbles in a mixture of childhood dialects. She
forgets the titles of these New World books but remembers the
feel of new prose unsullied by history.

When Max buys a book he keeps the receipt for the
family accountant. It is for him to touch, his father to critique
without reading and for his mother to devour. Eventually all
the books end up on the same set of shelves. This ritual will
continue for Max even after marriage.

Once in awhile his father calls his mother a Nazi
for lacking clear thoughts. He equates this sloppiness with
destroying the truth. Once in awhile his mother will not ride
the subway because it has an end where the track leads no
further, nudging up to a thick iron gate. Both his parents shift
the topic of discussion away from transportation (which should
never appear to be free) to food (which might disappear at any
moment) or to real estate (which can never be overvalued).
These are the staples of survival in the New World.

Every once in awhile his mother will stop eating. It is a
reflex that usually follows a short discussion with a realtor. She
wants to die of starvation as a millionaire. If she starves long
enough she will be rich. She cannot admit that she has lived
her life here and she regrets not moving to Israel before the
establishment of the state. Secretly she despises that grubby
little country fighting for its existence, hates the donations
exacted from her, multiples of eighteen dollars sucked from
the collective guilt. Mostly she resents that they have a struggle
over there, and a meaningful one to boot. Here the struggle is
over. Eventually she realizes that's what she resents the most—
not having to struggle, as if the peaceful world has disavowed
the traumas of the past.

In the end she has to admit that peace is a good thing and only then can she perk up, eat, smile and get on with it.

For forty years the city has bulged and grown but in her mind she still lives at the suburban limit and never goes north. The highway might as well be the gateway to Siberia. This is why Max is expected to open up shop down the road, to find a place to live on this side of the border. He couldn't challenge the tyranny of time that has stopped or the arguments of the living and near-dead if his life depended on it.

MILLIE, MYRNA, MYRTLE AND MAX

"They are sending Dr Max away," Myrtle says.

Myrtle has spent many years on her bum in Locating pulling switchboard plugs out of their sockets and shoving them back in. She listens in on conversations and knows the answers—where the patients are going, when they are coming back. She giggles into her chocolate, keeping her information hush-hush. The only people she tells are her lifelong friends Myrna and Millie from the Stop Gap across the hall. Myrtle sits and chews chocolate in her little box, her bottom expanding quietly while Millie and Myrna serve the public daily from ten to two. The three girls have been steadfast friends from grade one, when Miss Macdonald arranged the class in alphabetical order according to first names. They began their friendship that year halfway down the third row.

"Dr Max is going away," Myrtle tells Myrna and Millie. She pivots forward on her stool and speaks around the doorframe.

Dr Max is what they call Max. Kuhn is a funny name they do not understand. It sounds vaguely dirty, even dangerous, as if it could creep up the insides of their clothes. Myrtle cannot say Kuhn without going red and splurting chocolate. If she can't say it, neither can Myrna or Millie.

Myrna and Millie stand in their tan jerseys at the cash. People often confuse Millie and Myrna, despite Millie's tiny beaked nose sticking out of her pink flesh like a carrot in holiday jelly.

Someone has scribbled "M loves M" on the wall outside the confectionery, in black eyeliner. Myrna, or perhaps it is Millie, takes a yellow j-cloth and breathes into it heavily as if preparing to wipe her glasses. "One sicko or another has painted a black heart on our portion of hospital wall." She applies elbow grease to the scandalous graffiti inside its black heart. The twin Ms stand above two blood-red lines. Myrtle is certain this presumptuous touch holds a faint smell of roses. As she rubs, the stain spreads, then begins to dissolve from black to blue and finally merges with the wall's smudgy green.

"M loves M," says Millie.

"A bad joke," Myrna says.

They implicate a disgruntled patient from Forensic or Geriatric or that no-good Dr Max himself, who is forever calling up Myrtle to intercept his early-morning pizzas. There is no use in believing Myrna has printed the stark black letters herself; her love for Millie plays on inside her mind and nobody ever guesses.

"Poor Dr Max," they all say in unison. The three women sweep past Forensic and Geriatric, along polished floors, through the tunnel. For once they leave their posts open to the world. They are off to see Dr Max for themselves, to take him up in their arms and swing him back and forth like a baby, to hug the child of their dreams, their fathers come in from the fields. Their bodies spread toward him down the hall and along two sets of corridors painted institutional green, past the vending machines that misfire often enough to deprive a gutter-bound depressive of his last quarter while rewarding the manic who bashes the resistant metal with closed fists. Particles of dust eddy in great circles. The three women are swept urgently along too-smooth walls the colour of an indescribable secretion. Cans of New Coke rattle in the vending machines. The concentrated smell of electric wiring gently burning skin wafts into the hall. For once the dust motes are shaken from Millie's mousy-grey hair.

Much to their horror, where the ground pulls above the window and the tunnel dips under the earth, they come face to face with Dr Max. On his stubby legs he looks unusually small.

"He is preoccupied with some woman or other," thinks Millie.

"He is afraid the boss is going to beat him," thinks Myrna.

"He is considering how to keep Marjorie Upton's hands off of him," thinks Myrtle.

Or indeed (they steal glances at each other) Dr Max is troubled by the business of the world: who to discharge and who to keep. It is the time of year when the ice breaks up and aspiring depressives throw their bodies into the river. The three women are certain he is a little messiah. So what if he is a jew, Myrna concedes to Millie, who has difficulty on this point. Millie thinks jews wear horns like Fred Flintstone although where they get them she doesn't know. She has been to the central mall that snakes through downtown, where the jews own half the shops, and has seen no horns. Myrna, on the other hand, knows better. She has lived upriver where they have a synagogue that looks like any old church. For her it doesn't matter who produces the messiah or whether he has stubby legs.

Myrtle nods to the right and to the left, much as she did as captain of the high school grass hockey team. She was captain of the team way back then and she is captain now.

"Without Max, who is going to do all of the dirty work?" she wants to ask. Who will wake up in the middle of the night to relieve Marjorie's conscience?

Myrtle knows Marjorie Upton's sayings by heart. "We need a signature," Marjorie whines, and Myrtle mimics her. Marjorie Upton goes over her work at three in the morning, imposing order on her world while her patients are drugged to the hilt and the corridors are filled with the mellifluous snores of the complacent and near-dead. They are all women—similar women, Myrtle and Myrna and Millie and Marjorie—but Marjorie Upton has risen above them. She is beyond gossip and friendship and has not grown fat. Myrtle listens to calls from Marjorie. It is her opinion that Marjorie is on the verge of a breakdown. She is always on the verge of a breakdown. Dr Max's letters, the ones that spread out after his name, those MDs and FRs and CPs and QRSs run all over her ward stationery and threaten her control. Myrtle is convinced that the letters after his name represent extra bits of brain that have leaked out. Somehow Max's extra letters do not make him stupid, they make him crazy. Anyone can see that. Why, just the other day Max called her up in Locating and said, "G'day, g'day, Myrtle," just so she would unlock the front door and brave the spring downpour for one of his breakfast pizzas.

Suddenly Myrtle trips. She has been pushing her body sideways and the tension has broken her shoe. She sighs in immense relief as Max looks up from his little black book and says, "Hi, girls."

By now Millie knows that something important is happening. She is just late enough—a half-step behind Myrna and two full steps behind Myrtle—to feel part of the threesome, to say she is here. Her life on the Stop Gap cash has led to an ever-deepening reliance on Myrna so that if Myrna succumbs to illness or visits her relatives in the Townships, Millie will turn in on herself. And if Myrtle doesn't come to work, Millie will die right on the spot. She cannot fathom having a breakdown. A slowdown to nothing, yes, but breakdown implies some kind of greatness and she is not great. She will leave all of this greatness to Dr Max, who is looking right at her. She has nothing to say. She cannot explain how she rounded the corner beyond Geriatric and Forensic and Maintenance and Administration and Records with such a fierce ache. It is an ache very close to love and she has no word for it. Millie has no idea where it comes from or why it has left. Looking at Dr Max now—short, quiet, preoccupied with a pen and some notes he is extracting from deep in his clinic coat—it is hard for Millie or her two friends to fathom the forces that have shifted their collective 690 pounds through the halls.

Myrna notices the ache pulsing in her thighs. She has not run a single step since grass hockey.

Myrtle feels the full weight of her everyday emptiness. The ache of disconnection has driven her a full city block from her tiny Locating box, across the expanse of hospital, into the tunnels. It has concentrated itself in her body and broken her shoe.

The three stand there looking alternately at Dr Max and at their feet. Myrtle's broken heel is a perfect decoy. They cannot take their eyes off it. Myrtle is the closest to understanding this. She is, after all, the communications expert, and the fact that it is her shoe is predictable. She is the captain and she knows what to do.

Millie thinks of turning to her friends to request the kind of explanation that has earned her innumerable sarcastic responses over the years. She doesn't have to say anything in order to hear, "You shut up, now, Millie. Wait your turn, Millie. Be a good girl, Millie. Don't be silly, Millie."

Myrna, who is the most philosophical of the three, stares dumbfounded. She knows the sort of thing going through all of their heads and knows it to be insufficient to explain events. This is not a clear thought, only a rustling around her middle. She adjusts her body, tucking her shirt back into her slacks. The gesture is very comforting to her, as if she has just tucked the truth safely away where it belongs.

"You are looking well," Myrtle says to Dr Max.

Max frowns, displeased with something he has seen in his book. He has not heard her. He slams the black binding shut and slips it into his pocket alongside the *Manual of Medical Therapeutics*. The paper's edges, frayed by the nudge of elbows and the sweat of fingertips, split into tiny fragments and fall all over the floor. Hordes of white coats flap by. The elevators whiz up and down ten flights. The intercom system crackles, "Dr Max Kuhn. East Six." He scratches some more in his little black book, then looks up into their three faces.

Max does not run off and answer the call to duty. The hospital is full of people trying to get from one place to the next, blood and lab reports clomping at high speeds through the tube system overhead. The computer is even quicker, but Max just stands there. He is looking at the women as if reading their histories on their faces and writing them down in his little book. Surprisingly, even Dr Moussakanski flaps by in the tunnel and seems worried by the intercom calling a Code Ten, which is important, Myrtle knows—an arrest or a death. Maybe the Code Ten means someone is dying and the relatives want something to happen fast. Or that someone is dying and they need a priest. Or maybe the nurses are nervous and need a patient checked out but the patient isn't dying quite yet, only thinks he is. Dr Max stands before them with his finger scratching his stubby nose so that even if the Code Ten is important, the very last and highest and scariest of all codes, *it isn't as important as they are.*

"Dr Max," Millie says, "is it true that you are going away?"

Millie says this into the back of Myrtle's hip and sufficiently out of Myrna's grasp so that if her lifelong friend finds fault with Willy-Nilly Millie she will have to reach right around Myrtle's amazing middle to get at her.

"No," Max replies. He has no intention of going away. He has a number of journals to review and an entire book to read. But not to worry, he will find time to ride his bike along the river and through the greenbelt. He will find time to waste. In fact, instead of standing there talking to them he has to get off to the ward to look after the code. He smiles. The elevator door closes on Dr Max and a sea of other white bodies.

As they disperse, the women believe he notes them with clinical interest: how they have escaped their boxes and how they tromp back.

MAX ON CALL

Max is on call the night Moussakanski slashes open his belly.

Flickering light from the television, sound muffled, casts a changing pattern of shadow on the walls of the on-call lounge. Between calls Max is shooting pool. This is what they do to pass the time. He lifts the cue into position. Then the beeper goes off. For a moment it rests on his belt. Then he leans forward, cue striking the ball; the beeper catches on the edge of the table and falls with a soft thud. The beeper hits the floor, spraying plastic and triple-A batteries in more than one direction and the ball drops in the pocket. The table, donated by a manic and inscribed "My One and Only Home," lists to one side. Max leans the same way, ready to swing his arm and dial Switchboard. He balances, waiting for Myrtle to stop doing her nails, waiting for her to stop gossiping with Millie or Myrna on another line, waiting for her to stir up her body and plug in the wire. The corner pocket draws balls down. Max hits up-table as if hitting uphill or upwind, but the balls give in to the force of Myrtle's gravity pulling them back. He thinks on one foot, balancing against the cue.

Thirty, forty, fifty rings. Switchboard isn't picking up.

He could write a case history waiting with this cue in mid-air. He could formulate, diagnose or go right off to sleep before Myrtle answers.

In his mind's eye he throws the beeper full force into the wall above the refrigerator. He manages to dislodge the batteries and a modicum of plaster.

Sixty, seventy, eighty, he continues. When I hit a hundred, this beeper goes splat against the wall, he thinks (the real pieces are still dispersed on the floor, waiting to be reassembled).

He counts slowly with the other House Staff staring at him, white coats flapping.

There is love and hate in the beeper, he protests, waiting.

The beeper is full of blood and that is what he wants to splat against the wall, the love and the hate, the late nights and Myrtle's body.

"Answer the phone," he says out loud. "Someone could be dying."

Myrtle knows all the locals. She looks on her board and knows who is calling and who is calling her back. By now Max is ready to walk in on her in her Locating box. He knows what she will say. "I knew it was you all along, Dr Max. Next time use the phone. That's what phones are for. We can't have all of you doctors ordering pizza and barging in on me every two seconds, eh?" Myrtle endeavours to pay him back for the first time he gave up waiting and went down to her box. She saw him looking at her, his naked expression. He had seen too much, heard too much in her cajoling, raspy voice and seen too much in her humpty-dumpty face—chocolate on her chin, pink fingers wrapped in a dozen tangled wires.

He rounds the table, shoots balls directly into their pockets and waits. Perhaps the demented guy is up there pissing onions into Marjorie Upton's disinfected corners. Or perhaps the old Italian, gaunt and pale, is bleeding from his dissatisfied bowel.

Then Max gets through. As usual his speculation is wrong. The call is from Emergency. A look of contained joy appears on his fleshy lips, demanding utter reverence.

Moussakanski has cut himself from stem to stern with an Exacto knife.

Myrtle gets the story out of the burly emergency nurse, who is dying to tell all. As Max lets the phone ring and ring and shoots pool balls aggressively into corner pockets, Myrtle locates Myrna and Millie on separate lines and holds them in suspense. When Max approaches the end of his patience she prepares to cut them both off. "You're joking," they gasp in unison. They quiver in spasmodic delight. "Do you think Marjorie knows?" Millie says. "Do you think it is because of Marjorie?" Myrna says. "No, no, of course not, and you're not to tell a soul until morning," Myrtle replies to both at once. When they all hang up Millie goes so far as to reach back over her teak end table for the receiver again but halts, thinking Myrtle will want to tell Myrna herself, and besides, it is well past ten and Myrna never stays up for the news. As for Myrna, she now sleeps soundly with her forbidden treat snug within her folded arms, thinking of how she will let it slip to old Millie as they hover like hens over the cash in the morning.

In the emergency room Max takes control. He calls Dr Alexandra Tuttle to assist. This is what he tells her, but what he really wants is a steady witness.

"Keep the field clean of blood and cut the thread," he orders. She has forgotten how to do these things. He collects gloves, silk twine, antiseptic, anesthetic. He puts a surgical mask on his nose and tells Dr Tuttle to get boots. He does not know if boots are necessary and he is sure there are none in the department but he says this anyway.

He asks Moussakanski if his tetanus booster is up to date.

He spreads the lips of the long gash.

"A half-inch through fat, no bowel," he says.

Tiny yellow beads of pink-stained fat stick up here and there. The cut forms a small trench and fills up red.

"No bowel, eh?" says Moussakanski.

"Sixteen inches long," Max says. He wants Dr Moussakanski to know he is not listening closely.

"Did I cut the bowel?"

They ignore each other and Dr Alix Tuttle doesn't say anything either. Moussakanski does not recognize her behind her mask. He doesn't see her frightened eyes.

"Lie down," Max orders with quiet authority. Blood is leaking into his teacher's crotch.

"Keep your head down," he says, raising his voice. "If you jiggle your legs you will contaminate the wound and there will be pus there by the weekend."

Max does not know where he has learned these things, especially the visceral sense of having fought in a war.

Every so often Moussakanski challenges him.

"Silk?" Moussakanski asks.

By now Max is on to his fourth or fifth stitch, opposing the edges and pulling them gently upward, puckered in an open kiss.

"Silk," Max acknowledges. "Silk from the Sixties," he says for no reason whatsoever. "It's all we have. A good thing, too. Easier to tie knots. You wouldn't want this coming undone. You wouldn't want your guts hanging around your knees."

The gash begins in the right lower quadrant, two centimetres inside Moussakanski's knobby pubic bone, and describes a very gentle S snaking up his abdomen to the right of the umbilicus where it loops into the second curve and heads straight for the heart. Max works from the bottom up, zipping in slow motion what Moussakanski has rent in an agitated second.

Moussakanski is almost serene while they work their way up his belly. It is an old pain they quell within him, a pain as old as his grandfather chasing him with his wrinkled hands and coattails flapping, mud splattering all around. His grandfather bought fruit and sold it in the market Mondays and Thursdays. He chased Moussakanski through the mud, exclaiming in his screechy voice. Moussakanski saw himself grabbing his *zeydeh* by his slim ankles and twirling the old man around his head. Chicken sounds were the sounds of his *zeydeh* haggling and praying. Life and death rested in the price of apples and a mad love of god.

Zeydeh raised his hand to strike but nine-year-old Moussakanski—agile, slender—slipped away and the old man with his bony, bearded face and crazy eyes struck air and landed in the mud. He slipped into the earth as if he belonged there. From the dirt Zeydeh cursed god and nine-year-old Mendel Moussakanski. The family was poor and Mendel strong, a throwback to Simple Jacob who carried his family in retreat from Chmielnicki, striking Cossacks with his fists. Mendel wanted to be a porter, to mix with ignorant street-fighters and beasts of burden. He wanted to carry a knife and protect himself, to trudge from here to there under his own power with new boots and a hundred pounds on his back. A wild beast and a goy, his *zeydeh* screamed at him, resigned in the mud.

Later, when the ghetto burned, Mendel ran—blond, invisible, a pale skeleton. Zeydeh's curse kept him agile and alive. He knew how to cross walls unseen, to drop twenty feet onto his haunches and roll unhurt, a loaf of stolen bread tucked safely away. He disappeared into shadows dressed like a girl, carrying messages across the wall. He was chased by his own breath, his *zeydeh* cackling as he outran tanks and soldiers and stepped over the dead flesh of his brothers. *Vilde chaye! Goy! Shandeh!* His bones would rot. He would consume the flesh of his own children.

Mendel ran with the devil's fire. When they came to the door he hid, sliding his slender body through a crack in the window, hugging cold stone in the shadows outside. Three steps and he was over the wall, gunfire crackling in his ears. The old man slumped onto his thin beard, his jaw cracking on wood, his hands limp as fringes at his side. The soldiers tore open his mother, her bald head bared, her wig thrown into the sink. They tore at her, opening her up from the inside. Later they would throw her in a heap in the corner, her bones tinkling as they fell one on top of the other.

For a year he kept them alive, stealing potatoes, going over the wall for bread. He went through the security check with Bella, two girls shopping, or through the sewer and over the walls with Bella, two slim boys running with the rats. Bella slipped her hands down bare thighs and he slipped his hands into foreign pockets. One day he stole vodka and they drank in the sewer. They pressed together in blind alleys. They made love on the metal stairs below the manhole. He dug in his heels high above the city and his head spun up to the sky.

DR Z WRITES SOME NOTES FOR MAX

Dr Z writes, *Max, this is how to think about the job in the office.*

Dr Z writes and Max must be imagined somewhere scratching his head.

Dr Z's scenario number one: *someone has not shown up for an appointment so there is time.* This is the only perk of the trade, besides bottles of whiskey and Italian candy at Christmas. *Take the opportunity. The time is not yours, then it is half-yours, then it belongs to you alone. Write this principle down on paper at the head of the list of office policies A to Z. File the list away. Don't rip it up.*

Okay, Max, you have a minute before you have to get back to the rhythm of work. Look around to get your bearings. The giant creeper in the corner has revived. There are tiny droplets on the edges of the leaves. The plant is thriving, having chopped itself down to size. There is a herringbone pattern of light and shade on the carpet. Not much else. Dr Z wants to set a good example for Max. He wants Max to see what's going on. *Missed appointments are to be taken in stride. It is not worth getting worked up over them. They are an occupational hazard and contain a valuable warning. Max, even you will not always be needed. Sooner or later someone will come and close up your shop.*

Confrontations with strangers: The patient has drummed up a formal complaint. It is being sent to lawyers or the College, perhaps both. Hard to imagine, someone bringing a complaint against Max but Dr Z knows better. Complaints are generated in the unconscious and it does not matter who is right or wrong. Max already knows that confrontation is best avoided. Max does not need to be told but Dr Z would do well to remind himself. Only if he remembers this will he be able to sleep at night.

On giving advice: Counsel freely. On this point Max and Dr Z are true brothers. Both are fond of relaxing and enjoying themselves.

Dr Z reminds Max, *if you don't know what you are doing by now you will never know. You might as well have a good time. Don't forget to discuss relatives and lovers you have never met. Speak as if they can hear you even though they are not in the room. Comment on the mental state of everyone mentioned, even if they appear in the movies. Don't hesitate to repeat yourself. Keep the tone conversational, as if doing nothing out of the ordinary. Your own words will come back to you dressed up in strange clothes so you might as well get used to it. If you don't stiffen or raise your voice you can say just about anything. Stop in mid-sentence as if to collect your thoughts. Stroke your chin and scratch your eye.* (Dr Z has tried out this strategy, both in the office and on the page with Dr Max, and it has not let him down yet.)

Phone conversations: By now Dr Z is forgetting Max and thinking more of himself. He is becoming tangential, having reached the point where nobody could possibly pay attention. He tells (himself? Max?) to *remember the basics, that a receiver can be hung up. When in doubt, say nothing substantive over the phone and offer an appointment. Having something to tell increases the chances of making it to the next session. What is good for the doctor is good for everybody else. Both sides must remain in the picture, like a marriage. This has everything to do with the phone lines so do not take them for granted. Maintain a conversational tone despite invective and raised voices. Write in the chart: sentence fragments, quoted words. Classify as necessary—good, bad.*

Case scenario number six: Dr Z is way out on a limb by now. He can hardly imagine whom he is speaking to, can hardly listen to himself. Nevertheless he goes on. He is on a roll. He will edit the roll later, wondering how he got there in the first place.

He writes, *when visitors are late, (about twelve minutes), assume they are not coming.* Twelve minutes is more than a policy statement; it is a length of time sufficient to generate a feeling which no longer belongs to the expected patient. After brief consideration: *hope that the feeling is correct and comes from yourself. Then, if you must, take out works in progress.* Drawings of the Beltway. Sketches by Max. *Hunch your body over them in case somebody slips in when you are occupied. You will not want anyone else to see what you are doing. On the other hand, it is permitted to read the paper or a journal. If Bach is playing it is sufficient to sit distracted and stare at the wall. Don't forget to close the waiting room door. At twenty-two minutes past the hour, replace the drawings, fold the journal, turn the radio back down, and take to the streets. Walk, sipping coffee from styrofoam through the hole in the plastic top. Styrofoam means you are between here and there, that you will neither sit still out there in the world nor return directly to the office. In other words, sometimes you are allowed to wander freely at your own pace. Secure your right to observe the sights: the neighbourhood streets, the mist on the river. Be happy in your work and be grateful there are places to wander in the in-between times.*

Talk about the weather rarely and only under duress. The weather is a defence. Sidestep it as best as you can, gently. There is little time to waste.

Make sweeping statements.

Generalizations are not unlike real love. They are out of style and cause embarrassment all around but once in awhile you have to reach for them. If you don't know what you are doing, feign ignorance.

Reinforce what you say with body language, for emphasis. This helps cover up while waiting for a response. Then everybody can breathe easier in the time in-between.

Don't forget that words conceal their own meaning. Having heard something once you must neither stop listening nor take it for granted.

And if you must lecture that insight is a modern defence or that an attractive body is one that is attractively clothed, do it softly. You, Max, might be thinking about your friend Alexandra but push on nonetheless. You already think of her too much as it is. Remember that arrogance is part of the job. It is a reckless trigger that spurs healing.

Case scenario number eleven: quote from the movies and the street. Most of what is known comes from there anyway, and you are far more knowledgeable than I.

Shun false modesty; it takes up too much time.

Feign ambivalence when you speak about medicines. You are a physician and there is no good reason to get worked up about it. When tense, divert into physiology and pharmacology. It can be a pleasurable release.

At times it is necessary to raise your voice. Be deliberate; patients are not programmed to receive correct information.

You know that alone you are nothing at all, so do not be quick to dismiss your mentor Moussakanski or his right-hand man Miss Upton.

Take note of spontaneous clinical remissions and do not fret, Max. Things are bound to improve, whether you are there or not. Even Dr Moussakanski knows there is more than one way to split open a brain.

Dear Dr Z,

It's me, your friend, Max. The real Max. The Max you went to school with. It's time to stop this silliness. You know as well as I do what you are doing. I am grateful you haven't changed my name. I feel recognizable, though, and just sufficiently camouflaged that your stories do not damage my professional career. I must admit, most of me is you in disguise. I do remember one or two fat female bodies in Locating and Dr M's famous temper. I remember just enough to wonder where you came up with the rest. Funny thing, after reading your column I find it progressively more difficult to distinguish history from your version. Did the head nurse's face really droop like a scrotum? Was she truly uppity? Was there a broom closet on her ward? Indeed, Moses Kanski was fascinated with differential diagnosis to the exclusion of reality, and his wife Alexandra, if memory serves me well, had read more novels than I ever knew existed. I am sure they would both be delighted to find themselves in one.

Now, the real reason I am writing. I am, you remember, a real person. Being alive, I would appreciate it if you would summarily kill off my fictional counterpart. Although not disappointed with his exploits to date, I am somewhat squeamish at the prospect of what I might do in the future. Furthermore, I suspect I shall not see you until this process of distortion has been terminated once and for all. In the end, better an attenuated real relationship than this middle ground. Max could go up and down elevators followed by fat women forever and where would that leave us?

Now, before you take all of this to heart, I would like you to consider a drawing I did for you years ago. While shaving, I ran out of blades and came to your wife for acute intervention. You were too lazy, bearded yourself, and categorically unable to distinguish one end of a blade from the other. But your wife, well, that was a different story. As you remember, she helped me out, and I suspect the drawings are still kicking around your basement somewhere. You could call the chapter, "Max with Half a Beard from Many Angles." Nobody, I am sure, will expect too much more from a man with half a beard.

As always.

Dr Max K

P.S. There is a conference in the early spring. Resort in the Townships. On respiration, movement and identity. You could probably stretch a business pretext. I would like to see my drawings again. Bring them, your wife and your skis.

THE END OF MAX AND ALIX, ALIX AND MAX

The sun shines. Winter snow is reduced to sloppy brown corrugated piles on dead grass. Even the oak and poplar look dead. The wind is sharp and the earth is a frozen brown. This is the eclipse of winter, the beginning of the thaw before green.

On the river paths Max kicks through rusted pop cans and paper debris. His bicycle splashes brown, salty sludge over the cracked sidewalk, spotting his jacket and trousers, wetting his shoes through.

He remembers cycling over the crossing and past the university on the first day of classes: the mood joyful, all those new clothes colourful and clean. Then men in forest-green shirts with late-summer tans dragged a bloated corpse from the water.

Now the icy April wind blows into his face. He opens his coat a few inches to let it tease his chest, sucking the warm breath away. The months have slipped from fall to spring.

He goes with Alix into the hills where dogs romp and crash through sumac and skiers climb to higher ground. Snow forms pale-blue crystals that soak his feet up to his knees and crumble to mush in his warm hands. There are chickadees about, and the occasional woodpecker.

Alix takes him by the elbow, her head slightly bowed. She leads him up the trail toward the receding horizon, the sun bright through birch and alder. He tells her to shush up so he can listen to their feet scrunching and squishing, outrageously echoing up the incline. He hears a dog barking a mile or so away, and children's voices. They come to a pile of wet leaves under a majestic hemlock. She turns around and he laughs. Wet feet and she wants to go back. A rift opens between them.

The body, he remembers, was pale blue and bloated, hair scattered and coarse, mud on the face and clothes.

He kicks through sludge, the noise of wet muck against his shoes. A squirrel crosses their path; a hawk circles overhead. He inclines his head, listening for the underground stream. He thinks of spring fields with their carpets of white trillium. Her grip on his hand tightens. He looks into her brimming eyes and starts to run but she will not move. She flails at his back with the branch of a dead sumac. Something wet trickles past his ear.

The forest is silent. Blood rushes in his head. He sways from side to side, falls. There is a sweetness in the blows and a fascination in that sweetness. Is this what he has seen in her hard eyes and sturdy legs?

Her acne scars are livid and her face is on fire. He sees tiny black nose hairs, and white flesh protruding between undulating buttons. She plants her legs and sways as if he wants to push past her or throw her in the snow. He is laughing despite the blood.

His face is mottled from the pain he doesn't feel. The noise in his ears becomes the wind in the leaves and he is swaying above the ground, legs numb and wet, the wind blowing down onto his chest before he falls again.

He sees into the swollen eyes of the corpse as it is dragged from stale civic waters, while colourful faces dance and voices sing nearby.

She is gone now, limping down to the car, carefully protecting her leather shoes, her black skirt pulled up. A shadow against blue snow. He hears the sound of an engine turning over, the gentle four-cylinder hum reliable and contained. The slight pulse of noise quickens and disappears. The forest is empty of her. As if she has not been with him. As if she has never touched him. As if she has not gotten inside him, digging into him, striking him.

Welts rise under Max's shirt. He lifts his hand to his forehead and brings away red-tinged earth. He cleans his face with snow. He has seen bears up here rummaging through garbage. He has seen deer, loons, beaver, but never this. He walks on, following the sounds of a reckless, bounding dog and children.

He will see her at rounds. She will be aloof, tight-lipped and professional. She will be clothed. Perhaps that is the problem. She will be clothed, mixed in with the mundane miscellany of needles, orders, nursing protocols and signatures below the x-ray board, beside the softening mush of elderly brains. She will be there, mixed up with those familiar words: basal ganglia, mammillary bodies, fornix, cingulae.

He climbs higher into the hills. The sun is directly overhead, almost warm on his scalp. The mud on his knees has dried.

Back in the office he thinks of Alix, picks up the phone, puts it back down. His life is full of drama and people dying, routine traumas multiplied by tens and hundreds. He handles the routine but with Alix he goes limp and puts down the phone. There is something in him that cannot expand toward her.

He watches dusk approach, his back to the farm and his eyes on the river where more than one of his patients have attempted drowning. It is easy for him to shut off and classify. He is deadened by so much feeling, by those who scheme to create remarkable events to feel alive. Sometimes such violence is an attempt to bring a listener to life so that when he listens the staged dramas stop. He doesn't know what this means but he continues to listen nonetheless.

He meets Alix at a café around the corner from her house. She chooses the corner and he goes around it in anticipation. Noise and smoke cast a haze over his observations and her body. He mentions Beltway accidents and she talks about movies. Why does he insist on ruining the afternoon by bringing up blood? Why does he have to remind her of severed limbs and red-stained glass?

Eventually he says, "This is the difference between us and them. We are not allowed to talk."

Max is fascinated by the spirit of the Beltway. It is no coincidence that the westbound lanes invite the weak and weary to cast their bodies from its overpasses. This cannot be stopped. The road demands its toll of semi-reluctant civic flesh. Voices have been heard circulating on the ward that the road is possessed by the spirits of the dead.

"Never discharge a patient preoccupied with over or underpasses," Max says.

There are patterns of current and flow. Max seems intent on proving his insanity to her. He himself has been drawn into these vortices more than once, pulled in by a perverse imp where the lanes widen west. A car occasionally shifts to get by its invisible barriers of sound, space and light. He can see it coming at exactly a hundred kilometers per hour, sitting off to the right, until the tension dissipates and he relaxes in his seat. Vehicles fly over that stretch of concrete. To and from suburban sites, eleven minutes from downtown. The radio pulses with the news of the route in and out; words are coined, a language of motion and routine transformed by the spirit of the road.

"I can hear the hum from my apartment if I open the window or walk the streets," he says. The mind blocks it out. He makes an effort to bring the hum back into his consciousness. If he wanders north from home along tree-lined streets the sound swells hundreds of feet from the barrier. Late at night mechanical noise settles over the district like a damp, warm blanket.

He tells Alix that his obsession with the Beltway creates an honest link with his patients. The average obsession takes an enormous amount of energy and dedication, and eventually he finds out things other people never find out. For example, patients show Max their drawings, graphic designs meticulously tracing nuclear dust through precise orbits. These drawings resemble medieval depictions of the zodiac or cabalistic sketches of the human body expanded to include the universe. The details are hidden, ages numerologically transformed, names condensed and combined. Under it all, Max knows, lurks an unspoken loneliness.

By now he is lecturing her. A waiter comes by and offers Alix a drink in a glass shaped like a penis. The penis-glass is a prop, a decoy. Max gets the message. They want him to lighten up. He lowers his voice and smiles apologetically but he is not about to give in. He is defending a position she would medicate in the clinic. The tension provides him with a perverse release of pleasure.

His own drawing is impressionistic. All of the lines are straight and display an apparent geometric symmetry. Overpasses, underpasses, exits and entrances cut swaths across it. He has documented danger spots, weak points and the sites of accidents and blood. The Beltway thus represented is an enormous oblong spaceship with tentacled feet, a one-sided centipede shaded with scribbled commentary sending its feelers down into the earth. Further out it is just a road. The transition points are the areas of danger and these are always moving (more or less) depending on construction, traffic flow and the time of day. It is no coincidence that motorists racing along the black stretches to suburban homes are reminded of their childhood loves when they cross these nodal points, remembering when it was possible to describe love and everyone knew what you were talking about.

Max admits to being a sop. He tells this to Alix on their way back to his new apartment. After all, even he needs forgiveness.

"Sometimes I adore this city," he says, maintaining the rhythm of his step. The sight of brown spring mud reaching up stone walls brings tears to his eyes. In May he cries when the tulips lose their heads. He doesn't exactly remember the muddy canal system filled to the brim or the brilliant tulips, but only the signs of change and loss.

He confesses that after his fifth or sixth beer he can make a joke out of his obsession. Out in the fresh air it is more apparent that he is not drunk; the beer has allowed him to talk in Alix's presence and to be forgiven, that is all. She knows alcohol shrinks the brain, even his.

This is what he thinks about the Beltway but doesn't say. That the road breathes at night like an enormous beast. It aches from being stretched and widened. It groans to release the pain. It loves rush hour: all of those cars bumper to bumper, crawling, massaging its hot flesh. And it loves midnight, the occasional speeders flipped along serpentine curves so broad that they lose their lateral bearings. He has seen motorists slam to a halt and pull off to the side, flashers blinking, to breathe, rest and pray.

Back in the apartment he is quiet and Alix has nothing to say. She would like to outfit his wardrobe, censor his thoughts, teach him a thing or two about administration. Sometimes it is best not to listen. It is a principle of hers never to be caught with her pants down. The drink and the glass shaped like a penis have suggested this thought to her. She wants to throw out everything brown and polyester in his wardrobe. She had a dream about Mozart in beige double-knits, expressing a loathing for clothes and classical music. She holds Max to silence by waving a dirty sock in front of his nose.

He imagines she is like this with her patients.

"Look," she says, sitting forward on the edge of his bed. "In the west end the road slims up from four to three to two lanes. It makes perfect sense, like pouring water too quickly up a glass. Pour too fast, it's going to spill suddenly *right there*."

She stops speaking and looks at him. He is entirely predictable, the same after one beer or ten, the same off and on the job, as if reality had no bearing on him whatsoever.

All along he has been thinking other thoughts. If she tries to seduce him there may be some surprises. The shape of her rash, for example. She will undress like a cripple protecting a deformity. She will destroy his clothes piece by piece, shredding them in a pile on the floor. He has no drapes on his windows and his patients will be watching, cheering him on.

A storm slinks down the valley, a pink rim on the horizon. He stoops to put on something by Vivaldi and hears her rustling behind him. He imagines her picking up vinyl and smashing it on the nearest hard object. He hears the elevator door open and shut, its motor rev up and the elevator cab pull away. Vivaldi; what could be wrong with Vivaldi?

Sometimes he finds it impossible to understand people. They talk, talk, talk and suddenly there is no occasion for talk, only pregnant glances and mute gestures. Sometimes Max thinks out loud and nurtures the illusion that someone somewhere is listening. This may be the beginning of paranoia—a final effort to conjure a listener.

He bounds down the stairs after her at an ultra-confident "on the way to an arrest" speed. Thirteen flights to the lobby. He arrives in time to catch Alix by the arm on her way out the front door. "You are going," he says with perfect ambivalence.

She holds his gaze. She looks right at him and throws him off guard. What the hell. Maybe she is right to look at him like that. He does know something about her. And she has a right to be curious, to be accusing. That is the source of her rage, that he has seen her. He remembers a moment in the market, between the fruit stand and the tea room, when he reacted to a hesitation in the crowd to his immediate right, just beyond their peripheral vision. He had detected something in the movement of people in space and the suspension of the flux of traffic and congestion. He had steered her away, pushed her around moving bumpers, dodged traffic.

She had screamed, "Are you trying to get us both killed?" just as a man stumbled by on wobbly feet, knife drawn, pink saliva halfway down his work shirt.

Max takes her by the arm. Maybe this is what reminds him of the derelict with the knife, the way he grabs and pushes her around. He drags her into the stairwell by her sleeve. She has violated a major tenet. She has put her feelings into him. This is a maneuver best reserved for psychotherapy. He wants to bash the grey concrete with his closed fists so he will not bash her head into grey concrete. Instead he huffs and puffs and appears ridiculous.

He says, "What the hell," and "What, what, what." He grabs her sleeve and lets go. He does all of this for her, oblivious to his own needs. She wants a show of passion but even this is not enough. She breaks away, dashes around the building to the playground where the wind gusts off the farm, around concrete, bitter now even in spring. She is in mud up to her ankles, laughing, quoting from more than one movie she has seen of strong women in flight from weak, violent men.

Then he sees what is going on. It is the mud on his pants and hers, the colour brown that brings him to his senses.

It requires very little effort to scamper three or four branches up the nearest tree. He calls to her to take off her shoes; they are caked in heavy mud and she can achieve no traction on the branches. She is blustering about, losing energy. She needs a script, stage directions. She needs him to chase her, flailing.

"Take off your shoes," he smiles.

She looks at them and sees the mud. This is familiar territory, a repetition. He can see himself washing her feet, drinking tea in the bath, the mirror steaming over with Vivaldi in the background. He wants to break the pattern, to change the replay. To skid into snow and come out safe for once.

"Take off your shoes," he says. His words appear to come from her.

"It's cold," she says.

"At least climb a tree."

She won't. She is growing up and will remain forever rooted to the ground. Her energy cannot lift her.

"You believe too much in your own weight," he says smiling.

She swings on the play structure below the lights of the west block of the hospital. She can only behave this way because she knows they will meet on the wards at nine sharp for rounds. This must be what it is like to be married.

She lets her hair down and slides forward on the swing, kicking, arching at the sky. She has forgotten him, or so it seems. She cannot stay limp for long. She cannot sit and do nothing. So she kicks at the sky. She thinks of her patients because this is what she tells them: "When in doubt, do something—anything—to keep going." After years of memorizing biological circuitry and copying her notes late into the night, years of believing that it will all come together, the end point continues to fade away. She remains both confused and comforted by night rotations and shifting environments.

She has become a dark woman, a woman who is no longer young. She forgets her father is still a trucker, her mother a waitress. She forgets her brother is a drinker and failed landscaper who lives in an east-end project where the routine includes beating the *conjoint* and the dog. She only half-remembers her sister is on the street, in and out of shelters, a sister who shows up in the emergency room looking for provisions and a place to stay. She forgets the greatest pain, her mother's amorphous body spreading across the sky. Alix has relied on her brain to get her out of the Valley. She does not know why she clings to her depression, why she needs the long sentences and technical jargon to muffle the "ehs" and the beer and the scarred faces that are hers.

Eventually Max picks her up in his arms and carries her inside. The lines are gone from her face. Her skin is smooth. A softness suffuses her whole body. She doesn't try to apologize. She has no energy. She cannot walk; she must be carried. He makes tea and sets her naked in a warm bath. He rinses her feet. He has been thinking of her feet for what seems like hours. He is surprised by them, never having thought of them before. He watches her body: her breathing, her head resting backwards, her hair dipping its strands here and there into the water, her hands quiet beside limp breasts. He has no information to gather, no instrument to touch with. He can only look.

As Alix sleeps he decides to take off his beard.

It is a beard of convenience, of nonentity. The beard makes it easier to jump out of bed and race for morning rounds. With a beard he has one less item to worry about. He can trim things up every second or third day and does not have to keep track of his razor.

He sets up the event. Baroque on the stereo. Scissors. An assortment of razors on the lip of the sink. He plans to do half a face at a time. This is a tactic to divide up the work, to make the job seem possible. It eventually dawns on him that he is curious about his own face. He wants to see it and wants to see it covered up at the same time.

He watches Alix in the mirror, her features slack. He feels at home with her for once. The tension between them is gone. He is free to chop at the hair and trim it, to pull the skin of his cheek flat, to draw blood. The going is slow, methodical. The rhythm of snipping and cutting stirs up his brain.

Max always wanted to be a doctor, his voice says, snipping at hair. This is what he tells people and it is perfectly true. At first he wanted to be the man behind the scenes, watching, protecting, an invisible presence. Then reality got in the way. He saw the price to be paid, his calm sullied by angry social workers and patients haggling for money, food, cigarettes. Patients, poor souls, were expected to give it all up: the alcohol and cigarettes, their buddies from the street. That may be all they had but he had little to replace it with. He often overhears conversations in bookstores or on the bus. "So-and-so killed himself." Undoubtedly he saw his doctor a few days before. Undoubtedly the doctor gave him some pills. He wants to jump in with both fists flying (hair flying now, not imaginary fists) but he does what he usually does. He sits, thinks, does nothing.

His mind replies with a clinical case. A patient presents with a sprained ankle. On leaving, the patient mentions a broken life, makes the usual ultimate request for the physician to recreate the world in his absence.

Why do they blame him for the abuses of people he has never met? Love him with a love he does not deserve? In sleep he goes from dream to dream, from the Beltway gods of vengeance and mercy to cutting through brain. The gods play catch with his body and he floats above pavement. He wears a black robe and his side-locks fall to his shoulders as he dips to and fro. He has stolen a body from the morgue, looking for remnants of a deceased soul.

Blood drips down the right side of his face in tiny spurts. Alix snores. Her blanket has fallen below her breast. She pulls it up in her sleep and turns over. Watching her brings him back to his own reality. He touches the smooth part of his face. He laughs quietly. He remembers going into a deli with a bouquet of flowers for Alix and the woman behind the cash (a plain, harried woman) had flashed into life. She said, "Oh, how wonderful, roses," as if they were for her. She had taken the flowers and drawn them to her face in a broad gesture before Max had a chance to grab them and run back to his next patient.

He looks at Alix asleep, at rest, so different from her articulate, functional self flying up and down the wards, barking orders.

As he snips, he thinks of Dr Moussakanski. During rounds Max had sent his mentor a folded message. Max thought of the note as a peace pipe. He had sutured Dr M's belly with the correct twist and twine; now he tried to suture together the correct conciliatory words. He wanted to let Dr Moussakanski know that he understood why a troubled scientist would take a scalpel to his own flesh. The paper was passed to Moussakanski during the noon department meeting, between Budget and Mortality statistics. The talk went back and forth: M-and-M rounds, death, sickness, bed occupancy, money, as Moussakanski smoothed and then crumpled the note in his sinewy palm.

Later Moussakanski stumbled out of the inner office in an agitated trance, brushing by his bewildered secretary. He shot forward and handed Max the paper, nose hairs almost on fire, cheeks red. His white coat flapped as he said, "Stick to neurology, Max. Stick to neurology and remember the basics. Physiology. Pathology. Morbidity. Mortality." He waved his left arm back and forth as if doodling in the air. Then he took out a black marking pencil and drew the letters M and M with bold, firm strokes on the mint-green wall. "Take your humorous apologies to the people at the institute," he said. Did they not spend their days sleeping while their patients spilled their guts to the opposite wall? Surely one of those cerebral types would be able to help young Max survive whatever was troubling him.

Alix stirs again. The bleeding has stopped. Max has a chance to see his own face: the exaggerated angularity of the jaw, the cheeks sallow from years of on-call, the fleshy neck. It is the face of a European gargoyle half-covered by beard, now half-revealed under pink streaks. He is suddenly overwhelmed by weariness as if he lacks the energy to remove the rest. This is enough to satisfy his curiosity. His face reflects his ambivalence perfectly. The clean-shaven side throbs. The flesh is pink, full, swollen. Little patches of brown thistle stick out here and there. A professional and a goof. A fanatic and a charlatan. A jew and a goy.

And the surge of self-doubt, where does that come from? He wonders if his patients see this and, if so, are they threatened or do they look right past him and only see themselves?

Max snips and scrapes. He remembers (it is hard not to remember) that his mother who routinely rails against the beard is coming for the weekend. She is bringing food, advice and a vacuum cleaner. She will push her short bent-over body back and forth with the Hoover, close to the ground. She will be overjoyed and pinch his cheeks like caricatures of grandmothers from the old country. For her, this is a real gesture. She means it and he knows he will have to eat all of her baking. She will be satisfied to sit on the edge of his bed, made for the first time in a month and with all traces of Alix removed (stray hairs,  perfume). His mother will close her eyes in bliss, believing the real Max has returned. "I can see your face," she will say, overjoyed. She will not have to push his hair out of his eyes. Her Maximilian no longer looks like that ghastly Freud who fills her husband's library from ceiling to floor.

The balance of energy is broken and he suddenly needs to sleep. But in the end he cannot walk around like a freak with one side of his face smooth and one shaggy, much as he would like to. He starts in on the other half of the beard.

The blades are all blunted and there is too much blood. He cuts and cuts and the hairs fall over everything: basin, soap, floor, his neck, shirt, shorts and socks. He turns off the record and turns on the radio, then turns it off. He waits with his face, waits for Alix to wake up and comment, waits for his mother to come and grab his cheek and his father to hesitate that extra second as he surveys his son with that look of conditional approval in his eye.

He turns the radio back on and catches the last seven minutes of *American Pie*. Leaning into the wall, he feels a surge akin to pushing his back into the frayed upholstery of his father's rusted station wagon after a weekend of on-call and bombing down the Beltway off-ramp.

He is stirred up. He turns the music on and off and back on again but the song is over. He is trying to erase it retroactively. He wants to live in a time when people sing slowly, when he can hear the notes: all of their beginnings and ends.

He begins to swear out loud, losing track of himself. The meaning is elsewhere, in the surprise and the denial of feeling.

He puts on his jacket and goes out. Tears stream down his face. He is comforted that Alix is there inside, resting, suspended, not moving. He does not want her to see him like this. What the tears mean he doesn't know. In his head she says, "Therapy, Max," and for once she is right. No doubt he needs a good dose of his own medicine. And he says back, "To hell with therapy," for no reason other than that it is a reflex, something to say back and smile.

He won't give up these moments. They are rare enough as it is.

In the end, this may be all that matters. All he remembers.

THE END.
MAX, ALIX.
ALIX AND MAX.

Three:
Dr Bill

A KIDNEY STONE BRINGS ONE STORY TO AN END AND BEGINS ANOTHER

There is a time in a life, in a novel or a movie, where a juncture appears. Something has come to an end. Something else is required. The story must be careful or it will break. It is no longer reasonable to call me Dr Z; Max is forever gone taking Moussakanski and Alix and all the M characters with him and Dr Z is, well, myself again. The natural flow of events is threatened. The story is over but there is a reluctance to let it die. Novels are put away and people walk out of the theatre. In real life, there is a suicide or an unlikely affair. Perhaps this process stems from an error in observation and invention has become a conscious act. Perhaps nothing is required and everything is already known. Perhaps, perhaps. Maybe you have to stand back and watch what unfolds. Maybe you can do little else.

The pain I suddenly experienced had nothing to do with either Max or Dr Z but somehow brought them both to an end. It struck suddenly as I was walking with one of my patients to a psychotherapy group. I crossed the driveway in front of the emergency department bent over on my left flank. The emergency department was a simple coincidence. I had to cross there to get one floor down to the group in the extended care unit. Despite denial (that it was just an abdominal migraine or constipation), the diagnosis was clear from the telltale tingling in the tip of my penis, a signature of uretero-vesicular spasm. I looked over my shoulder at the EMERGENCY sign and soldiered on in the opposite direction.

I was too preoccupied with my body to process the response of the group and after a few minutes I was forced to dismiss them. My shift from doctor to patient was sudden but everybody made the shift with little difficulty. Only later did I think of Beckett's uriniferous heroes, his hallucinated men in greatcoats branded by that smell.

For three days I hovered, moving in and out of a state of childish bliss. The pain, the drugs, the loss of control were terrifying and comforting. Everybody who came to visit called me by my first name, which is not Max and does not end with an X or begin with a Z. I was reminded of something human in myself again. The routine blessing for the gift of the body, *asher yatzar*, thundered in my head: Beware, should god close but one of those passageways. In a morphine-induced haze I imagined the good urologist in a clown suit and I am certain I frightened more than one of my doctor friends each time I returned to the department. The stone was obdurate. It would not pass.

When you are ill something wonderful happens. Others consider their mortality and give a piece of it to you. It doesn't take long. What you remember is a greeting and a face.

On the second night after the basket extraction I awoke at dawn. I had been dreaming but was roused into a state of somnolent wakefulness with a blazing half-hour replay of my prior experience. I thought, Is there another stone? Is it not over yet? and went back to sleep.

My saviour had presented itself in the form of a metal tube with a distressingly firm elbow. It was wide enough to thread a pickle grabber through. The stone was harder than you can imagine, with symmetrical grey spikes capable of ancient torture.

For weeks I could feel it there, a visceral flank memory. I stood above the toilet, my stream spraying in all directions, steadied by cold parental hands on all sides.

My children kept their concern to themselves and my mother was busy in the next town. First came the jokes about doctors in denial. Then about men being babies as they approached their years of infirmity. Family life did not miss a beat: the television with its relentless laugh machine, the same half-lies about homework. The sweet sounds of my wife channel-surfing.

The next night my eldest child awoke crying in bed. She had a monstrous spasm in her right calf. I know what this is like; it runs in the family from my maternal grandfather on down. The window was open and her legs were cold.

I said, "The window is open. Your legs are cold." And she responded, "I'm hot, I'm hot. Open the window!" She kicked off the blankets. "Your legs are cold and in spasm," I hummed to myself, over and over. I no longer expected to be heard but I spoke nonetheless. I rubbed her legs, covered her up well and she went back to sleep.

In the morning she was her usual self. On her way out she kicked the French door to balance the tension, opened it at precisely the right moment and slammed it shut behind her in a flurry of video-coordinated acuity. The house shook on its foundation like the visual scatter of a commercial.

My middle daughter, smiling, reaches for something at the table (the salt or the sugar) and topples her glass, which drains its fluid contents through my toast, down my leg and into my shoe. She watches it, still smiling, not moving. I say, "Please get me a towel." I can see on her face my expectation of an apology, my implied accusation turned on its head.

My youngest daughter and her friend Antonia are playing pictionary on the washer and dryer with black, blue, green and red markers. They are sitting cross-legged writing on the message board while the television mumbles in the next room. Thank god for small miracles.

Dear Dr Z,

I am writing on behalf on my son Freddy. An unexpected transformation has come over him since you left. We continue to present almost weekly at the emergency department but at that crucial moment when the possibility of admission comes up he smiles, cocks back his head on his knobby neck and says, "Mom, let's go home." He is spending his time looking over his shoulder at the sky instead of at the ceiling and four walls of institutional pink. The emergency is an odd habit, no doubt part of his obsessional thinking.

He has begun riding buses again. I suspected as much when I came back from work one day and he said, "Dr Z was following me in the market." I thought at first he had seen you there, perhaps visiting old friends or clearing up some of your business affairs. Then you followed him along the canal on rollerblades and across the greenbelt jogging home. It was the way he said it that tipped me off: "Dr Z was there behind me."

You stalked him to his old school to visit his childhood principal, long dead. To the beach where he broke his ankle at age seven jumping off a play structure. To the garage to get the snowblower going. To the driving range, the putting green and the links themselves. You have hidden behind birches and under the tee-off mats as he gradually resurrected his adolescent swing. You have advised him, your various voices coaching, cajoling, criticizing, "Loosen your wrists, keep your head up, put more weight on your leading foot, hold your elbow in, straighten your take-away." His mood has begun to brighten and he has broken a hundred for the first time in a decade. As if that wasn't enough, you have begun to follow him when he is not alone, undoubtedly a sign of your perseverance or lack of embarrassment. It is as if when you were there, you weren't, and now that you aren't, you are. Freddy likes paradoxes of this kind and suspects that you do too. He often looks at his feet first, remembering your dictum, "Medicine helps you keep your feet on the ground, but where you go with those feet is up to you." Then he looks over his shoulder, smiles and moves on.

People no longer slink away from him when he walks on the street. They smile condescendingly, amused. They often look back just like he does, to see what my Freddy is seeing there, but that is all. He has been helping at the course, collecting balls from the water hazards and bush, mowing, trimming back the trees. He has caddied nine holes when they needed someone; he knows the course like the back of his hand. He doesn't have to look at the red, white and blue markers to know exactly how far it is to the pin, how the fairways roll, the hidden traps, the breaks in the greens. He gets on best with the elderly, who don't mind his odd answers—which are always correct. They respect this correctness and they pardon his eccentricities. When asked, "What are you looking back at?" he no longer says that Dr Z is following him. He says, "Dr Z suggested I flatten my swing," and leaves it at that.

You, Dr Z, have been whispering in his ear and he quotes you to his friends. You have developed quite a reputation. They suspect you are a pro from one of the more exclusive clubs upriver, someone who trained Freddy in his deferential art before demoting him to the public links. He is making steady money and will soon take his older sister to the usual Florida tourist traps and play a few rounds down there as well.

I am a little concerned about the weather and his reluctance to remove his navy windbreaker in all seasons of the year. He may burn up after fifteen holes in the late-August heat, drop from exhaustion or have another seizure. His tantrums that we all remember so well persist if you challenge him, but he knows he can get what he wants in better ways and now rarely misbehaves in public. I offered to bring him out to see you, but he just rocked in his chair as if he was the parent now and would have to pull it all together as the master of the house.

I don't know how this works—one spirit tailing another, whispering from behind trees, putting thoughts in his head. His new doctor has tried to explain the changes, something to do with dopamine and the frontal lobe. That may be. Last week Freddy said, "Dr Z is in my frontal lobe," but quietly, so only I heard. As for dopamine, we have nothing against it.

Hope you are well out there. Freddy wanted me to enclose this photo. He is standing on the seventh green, on the short par three. He sank a twenty-foot putt, his first birdie. You shouldn't have to ask who took the picture. As Freddy said, it was you zooming in on him from the stand of poplars off the eighth fairway.

MY SON THE DOCTOR

"Dear Dr Z,

This is your mother speaking. Not a patient. Your mother. Me."

Breath sounds.

"I know I am not one of your patients or ex-patients and this is just an answering machine. But since we now live in the same city and I rarely if ever see you, I will, as they say, leave you a message."

More breath sounds and the scratch of tape going round and round.

"You can tell this is me, the real me, because this communication is not italicized and for once the letter sounds like someone else, not you."

More breathing.

"You almost lost the trust of your reader there, number-one son. Your reader was thinking, '*Dear Dr Z is talking and the letter is not italicized. More to the point, Dr Z is being inconsistent; I cannot trust him.*'"

Yet more breathing.

"You cannot deny that I have a good point. If you want to

hear more, meet me at the coffee shop on the corner tomorrow at 7:30 in the evening."

Pause.

"Do not bring your wife or any of your adorable children."

Further pause.

"I have had the pleasure of their company lately, in contrast to yourself."

Significant hesitation.

"The purpose of our meeting: your new career. Be prepared."

She barrels in twenty-five minutes late. I have had little to do but stare out the window at pedestrians in the dusky light.

"There you are," she bellows, as if it is I who have kept her waiting.

She has been reading the *Medical Inquirer*, she begins, without sitting down. I have previously played this moment out a few times in my head, offering her coffee or cake, asking if she has eaten. As it is, I look at her and wait. I do not wish to interrupt.

"*The Medical Inquirer*," she says.

I look at my hands.

"You have been writing for that third-rate magazine for quite a while. I hope you don't think that your thin editorial skills represent real work. I have a bone to pick with your fictional family."

Finally I speak.

"My what?"

"You heard me. Your fictional family. Those people you have made up and adopted for parents. I know that your father, may he lie in the earth and shit in the sea, is dead so he's not much use to us at the present time. I should have rid myself of him years ago, but that's another story."

"Another *story*?" I say.

"Don't get me off track."

Her voice has lowered and intensified at the same moment.

"My son, Max," she needles me.

"My name is not Max," I say with little conviction.

"You may know that. And I may know that. But your readership doesn't know that. And when they find out... "

"They don't have to find out."

I don't know why I say this. It is obvious to me who I am and who Max is and I don't believe anyone other than the occasional postgraduate resident or colleague reads the *Medical Inquirer* anyway. Somehow I am supposed to rise to the occasion.

"When they find out... "

"So what if they find out?" I manage to say. It doesn't matter. She is going somewhere and these are introductory comments.

"Now, take this Max," she says.

"Max?"

"He's a friend of yours? Right?"

"Mom."

"I know. He's your hero. Your alter ego. A biographical self."

"So?"

"So? I'll tell you so."

Finally she breathes. In-out. Counting. Making us wait.

"He's boring."

"Boring?"

She has thrown me off balance.

"Right. He is in love with an ugly woman and does nothing. He works at the hospital and does nothing. He sits in his office and does nothing."

"That's me, Mom. That's me in the office, not Max."

"Don't interrupt. There you are, falling in love with an ugly woman, going up and down elevators. Then there's that scene where three fat women come barrelling around a corner and almost run into him. They don't actually run into him. They don't actually have anything to say to him. They don't want anything from him. They don't touch him. He hardly notices them. Then he goes up an elevator. That's the punch line: *he goes up an elevator*. What kind of a story is that?"

"Sounds good to me. It's a plot. He stands there. Then he goes up in the elevator."

"Plot. Shplot."

"Maybe not a good plot," I say, "But defensible. He's on the way to a cardiac arrest."

"Stop the deprecation. It won't work. Bad work is bad work but this is no work. Something has to happen."

"You're not going to tell me what to do with the plot, are you, Mom? Not that. Not in all seriousness. Please."

She takes a breath.

"No. I'm not."

I know enough not to be relieved. I wait.

"No plot can fix what you have or haven't written."

She is smiling now. She has been wanting to tell me her side of the story for quite some time.

"Forget it. Your story is dead. It's going nowhere. It will peter out on its own. You don't have to worry."

"Mom?"

"Consider the narrative in light of your most vile patient, a child molester, say, or a murderer. The person you don't care about, who will vindicate your hate and go out... "

"Mom!"

"And blow his own brains out."

"That's enough," I say.

When she sees I am significantly offended, she smiles protectively. She has begun to joke.

"Listen here, Max Kuhn."

"Dr Z," I intone halfheartedly.

"Okay, right. Dr Z. Now, your fictional Mom is a holocaust survivor and your real family arrived here almost two centuries back, before the first great war. Your fictional Papa is a Viennese post-Freudian academic neurologist and my husband, your father... "

"Your ex-husband."

"Your real father, let's not beat around the bush, was a failed hockey player from the Prairies who played for the Red Wings farm team and destroyed his knees. Your father was a guy who walked around turning the television off and on with his ring of keys."

"I know, Mom."

This kind of talk is rare for her. One of her children is subjected to such an outburst about every five years, releasing the pent-up energy of a frustrated life focused on expectations that her progeny will achieve perfection.

"Now, let's get back to Max. I didn't send you to medical school for thirteen years so you could observe yourself going up and down elevators and falling in love from afar with unattractive women. I was hoping this wasn't true."

"Mom, it's a story."

"Yeah, yeah."

"I'm married. I have three children. I was married before I hit the clinics. I have an attractive wife. Do you hear me? Attractive."

"You can find her attractive, if you like. It's up to you."

"She does not have a skin disease. And I have no time to write."

"Don't contradict yourself. You have no time but you manage to write. My son, the little miracle. Now, let me get on with my point. It's just a story, right? Maybe a story put together about a friend of yours. Maybe more than one friend. Maybe you had a friend a bit like Dr Z or Max and you gave him a few more brains. Or if he was smart, maybe a few less brains. I know some friends of yours with names that begin with M or end in X. And maybe you had a supervisor like that Moseskanski fellow, whatever his name was, and maybe you didn't. Maybe you liked the idea of a survivor who really is a Nazi at heart. Which is a nice idea, I have to admit. It has a ring to it. It made me stop and think a bit. And maybe this Moseskanski fellow was nastier in real life and you wanted to transform him in your own memory. I can accept that. And maybe you were attracted to an ugly woman. Fine. It's a concept, as your brothers say. I have been called worse than ugly in my day and your father was attracted to me.

So here you are, imagining that maybe somebody else could love the woman who was ugly, which didn't necessarily mean that it had to be you in real life. Or maybe you know how that ugly woman could become beautiful, which I believe to be closer to the truth. So there is this ugly colleague of yours that you live with day in and day out on the wards and you start to notice how she moves and how she eats or doesn't eat and how things fall out of her clinic jacket when she stands up and how her body pushes against that restraining white cloth, and when you see her you think you can reclaim her somehow, make her a little beautiful, and what better way to make her beautiful than to put her in a story.

And maybe, here you are working under some rigid head nurse that you call Uppity Upton and after you and maybe somebody else has suffered working on her sanitized ward, really suffered with her for six months or a year, maybe even killed themselves, it was so difficult to work with her and that Nazi Moseskanski, you decide to first destroy her, then you realize, no, that's not it. That's not worth it. Anyone can do that. You can just spit at her behind her back. Or give her the finger. Better to have her boss screw her in a closet in a novel. Slimy, if you ask me. But, I can understand how first you have to make us hate her, then make us like her and then make us understand her."

"Mom, you said—"

"Don't interrupt me. I'm leading up to something. There you are sitting in your office all day, day in day out, doing nothing except listening, and suddenly you decide to say, Hey, what about me? I'm here too. I've got a story to tell. And I'm going to force you to listen to it. So you go about paying everybody back, paying them back for what they did to you, which is to burden you with their stories. So you burden them back and bore them to death. When I came to the part with the gun I thought, oh yeah, something is really going to happen. At least the gun will go off. Maybe it will shatter some glass or pop a tire. Maybe the police will come. Maybe the bullet will hit you or Max or the ugly intern I hope you seduce soon and graze you on the arm or rip your trousers or splash mud on you. Maybe the vehicle with the two women in the front seat

will veer off the road and smash into a lamppost and throw the
body of the man with the gun through a window. Or maybe,
just maybe, one of those hookers of yours could actually slap
one of those pushers or pimps or police officers that you are
always looking at beyond the brick wall (which hasn't moved in
a hundred years). And I'm not quite finished."

She takes a few breaths. Indeed, the wind has gone out
of her sails and she is thinking at her normal pace, which is a lot
closer to the pace that most of us think.

"I quite enjoyed your stories but I was disappointed."

"Disappointed?"

"Yeah. I'd like you to write about yourself."

"Myself?"

"Us," she says.

"Us?" I know I sound like a parrot and a fool but what
else can I say? This is my mother.

"Right. We have a history. My father was... "

Now I get it. My friend Dave is doing a screenplay on
Grey Owl and my brother is producing it. Another brother is
working on a script about planting my father in his grave. A
further script has been commissioned about Mom's father. It
is full of lies and bombastic sexual encounters shot against
muddied vistas, complete with cigarettes balancing precariously
on fat lower lips. It will be shot in the old world as it teeters into
the next. In our next life we are all moving to Hollywood.

"I thought you were working on a script," I say.

"It is commissioned."

When the punch line finally hits, it is me who inadvertently
delivers it.

"They won't get it right," I say. "Food will be scarce and
they will call him Wolf instead of Bill. His chest will be too big

and his moustache too long. He will betray your mother and smoke out his puerile guilt behind the barn."

"You are right," she says. "They will dress him up in buckskin and call it *Wolf at the Door.*"

She is not laughing. Suddenly she is not ignoring me. I get the funny sense she has not been ignoring me all along. We finally order coffee and cake and she seems to be avoiding my gaze. We dance around the usual topics: the weather, my children, why they don't visit, why they visit more than I do and how I married such a wonderful woman. She tried to warn my wife off sixteen years ago, she reminds me, but who would listen? By the time the topic comes back around, it has already sunk in. If I can write about people I don't know, I can write about family.

This is my mother's lasting connection to her father: a frozen metacarpal-phalangeal joint on the first digit. She is the middle daughter, the only girl with a physical deformity, the girl with frozen thumbs. Like her father and me and her first grandchild, she is prone to muscle spasms. Her toes curl under her feet and she has difficulty grasping a tennis racket and opening doors.

"Your father died when I was two. I know nothing about him." I say in my defence.

She knows I cannot write about the people I know, only people I don't know.

"Make it up," she says.

FIRST MEMORY

This is how I remember my grandfather Bill.

It is a single memory, on King Edward Boulevard, facing west. He is walking away—his broad back, his bald head. He smiles at me over his shoulder and walks away. That is all. He hesitates but does not come back. The mixture of my own fear and his confidence in me makes it seem like a strong gesture on his part.

He is going away; he will be back.

I am behind the wheel of his vehicle, looking along the street where it curves up and to the left. I know this is impossible; I must have been in the passenger seat but somehow I crept behind the wheel and got up on my feet and looked straight out the windshield as if I were him and, like him, about to drive. I stand up, look and wait.

This is the view into the future. Where I will ride my first bicycle. Where I will walk to school. Past the retarded boy's house who will drop my brother on his head and set the telephone pole on fire. Past my first love who will betray me on her sixth birthday. Past the old lady and her frightening dog where the world will end.

These thoughts cannot have happened then, I know now. It may not even be my street, my house.

It is just an image: early afternoon, the curve in the street, a look forward in time. Memory does strange things when it edits ordinary circumstances.

ORDINARY CIRCUMSTANCES

My kidney stone passed a month ago but I am not quite on my feet. I have six inches of tortuous phlebitis creeping up my right arm from the venipunctures and I am too weak to jog. It is important to drink and urinate constantly and I am supposed to avoid spinach and hard cheese (an injunction I ignore). My patients have forgiven and forgotten, my family has stopped quipping about the weaknesses of men in pain and I have been in touch with my mother.

The manuscript is back. My mother is making a movie about her father, Dr Bill. The work has been commissioned but the result so far is disastrous. Nothing is correct and no one will promote it. Producers have read the script. They have been polite, pointed out flaws, made suggestions. My mother will not give up. The writer she has hired does not know what to do and wants more money. The writer is busy in California working on a television series and my mother has been leaving lengthy monologues on my answering machine that begin, "Dear Dr Z."

Dear Dr Z, if you know as much as you think you know you will pick up the phone and talk to me.

Dear Dr Z, if you ask me you should stick to medicine and keep your nose out of this family project. Call me back right away.

Dear Dr Z, if you loved me like you are supposed to, you would help with this production. You could put your beautiful mind to it. You could make it go right. You could pick up the phone.

So far the project is all wrong, I tell her. I do not know if this is true but I say it anyway. I have a habit of emphasizing my diction to get her attention.

"He is my grandfather," I say, as if that gives me special rights, special rights to lie. I will ask her questions and write the answers down, I threaten, but this does not happen. I know more than she suspects.

I know what little there is. There are pictures and I know the three sisters, can imagine them as children, his children. There are plaques in the synagogue, a box in a local museum with newspaper clippings, the memories of the elderly. It will be a family story. It is a family story. It will be for us, not for Hollywood. I am at an age where many of my friends have produced similar manuscripts and filed them away for later. What is later? I don't know but there better be one.

Dear Dr Z, what do you know? Your grandfather Bill died when you were two. Had he stayed alive you would have done something with your life, believe me. He would have seen to it.

Dear Dr Z, why would you want a memoir in a drawer somewhere? What purpose is there in that? Who will read it? What's the point?

I am screening my calls. I listen to her go on and on. Her diatribes have become strangely supportive, even conciliatory.

If my grandfather could produce a churlish manuscript for his family, so could I.

Enough, Dr Z. This is your mother speaking. It is time to write about something interesting. The discovery of insulin. The plague of Montreal. As your father used to say, stop futzing about. Choose a topic and stick to it. All the bouncing around is making me dizzy.

In 1905, when Bill was fifteen, he survived a Russian pogrom. His short memoir of the events is not heroic. We know he survived and how.

I read the document one spring afternoon in May during late high school. It was an unusually warm year and I was sitting on the suburban patio he never saw, with my Alsatian at my feet and my golf clubs leaning against the lawn furniture. It was painful to recognize the adolescent yearnings of the unedited manuscript, dictated to my grandmother and transcribed in her hand. What's more, the prose was abysmal. He couldn't enter or exit a sentence safely. He began paragraphs with a judgment, left unnecessary qualifiers floating, forgot pronouns as if making notes on a first draft, and repeated himself. The bullets, the betrayals, the arbitrary violence circled around a sob of disbelief that looped from phrase to phrase.

I read through the story quickly and gave it back to my mother.

"He's translating as he goes," I told her, "And she's fixing it up, chopping, reorganizing." She, that was my grandmother.

English wasn't his first language, my mother sniped back. He always spoke with an accent, she informed me. What did I expect?

"There is only one idea in there," I said. "He runs and he gets away. Others don't."

I was seventeen at the time, studying science and playing golf. What did I know?

"Just fix it up," she told me, even then. "Take the story and fix it up."

I went to the eleventh hole to sneak onto the golf course with my trusty half-set of clubs and forgot all about it.

The manuscript was folded in half and tucked away for fifteen more years. My grandmother pulled it out of a trunk when she was getting over her depression in the nursing home. For her it was a talisman, a sign of life's unfulfilled possibilities. She stuck it in a cheap yellow folder and gave it to my mother, hoping the process would bring them both back to life. My mother went through it with red ink, underlining the intense emotion, the action sequences, the violent sobs.

I suspected he wrote the short account on the Prairies as a medical student, or in the clinic between patients. He was a student and an intern during the first great war. That was the way I thought of him: in the lab reading, his head bowed over his desk, pen to paper, stethoscope to chest. The great war created a life for him. It opened up possibilities that he grabbed, created patients that he treated. For a long time that's how I thought of his manuscript: something he wrote down in between patients while others fought overseas in a war he didn't want.

FIRST SABBATH STORY

They assemble Friday nights.

Bill's wife Rachel dresses the girls up and lights two candles in the middle of the set table. She reads the words slowly, hesitantly. She does this for him, for a tradition that has come to her late in life. The silver candlesticks are from his family, not hers. Contrary to tradition, it is the father who sets the tone of this home. He likes to joke around when he is telling stories.

"When I was running from the Cossacks," he says. He laughs and so do the girls. Cossack sounds like something you get wrapped up in, something you wear to a school dance, a word from another culture. Other cultures are wonderful because that's where Daddy comes from.

Someone passes the tea, asks for a second cup.

"It was like Winnie the Pooh," he says. What was? The Cossack story. Everybody titters. Winnie the Pooh is boring to the girls but Bill continues to smile. Being bored is the right of those who live in safety.

"Remember when Pooh gets stuck in Rabbit's house? That happened to a friend of mine when we were running."

Rachel casts him a glance a shade cooler than usual. They have all heard the story before. It is like the blessing over the candles—it has to be repeated at appropriate intervals. Bill is a child and he is running. He cannot tell his children anything about the man who gets stuck. He knows nothing; only that he, Bill, was smaller and the other man was bigger. Bill did not wait to see what would happen to the bigger man. Seven or eight of them were trapped in the house when they found the bricked-in window to the lane. They were too frightened to notice each other's faces. They knew they were friends by design, that they were being herded into the same place.

"Pooh got stuck with his legs in and the man got stuck with his legs out," says Bill.

The girls are confused. Had the man eaten too much honey? Is that why he got stuck? Did his friends come by and read to him, like Christopher Robin and Rabbit? Did they all get together to pull him out later?

No, it wasn't like that. The house burned down, everything on the inside. The courtyard and laneway were spared, including the legs. The priest said it was some sort of miracle, those legs dangling against the brick.

"Like Eeyore," says one of the girls. He lost his tail and Christopher Robin pinned it back on.

Rachel says, "Why did they say it was a miracle, Bill? The man was dead."

The girls hush. It is their mother speaking.

"That's what they do when the church fails you," he says. "They find something odd and call it a miracle."

"Pooh's head got stuck in a jar," says the little one.

"Listen to Daddy," says her eldest sister. "It's a miracle he got it back out."

TWO PAIRS OF GLASSES

Bill wears glasses. He is funny about them. He gets them in medical school and is never without them. At the time he has only a single pair to misplace. Maybe his eyes deteriorate from all that microscope work. He soon has to remove his glasses to read. Then he needs bifocals but cannot seem to manage them. He gets dizzy and has to sit down to catch his breath, as if his limited sight uses up his air. He never adjusts.

"My reading glasses," he often screams, neither a question nor a statement, at no one in particular.

When he turns on the ignition of his miraculous vehicle, he knows nothing, enjoying the hum of the engine. If a fan belt slips he enjoys the crackly swish against the rad and waits for the smoothness in the rhythm to return. He expects cars to run by themselves. Such is his trust in the new world.

Like many, he comes to the new country in those few years between the pogroms of 1905 and the first great war. Like many, he stays on the railway until he reaches a spot where he knows someone and then gets off. He has family in a prairie town. This is in 1910 or 1911. The family has been coming out piecemeal. He imagines his brother Isaak in his cell in Irkutsk,

Siberia, although Isaak is already dead. With Isaak either dead or gone, Bill has nothing to lose. Another brother disappears to New York. His last brother, crazy Shimon, sticks to him at a certain distance. As does his sister Fanny. They all come to what he calls "the colonies." He is already in his mid-twenties and is working on getting rid of his foreign accent. The accent sets him apart from the other immigrants: Ukrainians, Mennonites, jews.

When the time comes, he walks to the Assiniboine forks on the railway tracks. "I walked to school along the tracks," he likes to say, meaning medical school in the next province.

During the war he is assigned to a clinic in a small town his Prairie colleagues consider "near the coast." He is told to enlist in the provincial capital. Then he proceeds down the hall and gets an honourable discharge—he knows the difference between good bureaucracy and bad bureaucracy. It is his duty to fill in for the country doc who has gone overseas.

He doesn't really intern: there is no time and there are no instructors.

He works in the interior town awhile and is transferred to a sanatorium nearby. That becomes his passion, respiratory medicine. He comes to the real coast for his social life. That's where everyone he knows ends up, the last stop before the sea. Eventually they offer him a job at the general hospital and he moves down for good.

He is often joking and serious at the same time and it gets him into a little trouble. Once he is frisked at the border when he says, "Just three monkeys in the back; see for yourself." That is his whole life, his three daughters in the back seat.

He likes the freedom of remaining ambiguous and relishes exercising that freedom. When the customs official pulls him into the building and searches the car he is not afraid. He remembers the past and knows he is in a different place. Here officials check things out and keep a straight face. They don't shoot you in the head and laugh about it later. He loves the three girls—his monkeys—no longer laughing in the back of the car. Over the years he drives that trip so often the border gets used to him and his jovial balding pate. When it comes time to smuggle streptomycin he goes across weekly, tossing the pill boxes onto the seat where the children sit. Like his kids the boxes rest there haphazardly, in full view. He has paid his dues and they let him through.

BRIDGE

Dr Syd moved to town the year after the second war and Bill immediately became his mentor, inviting him back to dinner that first sabbath. There was exactly a decade between the initial dinner with Dr Syd and Bill's death but it seemed like the stretch of a lifetime.

Dr Syd, at 81, seems young and eager. He scans his brain for other sources, people who will remember. He arrives repeatedly at the same conclusion: they are all gone. It is a disquieting thought and he will not sit with it very long. I have to ask him for details. He does not believe he is the only one who knows.

I, Bill's grandson, should know.

"I agree," I say. But I still do not know.

"The sisters?" he asks.

I say nothing.

"Bill was a smart man, a quiet grandstander," says Dr Syd, as if they are the same thing. "He would put up those old x-rays—the small ones you could frame with two forefingers and a thumb—twenty, maybe thirty in a row, and read them off in two minutes. His eyes would hardly rest on the film before he was on to the next one."

"Like shooting a row of hockey pucks into an open net from the blue line," he says.

"Bill often crossed the border and bought streptomycin. At first it was only available there, and then it was cheaper. He bought it for his patients and brought it back."

In the meantime he left the young Dr Syd in charge of his practice.

Dr Syd's face brightens when he mentions bridge. Do I know how to play the game? he asks.

I say something about suits and runs and Dr Syd says, "Okay. Bill didn't organize his cards in any order, not by suit, nothing. He just picked them up and left them random in his paws, sticking out at odd angles."

"And he played well?" I ask.

"Better than some," says Dr Syd. "It was a joke but not a joke. It was somehow easier for him to play that way. He was full of odd habits. His wife was entertained by his antics. She revered him. It was the Russian hysteric in him. He could have smoothed his accent away but he kept it for her, for the drama. She was a better player than he: controlled, more studied. She provided the foundation, he the flair."

Dr Syd looks at the ground.

"He gave her the opportunity to participate. And she gave him the opportunity to win."

Dr Syd says I can call him anytime. Memory for him is hardly more than a feeling. He doesn't want to work at it too much. My fourth conversation and this is all I have.

"Ask the others," he says.

"The others?"

"How about D?"

"D?"

"No, he came to the community later. In the Fifties."

I watch Dr Syd carefully.

"And P has just died," he says. "People don't live forever."

By an odd coincidence I know Dr Syd's sons. I ask how they are and the conversation takes its usual turn. And that is how it should be. To live in the present and the future.

My mother confirms that Bill played an odd game of bridge. Dr Syd was not making everything up.

"Your grandfather held his cards upside down," she says.

"Upside down? There is no upside down," I reply. "Upside down is the same as right side up."

"He held them so no one could see them," she persists.

"Who cares about that sort of thing? Nobody looks at your hands." This much I know.

"They try to look. Maybe he wanted them to look."

I don't understand.

"He used to shuffle the cards in his hands."

"Shuffle them?"

"Yeah. Move them around. To keep the order random and changing. What's more, he was a bid stealer."

"A bid stealer?'

"Come on, Dr Z. Don't you know anything? They would be sitting around, all of those doctors, Isaac S and Victor H and Harold K and Dr F the surgeon and Archie H that delivered even the likes of you. They were all ten or twenty years younger than him, some were even my own contemporaries. That's how he sold the house, to Dave Z, over bridge. Anyway, they usually had an extra one or two because they were doctors and always on call. The extras were called kibitzers; you know, the fifth wheels, the guys who moved in if you got called away.

He didn't want the kibitzers to see his hand, so he shuffled his cards around and flipped them over."

"A bid stealer? What's a bid stealer?"

"Three is easier to make. He would lock in routinely at Three No Trump and force his opponent to go to four or five."

"I don't get it."

"You come by and I'll give you an education."

"That's how he won?"

"Uh-huh. He stole bids and confused the kibitzers and won often enough. No one knew how he did it. He didn't play in a normal way. If you come over I can explain the game to you. But I can't explain how he played it. He played it his way. No one else ever played that way. Ever."

"What way?"

"His dog Smokey would sit on the footstool and give him advice. Smokey would walk around and around in a circle to get comfortable, as dogs do, then sit down and look the other way when Bill had a rotten hand. Smokey was the greatest kibitzer of all. Come over. I'll show you how to play. I'm your mother. I still know a thing or two."

"The dog was his kibitzer?"

"And that streptomycin thing. It wasn't cheaper across the border; it was just available, plain and simple. You had to register on the way into the country. There has always been trouble across the line, even then. They let you take ten bucks across, not a penny more. You couldn't buy much streptomycin with ten bucks. Mr H of Mr H's Apothecary in Blaine, a very proper man, slim and extremely short even in his top hat, had to help round up the money in the States somehow. I know what I'm talking about. I went with him more than once."

Lil, Bill's eldest, can't explain the cards either.

"He held his cards backwards," she says. "He would flatten them and hold them backwards. I need to have a pack to show you. One card on top of the other. Can you see what I am doing with my hands?"

We were on the phone.

"Lil!"

"You remember Smokey?"

"Smokey?"

"The dog. My dog. He would sit on the footstool and Daddy would consult him. 'What do you think, Smokey, should I play this card?' And he—the dog—would shake his head back and forth and Daddy would say, 'Smokey says I should play this card.'"

"Okay."

"He had a partner. I even remember his name. Charlie W."

"Was he a doctor?"

"No. Daddy didn't play just with doctors. Charlie W would light a cigarette and take one puff and forget about it. The cigarette would get knocked onto the floor and burn a long gash in the carpet. Mother had to have pieces sewn back in three or four times."

Daddy and Mother.

"Grandpa Bill sounds like a funny guy."

"He was too busy to be pinned down," she says. "Poker once a week. Bridge. He was a founding member of the synagogue, and the president. He gave lectures. He couldn't write and he couldn't spell. If he made notes he couldn't read his own writing. He had to throw his notes away. He had to be extemporaneous. He took his medical school exams orally. He couldn't write and they couldn't read his notes. He signed his name on his cheques with two or three up-and-down strokes. On one occasion the bank could read his name clear as day— William M—and they wouldn't honour the cheque. There was a new manager and Bill wanted to make an impression so he took five minutes or so and wrote his name out properly. They thought it was forged. You know how he got his job?"

"His job?"

"Yeah. He was the only guy in the province who could read TB plates so they had to lift the restriction. You know, on the jews. There wasn't exactly a restriction, but there sort-of was and it had to be lifted. I know; I worked for him two summers. I put the plates on the fluorescent backboard, the viewing screen. He took care of the mobile clinic buses.

"They would shoot the films with the patients' clothes on. Once he called me in to see a picture of a guy who was so poor he had a nail holding up his pants. They took the film again, with his clothes off, and the nail was still there, swallowed. He recognized my fifth-grade teacher from her x-ray plate. She was, how shall I say, rather broad, hardly fit on the screen. When Daddy died, six police officers held up the Broadway intersections for an hour to let the funeral procession pass. The whole community was there. That's how well he was liked."

Then Lil gives me a bit of a gift.

"When he went for a walk he always used his cane. His voice was high and squeaky and a friend or two used to imitate him. When you were born he came to a clinic meeting and he beamed so much, all the way up to his bald head, that he didn't have to say he had a grandchild. They read it on his face."

A DAY IN BILL'S LIFE

It is time to reconstruct a day in the life of my grandfather Bill. I know little about this. As Dr Z's mother has repeatedly said, I will have to make it up.

The computer screen is expanding and contracting. Perhaps it will destroy all of my notes.

My wife is on the highway coming south in the rain. Headed home.

The kids are in the kitchen listening to pop noise. They haven't watched television all night. Of this I am vaguely proud.

My eldest daughter has been sick again. Her illness is a little out of control and she is on medications normally reserved for the frail elderly. I suspect she is feeling better. Having found a discarded set of drumsticks she is rhythmically smacking some pots.

My middle daughter is downloading photos of her favourite movie stars, decorating cards and blowing up balloons. She is constructing the parameters of a birthday party. The birthday girl has yet to be assigned.

My baby, who is eleven, is making her lunch for school tomorrow. My eldest made dinner. My middle daughter was cajoled into baking the dead bananas into a cake. When the cake wouldn't gel, my middle daughter blamed her younger sister for not helping. Indeed, the youngest had been busy all day reading through a section of Talmud for school. She is translating The-Parade-of-the-First-Fruits, drawing a picture of the biblical procession. The parade is being led by a crayoned ox with a garland and gold-plated horns.

My middle daughter is really blaming my eldest daughter for being sick and my youngest daughter for being smart. I suspect she would forgive them if they weren't so busy.

In all of this there is no avoiding the topic of mid-life failures. They have been concealed within little successes and provide a kind of context of what it is reasonable to expect. I can rattle off examples in a flurry as predictable and impulsive as prayer. Each item brings with it a remarkable sadness. Poems and stories in the top drawer, abandoned. Careers occasionally glimpsed. The golf swing that doesn't quite integrate. Books not read, instruments not mastered. In medicine there is always the failure of insufficient research, of missing the diagnosis, of not conquering death. Then there are the relentless dislocations of marriage and, worst of all, the unspeakable failure of parenting. Some say it is important to fail your children and hope they will learn from it. Undoubtedly this puts us in the same league as a demented god threatening once again to flood out creation.

My grandfather Bill lived a life beyond irony. He was a success in a world that told him so. His was an almost-modern world, a world where the stride of a man with a cane revealed his inner world because it was his outer world, where statements could be made and supported, where he could assert and command belief from his children for the duration of their lives.

Bill liked to argue with his colleague and archrival Dr K, the surgeon. I think of Dr K as the bad guy whose son-in-law the dentist won Bill's house in a game of cards. Medical illnesses are social illnesses, Bill liked to say provocatively. Dr K would throw up his hands and wonder why Bill went off to do house calls in the middle of the night. Dr K did not see the enemy Bill could see in the weeping walls of those homes: the silent tubercle bacillus hiding in the mixture of breathless screaming and despair.

What can the tubercle bacillus do?

Invisible, it comes in on the breeze without a shudder. Bill tells his wife this and she smiles condescendingly, rejecting his tangential comments. She knows they are important but recoils when they are not clearly articulated. When they are alone, she is cold to him and turns away. The arbitrariness of her vanishing smile pulls down a shade, takes him back to the circumstances of "those three days" in 1905.

Bill's wife Rachel wears flannel to bed. And what does he wear? Looking back, his three daughters do not know and there is no one else to ask.

The eldest, naive and dumbfounded.

The middle, unfinished like her mother.

The youngest, bitterly shrewd, almost miserly.

How do you examine a chest?

You enter the room and you watch. You take in the walls, the surroundings, the air. You are sensitive to biblical curses, walls that breathe and grow unnameable things. It is this malevolence that gets into the lungs. The mycobacterium resists staining, resists identification. Invisible, it sits within its calcified temple in the pulmonary apices. Slowly the body's defences crumble. Bill knows what he will hear before the stethoscope slips into his ears, from the shape of the chest and how it moves. He is rarely surprised by the crackles, the dullness of pleurisy, the limitations of fibrosis, the hollow blowing of sclerosis, the quiet dance of whispering pectoriloquy.

He likes to demonstrate this to students. They are anxious and hurried, their hands on their stethoscopes even before they enter the consulting room. He does what he can to slow them down, to get their fingers out of those pockets. He knows how to quiet a room full of anxious students by dangling his hands at the sides of his body in natural flexion.

His daily scenes: his office, the wards, the squalor of rooming houses; wives abandoned up the industrial streets; and in the back of his mind his brother Shimon the dandy turned prematurely old and crazy, not opening the blinds where he lives with no light and little air.

How does a doctor see things?

This is how Dr Bill might answer. The physician detaches, watching. He hides there in observation. Patients live in his mind. They are folded into the details of his life and dreams.

These are Bill's sounds: footsteps in a deserted concrete hall, the relentless whining of the centrifuge, the faint hum of traffic on Broadway. The sounds come to represent his mind, a distillation of thought that has penetrated the people and their diagnoses, a feather moved by the mouth's breath.

His life reflects a remarkable balance. He is a happy man and has no complaints. But he knows there is something else. He is grateful for his past, of coming close to death, if only once.

Bill hunches over the wheel of his car in the same position he uses to peer down the barrel of the microscope, stretching the same muscles in the small of his back. He turns the key and checks for his glasses. He touches his black bag on the passenger seat. The antiquated loupe is still in there with his black stethoscope and reflex hammer.

Although uncoordinated, Bill is a friend of technology past and future. He has never owned a car you have to crank up on the outside, and for good reason. It would get away from him and run into something. He loves his tools but knows there are limits. He loves his tools even if he rarely uses them or if they have outlived their usefulness.

He looks out at his home, his safe bit of paradise: the treed lot, the stretch of grass. The neighbours (although a bit nosy) would never shoot him or burn him in his house.

He has a habit of turning right twice and going down the main street and in the back way to the hospital. He doesn't like to turn left against traffic. It is unnatural—an unnecessary risk. He thinks of his car as a farm animal that is used to its routine, sticking to its own rutted track. He expects it to be happy if it has a marked route. The routine eases his mind and reminds him of the country of his birth.

He has a patient or two to remember to fit in between his office and the ward. Mrs Lee, with her chronic chest. Mr Joe, actively spraying tubercle bacilli into the contained humidity of his restaurant.

Bill the doctor has a mind to show up at Mr Joe's with a hospital mask and gown and order some spaghetti one of these days. It is a fleeting image of no consequence. Still, if pushed, he has a habit of acting out these fleeting images of no consequence. Bill likes to eat vegetarian out and kosher in, but he would nibble a bite or two of ham so as not to insult his host.

Joe is a special concern. His restaurant is small and dank and his wife and three small children routinely spread rancid dust about with their kitchen chores. There is a steady stream of regulars to consider: stevedores up from the docks, workers after shift at the train station, secretaries en route to their east-end apartments, working girls dropping in for spaghetti before their shifts and coffee, usually free, afterward. Joe could easily hand the restaurant over to his wife but he cannot imagine himself idle and people talking about it. He would want to be there, to talk back. He has been minimizing his symptoms, ignoring them. And with the tubercle bug, Bill knows, you are often guessing. You couldn't say, "Joe, you are going to die unless you do something about this." Joe believes the TB bug is mostly a thing of the past. It was vanquished with the war, struck down by post-war optimism.

Bill the doctor is compelled to disagree. He has too much respect for the sneaky bacillus. It will get up and strike again. A single mycobacterium can mutate in the liquid caseum, generating a new link that, in time, would kill the strongest host. Bill doesn't care about the strongest host. He cares about Joe. Bill wants him in hospital where he could be dying one minute and miraculously saved the next, where the drama could be humorous and not tragic.

Truth be known (he barely notes the blue mountains above him as he drives down the hill) Joe's symptoms are puzzling. High fevers without night sweats. Middle lobe consolidation. No sputum. At least not yet. Perhaps Bill as physician has conveyed his indecision unwittingly. The plates have not grown anything—no bacilli, no regular bugs. Without sputum there is nowhere to look for offending organisms. The lesion is likely in the process of being walled off. As Joe says, "I'm not spitting blood. Yet."

Joe is right. And Bill thinks, Maybe that means he's not contagious. Or maybe it is cancer or a fungus or an infected noodle that slipped out from between his teeth deep in sleep and lodged itself in the right middle lobe. Still, risk is unnecessary. Bill will drop by at lunch, between his rounds and his office. He will drink half a coffee; that's about all he can stomach. It will soften Joe's resistance. They will talk. If he waits for the famous miliary pattern to emerge on the roentgenogram, it will be too late for Joe.

He glides down the hill riding the brake, thinking of the bacillus's cell wall. Unlike bacteria that take up the blue dye and succumb to the famous penicillin, its acid-fast barrier is a more competent forcefield. To Bill the tuberculosis mycobacterium seems to hail from a different planet, holing up in its fortress of pus behind a fibrocaseous wall of its own making. He knows it is just a question of time before the right antibiotic combination comes along. He believes in the twentieth century, but he also believes in something stronger, more resistant to the progress of knowledge.

He believes in the presence of mind of the tubercle bacillus. There will be battles en route: step-wise cures, man and bug honing their strategies in petri dishes and living tissues. Some of the bacteria's sister microbes only rarely seem to strike, floating around in the air as benign as dust, choosing only the most opportune moments. Under the microscope benign tubercular dust is indistinguishable from its pathogenic sisters. He considers this camouflage something of a clue or a warning, a riddle within the riddle where philosophy and medicine come together.

He slips right on Broadway, waiting unnecessarily for the light to change. As usual there is little traffic and most of it ambles on over the bridge downtown as he waits. For a few blocks he could have been in any American town, the broad nondescript

streets dotted with small businesses, two- and three-story walk-
ups, tall neon signs, the occasional pedestrian. The architecture
is haphazard, patchy. And then he is on another tree-lined street,
back into the calm of semi-suburbia and the hospital.

Bill's day unfolds in the usual fashion. Rounds with the
nurses. He checks back with the sicker patients—looks, listens,
gossips. He learns by listening to patients' natural speech: how
they get through a day, how they burn up their energy, how
they save themselves for later. At eleven he speaks briefly with
the intern assigned to his unit. Grabs a sandwich and chats
through his break.

He will be off the ward by one, driving further east along
Broadway. The obligatory left turn he needs to take onto Main
has haunted him all morning.

He tells his secretary he will be back in the office by
two. He asks her to call Mrs Lee, to see if she can get in by
bus. It is best for him to stay out of Chinatown's one-way streets,
especially in the rain. It is good for Mrs Lee's chest to fill up with
fresh city air, too. Better than the mouldy rot of the rooming
house. What Mrs Lee really needs is a ticket to Honolulu, he
knows. Bill's friends from the synagogue board have gone there,
had themselves photographed in the virgin sand and burned their
noses in the winter sun. A close relative of Mrs Lee has moved
her to Keefer Street, the first suburb, away from the mould of
downtown. There the air is cleaner, drier, fresher, the light of day
stronger. He hopes the change will stabilize her illness, contain
the rumbling colony in her lung apices, allow the body to rest.
His rival Dr K has recommended an operation. But Bill detests
the disfigurement and violence necessary to suffocate the germ
before the germ suffocates the host. Surgery reminds him of the
pogrom, smashing the chest in with a shovel.

At Joe's he drinks two full cups of coffee even though they are too strong for him, pats the children on the head and tries to tell them apart: ten-year-old Violetta and eight-year-old Nina and five-year-old Francesca who he thinks is seven. They are all daughters, spaced like Bill's teenagers a few years ago, but he cannot get the girls straight.

After Joe's he wends his way back to the office, relieved somewhat by all the right turns. He hangs his jacket back on the hook, puts on his white coat, checks his black bag. He touches his regular glasses on his nose to make sure they are there. He removes his reading glasses from his bag and replaces them as they were. He does this to identify them and to set off on the right foot. He shrugs his shoulders, does up two buttons of his lab coat and walks out of his office door greeting the nurses and patients.

He pulls charts out of their slots and reviews x-rays in his shotgun style, dictating the results to his secretary so quickly she can hardly record them. He hesitates only to allow her to catch up. He heaves a sigh of relief. Thank god those fluoroscopes have been dismantled, all of that unregulated radiation flying around while he looked anxiously for changes in documented lesions. He writes notes in charts that cannot be read. He scans temperatures, pulse and pressure graphs, respiratory rates. Interns, he likes to say, cannot count past the number three; they listen for five seconds and multiply by twelve; they cannot tell a story and rarely speak more than one language.

What he means but does not say is, They have never lived through a pogrom.

Bill moves through the day, puts his stethoscope to chests, counts respiratory rates for a full thirty seconds. He scribbles the results next to the nurses' determinations in lighter ink. He barely hears his secretary on the phone collecting biographical data, unless she raises her voice slightly to signal him to take note—there is a clinical point to be made, a curiosity to be considered. Mrs Lee has gone shopping at Woodward's, which is good for her lungs but puts his house call off until tomorrow. Although he appears to lumber he gets through the day confidently and quickly.

In the late afternoon he sits in his office with a book open on his lap, a journal or a classical music program from the theatre. Or Maimonides' *Guide for the Perplexed*, Friedlander's edition that he has scanned but does not know where or how to begin. He sits with his feet up and thinks of nothing at all. He sees a picture of tiny pink rods against the backdrop of the downtown vista and blue mountains.

THE POGROM: A MEMORIAL REPORT STICKING TO THE PLAIN FACTS

Bill knew of pogroms but had never lived through one before. He was vaguely aware of the wave that had been sweeping the Russian Pale for two years from the strain in his mother's face and the spontaneous curfew on his street. His town, Dniepropetrovsk in the region of Yekaterinoslav, was at the heart of the trouble, but no corner of the hinterlands was spared. Everywhere in the Pale the Black Hundreds were known and feared. Although remote and across the desolate prairie, the Dnieper valley was connected by river and rail to its lifeline, Odessa.

In Odessa there were newspapers and foreign languages, work, education and people. In Odessa there was life.

Bill worked there for a potter, although his journal locates his employer in the Dnieper town. This is one of many small details changed to suit his journal's purpose.

In Odessa he breathed the air of the outside world, where he was going, not where he was from. In Odessa, jews and others banded together to support the anti-czarist reforms. Like the others, he knew the little czar in his garden would eventually fall as the modern century got underway. In Odessa it was possible to believe that someone was listening. As his brother Isaak said, in Odessa you could jump on a boat and sail to America.

Contrary to his expectation and deepest faith, the violence, when it hit, included that great city on the sea.

Like many, he knew vaguely in his bones that his ancestors helped settle the Pale. It was hard to contain a people whose ancestors spread across a flat prairie where the snow blew itself away leaving the land bare, where your fingers turned black with cold and fell off, where the land produced grain if you worked at it and knew its rhythms. Over the centuries these ancestors had come to control the grain, from the farm down the railway to the outside world. The peasants worked the fields and the synagogue elders managed production. The peasants ran the railway that moved the grain about and the jews managed the goods and trades. They controlled the banks and mediated international finance. The peasants seemed to live in the past, attached to their slavery, and the jews in the future, where they would be redeemed by a god they had forgotten. Like the Hebrews under Moses in Egypt, you couldn't keep the jews down. The czar and his cronies were warned periodically with the occasional cartoon likening the czarist whip to Pharaoh's restrictive decrees.

It appeared that the czar read the bible, something Bill could respect.

While the jewish schools taught the history of discrimination that Bill half discounted and the catholic church relied on its theory of Hebrew machinations to explain itself to the people, the truth, he knew, was more difficult. His journal is filled with that broader sentiment. He was a citizen and his family helped build the land. His ancestors moved into the barren wild with the calculated permission of Alexander II and Catherine

the Great. That was long before the emancipation of the peasants. Now his people could negotiate more freedoms in the
Pale. They could challenge the university quotas and the regis-
tration licenses. They wanted to move about freely.

This is what one half of him knew.

The other knew that his beloved brother, Isaak, already
in and out of hiding, would end his days in a Siberian labour
camp, hand on his heart, a bullet in his head.

The experiment to settle the Pale had succeeded but the
little czar could not govern his burgeoning territories. Bill's account
mentions the failed war with Japan as if he needs more proof of
regional folly. The czar was undone by his greed, overstretching
himself this way and that like the man in the famous parable
staking as much land as he could traverse in a day.

If the czar had made it back to the doorstep of his home
by nightfall without dying of greed or exhaustion, Bill would
have been inclined to welcome him back in.

On October 20, 1905, the Black Hundreds whipped up
army and peasant alike. At this point Bill ignored his thoughts and
simply ran. The violence lasted for "those three days," although
Bill's journal deals mainly with the events of the first. It is not
clear from the journal whether the events described occurred
in the town up the river or the city by the sea. Perhaps the
location does not matter, that Bill intended it not to matter.

By the second day Bill was safe, in hiding in a church.
His escape hardly warrants comment. He knocked on the door;
he was acknowledged, possibly recognized; he was let in. This
is the origin of the family story: Wolf (as his mother called him)
at the door. He learned of two more days of violence from the
noise beyond the wall and the face of his protector. He waited
in the church, hardly lifting his head from the feather pillow. In

the journal he notes the more than seventy municipalities hit and begins to name them one by one. There are hundreds of towns, villages, hamlets he cannot identify. He gives up. His journal is a failed memorial. He does not know whether to list the dead or tell his story of survival.

A picture was eventually published of the dead of Dniepropetrovsk, a picture he could only imagine and never saw. Two rows of bodies separated by a path. To the left rest the bulky tarps. A single pair of feet protrude. To the right fifteen small lumps under cloth. It is impossible to look directly at the children, impossible to distinguish them clearly. The eyes of the viewer scan away, back to the gentle upward grade of the path, to the pair of feet.

Around the same time as the pogroms, newspapers flourished and Hebrew was resurrected as a living language. The second *Aliyah* gained momentum and the jews learned how to organize and defend themselves. As people say, something was won and something was lost. Little by little they spread to Europe, the Americas and Palestine. It is an old story. Those that stayed flourished for the time being. As for the dead, he was not among them, so he had a story to tell.

PHOTOGRAPHS OF BILL IN THE NEW COUNTRY: TRACKING BACKWARD IN TIME

The most famous picture of Bill (and the last in this album) presents him dressed in a three-piece brown suit, tie and wing tips. He is standing on the wooden steps of the hospital upcountry. It is an outpost hospital and the steps are rudimentary, rough two-by-eights on risers. His hands are behind his back. He is posing but he is also very much at ease. His face has begun to pucker with the intent of his years, with the seriousness of his work, with his stature. His eyes are slightly narrowed with the same intent or perhaps he is just looking into the sun. It is likely that he is married by now and has left his wife temporarily on the coast. Or if not yet married he will be soon. His wife does not mind the rumple in his pants and vest but there is still a touch of the dandy about him—a hint of narcissism, even arrogance, that he can make a difference if he should so please. At first it appears as if he is leaning into the four-by-four pillar, but this is a trick of the eye. He is simply leaning to one side, posing. His hair is beginning to thin but it is still there, still dark. He is a man at the height of his strength.

Another picture of somewhat earlier vintage is marked 1920. He has been thinking of letting his hair grow over his fledgling bald spot. His collar is starched and high. He has taken his glasses off. It is the same suit but the picture has faded across his chest.

Next in the album is Bill a few years earlier, without his moustache. His hair is parted to the side. His mouth is pulled in with the same expression only harsher. He is still young and his eyes are soft. Again he has posed for the camera, for posterity. His collar is very starched and much further up his neck than could possibly be comfortable. His tie is tight and off his chest, suspended in front of him for optimal visibility. It disappears beneath the pinstriped suit halfway around his neck. Nothing in the picture hints at the state of the world, the influenza pandemic that has claimed a colleague here and there, or the aftermath of the great war.

There is another shot from the same sitting, with his brother Shimon. The light is harsher and you cannot see the pinstripes at all. His collar is in the same position but his head is inclined, exaggerating his seriousness.

The left half of the photo is taken up by Shimon. Shimon's head is tilted at an odd angle. His suit is rumpled, suggesting he has cramped his body into an unnatural closeness next to his brother. His mouth is more puckered than Bill's and he is looking provocatively at the camera. He is almost defiant, his bushy hair falling over onto his forehead. He is younger than Bill, who seems slightly protective and disapproving. Some said that Shimon was crazy, others that he was homosexual. Here he seems the rebellious, presumptuous dandy close to his brother, leaning on him intimately.

Or maybe it is not Shimon. It may be somebody else, one of Bill's friends. Even the girls argue about this. There is already nobody left to ask.

The first picture is of Bill as a young man. He is posing with his moustache intact, reading in an extravagant forward-leaning pose. It is a typical setting for that era, designed to artificially evoke aspiring intelligence and style, wit and looks. His body is facing to the side. A book rests impossibly on the arm of the wicker chair. His other arm supports his head, which is aligned in the pose of reading. (Perhaps this is the shot he intends to show the selections committee when he walks along the railway tracks to the medical school in the next province, before he sits down in the lecture hall and refuses to leave.) His leg is crossed to complete the unnatural balance of the position. He is wearing a light suit and two-toned lace-up shoes with pointed toes. His face is broad and very handsome, almost Oriental. His skin is dark, and his hair, which is black and bushy, has been shaved at the sides. Behind his body is the fanned back of the elaborate wicker chair and a hint of a mural on the wall.

MORE PHOTOGRAPHS
AND WHERE THEY LEAD

Bill is already old at the birth of his second daughter. His face is round and there is a second chin. His shoulders have slumped and his belly is present. He is looking at his daughter, the mother of Dr Z, who has that remarkable alertness of some one-year-olds. His hair by now is very thin but still brown, lighter above the ears. He is wearing a bow tie set a little crookedly off to the right. He looks more like a grandfather than a father, a bit too old and goofy to be the dad. Nevertheless, the two smiles are very similar, as if the child has already had an impact on the father. There are houses and dirt lawns in the background, out of focus. His glasses no longer seem like a mark of distinction. They seem necessary.

Another photograph that is part of his new life was taken on his mother-in-law's front lawn. Bill's three girls stand close together with their heads one above the other, from smallest to tallest. Above the head of the eldest is the head of Harry, his wife's youngest brother. Behind the four heads one sees the house and the side of the house next door, bungalow-and-a-halfs circa 1925. The picture was taken about fifteen years later. His three girls are still children but they are growing up.

Geraniums, lilies and lavender frame the walk. The trim detail is still fresh. Bill's middle daughter is smiling and Harry, his head on top, is beaming like an English schoolboy. The camera has captured a restless symmetry that cannot last.

There are many photographs of Bill's eldest daughter. Not only was she the first, but as a young child she was stunningly sad and beckoning. Her ringlets frame her round face, which is his face at the moment he becomes old. She is dressed for the snow: mitts, pants, jacket with buttons over to the left, and hat, all matching. Everything, including the snow itself, has faded. Skeletal houses rest in the shadows. A parallel line of electric poles cascades back into the distance. Despite the faded black and white, the cheeks of the young child are full of colour.

The last photograph in the box is of Bill's eldest brother Isaak Morosov. It is dated February, 1907. Morosov stands as a young man, with a full head of hair and an extravagant eastern moustache. His right arm is bent at the elbow with his hand (excepting the thumb) in his waistcoat. His left hand is in his pocket. His pose is expansive, deliberate, beyond defiant. The sepia tones are smudgy brown and it is difficult to tell whether this represents the ravages of time or dirt.

Isaak is standing on an ill-defined bed of earth that might have been a garden in another season. There is a smudgy white building behind him, a wall with an open casement window swung out at ninety degrees. His body is blocking half of the window, but to the left below his elbow you can see the bars. You have to look closely to notice the outline of chains rising from his ankles, up the insides of his legs, coalescing and disappearing near his thighs. His feet are more or less invisible, camouflaged by the dirt.

ISAAK IN THE PALE

When Alexander II was assassinated in 1881, Bill's eldest brother Isaak was four years old. Two years later the first pogrom broke out in Yekaterinoslav. There had been spontaneous rioting and looting on the part of the peasants in Balta, Kiev and other parts of Russia. But rage was not limited to the peasant class. It was a powerful force with vague boundaries that encompassed the peasants, the new czar's followers and the intellectual class. By 1884 the enactment of residential and educational restrictions temporarily contained this rage. The military police enforced the law and the people were appeased.

Before he was as tall as her waist, Isaak had seen his mother cower when the uniformed police rode by their home. She hurriedly ushered him away from the activity in the streets. This was a daily event. There was little real threat but her reaction conveyed her fear to the boy. By the time Nicholas II became czar Isaak was old enough to be skeptical. He was neither religious nor an intellectual; he was Russian. Underneath the fancy arguments of the intellectuals he could detect the church's agenda to convert the jew or drive him away. If a few died here and there in the battle, so much the better.

As a child Isaak hitched around on the barges to Odessa with the Russians, drank vodka with them and sang Russian songs. When the time came he became interested in Russian women. He danced, sang, and danced some more.

Later, when Isaak applied to the working guilds the quotas kept him out. In Zhitomir he had no papers. He followed a Russian girl to Yelizavetgrad where he found work as an apprentice miller, but he was again sent home. The police were meticulous about their registry; there was no opportunity to negotiate. They could be kind or harsh, but they rarely bent. No one fit in better than Isaak—no one was more Russian—but even he couldn't hide forever and they repeatedly found him and sent him home.

Until the climax of 1903 there was little violence. Then, the events in Kishinev convinced Isaak to stay close to family. He had his younger siblings to watch; his mother was anxious and his father, a weak intellectual, could not be relied upon to act decisively. The Zionist self-defence movement was gaining momentum, and Isaak wanted to maintain contact with its centre in Odessa. The idea of creating a physical presence there attracted him. Bill was working in a pottery shop and his mother was contemplating moving down with little Shimon to keep Bill off the Odessa streets. Bill came home far too often for her liking, braving the trains and the roads and even the occasional boat ride along the Dnieper.

It was during these times that something dangerous and fundamental coalesced in Isaak. His mother said that he stuck out too much, more than he thought: he was a yid like the rest of the kinderlach and should stay close to home. But Isaak said that he was safest among his enemies and that he was Russian. He didn't know how to be anything else. Sometimes the eldest is like that.

He goes off into the world and proves there is no welcoming place there. And the younger ones, his siblings, take his challenges and identities off with them elsewhere in order to survive.

Isaak was identified in Zhitomir and Yelizavetgrad. In 1905 he was identified back home in Yekaterinoslav. It was then that he began to resist. He moved about the streets of Odessa, joined more than one self-defence organization and watched out for his family. But even here he did not feel at home. The city was too cosmopolitan. He was more Russian than the intellectuals and revolutionaries. He got into arguments with the Zionists, with the Hebrew poets and social philosophers. His eyes aflame with a focused madness, he challenged their softness, their desire to build something new in Palestine. He didn't trust the other languages like Hebrew, Yiddish, German. Yiddish was the language of maternal overprotection. He had failed his mother by not becoming a doctor or a banker. And Hebrew, the language of somebody else's hope, reminded him of his irritability and frustration in *cheder* as he tried to glue himself to the chair while his *rebbe* reprimanded him. His teacher could not make him afraid so the cane was useless and in the end Isaak could hardly read the *aleph beis*.

During the pogrom he roamed the streets looking for family and friends. He was not afraid, and was deliberate enough to look like he belonged. Judging by other accounts, it is most likely not known how he was caught and why he was sent to Irkutsk. His mother insisted he was recognizable as her *kleineille kinder*. His father speculated quietly that Isaak's whereabouts had simply been identified once more. This was an expression of the final straw spoken by the man who was hardly there. Many were sent away without documented reasons so Isaak's disappearance was not unusual.

Bill heard other stories between the time of the pogrom and when the family received the picture in the mail two years later.

He heard that Isaak had warned a group of *lantzmen* to get off the street but that they misidentified him as a member of the Black Hundreds. The flurry of flight alerted the military police.

He heard that during the pogrom Isaak fell in with. a group of childhood friends. They chummed about in the spirit of adventure until they found a storefront to smash. When Isaak hesitated they turned on him.

There were many stories of a swarthy bearded *mentsche* caught striking an officer who had been beating a woman with child. This version was reminiscent of Moses defending his brethren in Egypt and was considered ultimately unreliable, only a hope and a prayer.

In the end, nobody could verify or disprove the details of Isaak's whereabouts. Once in Siberia, the truth was best forgotten. There is only a face staring back defiantly at the camera as if the camera is the prosecutor looking in, the foreboding eye that would push Isaak back into the exile of his cell.

When Bill and his other siblings come to the new country and disperse, there is a vague understanding that someone has been left behind. By the next generation nobody knows for sure. Three remaining Morosovs with Anglicized names stick together: Bill, Shimon and their sister Fanny. Isaak is not mentioned. His picture is mixed with other photos in the box and forgotten. Fanny has a copy, a cropped version, enlarged. Shimon has another copy, but he pays little attention and it is lost with everything else.

Bill has the last picture, which sits at the very bottom of the box.

Someone has written "Isaak Morosov, Irkutsk, 18th of February, 1907" on the back. It is not Bill's hand; it is the handwriting of a later explainer, perhaps Bill's wife Rachel. She has used ballpoint in blue ink. The original Russian handwriting in black is no longer legible.

The shackles are so faded that the chronicler in blue ink is compelled to mention them on the picture's back, in case they disappear forever.

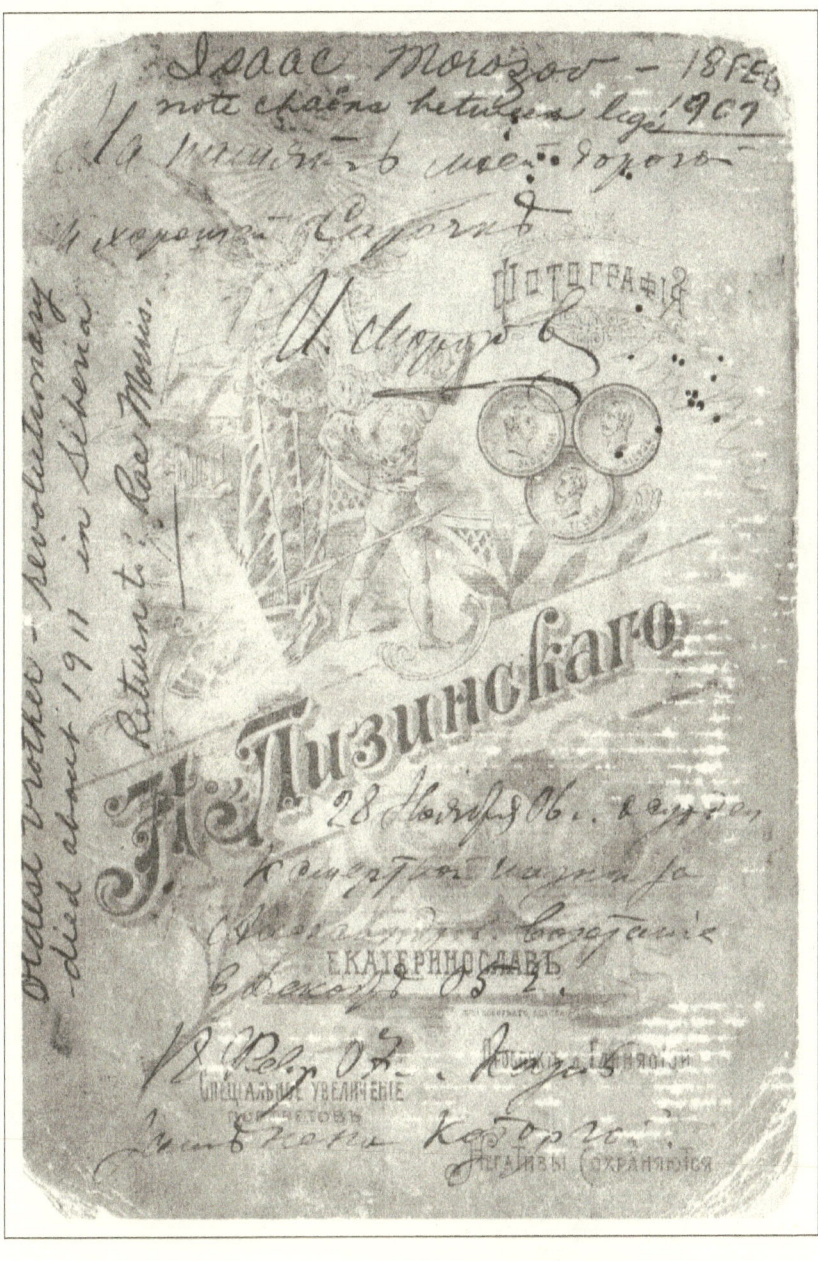

SPORTS

Bill learns to play golf. He plays with his friend K the surgeon and his own wife Rachel. He tests out his swing this way and that. He decides to play left-handed but he never finds his true balance. Sometimes he steps up to the ball backward and does no worse. He loves the fog of the Quilchena course more than the game. Of lost sliced balls he says, It is just a ball, but the cost worries him—the idea of something unnecessarily gone. An old man with a beard and a bicycle wanders the woods. The man with the bicycle finds Bill's balls and sells them back to him. It is a form of charity to buy his own balls back. Bill's swing is destined to fail, his mistakes ingrained. He has a lumbering grace that pulls him up, over and through in a closed, jerky arc. It is impossible to straighten out the trajectory of the ball. He compensates for it (reasonably) by twisting his trunk. On occasion the ball skims the trees and curves back to a perfect lie.

His wife drives 220 yards straight down the fairway but he tees off first. This is a family tradition, her deference to him. Without him the game would be impossible.

His tennis swing is similar but it works. There is no drift. His follow-through is weak and he insists on facing his opponent with his feet planted side to side. This position further stresses his back. He knows there is a better way but his mind is elsewhere. It is only a game; it is only his back. He marvels at his wife's strength, her accuracy. He, too, is reliable after a fashion. He sets her up and she slams it back. In doubles he plays the net, looking intimidating and intelligent. She plays the backcourt, running from side to side. She knows the game. Even with Bill as a partner they rarely lose.

When her husband dies she no longer plays tennis or drives a golf ball. She regrets not caring more for Yiddish, cards and mahjongg. She has few remarkable memories of her own childhood; they have been taken over by Bill.

Croquet is Bill's game. He can set it up in the back yard. Bumps and detours are to be expected. He plays with the children. (No one wants Mother to play. They will lose or she will let them win.)

He faces straight ahead and spreads his legs, bending them unnecessarily at the knee. He shifts his hands periodically. Sometimes he overlaps his small finger, like in golf. He hits the ball with the edge of the mallet, sending it flying sideways at an unpredictable angle. The ball is retrieved from the rose bush or the hedge by one of the laughing children. He rubs his eyes apologetically and sets it back on the border of the course. No one expects him to play it from its natural lie. The girls have learned to account for him. They do this readily, unconsciously. They adore him.

Bill has the habit of stopping inexplicably in the middle of any game—golf, tennis, croquet. That is enough for me, he says. The girls imagine he is going back to his journals and microscope slides, case reports and synagogue committee duties, returning to his work life.

It does not occur to them until much later that this is his life and that he is simply taking a break. He says good night to a patient and picks up the case again first thing in the morning in the same way.

Bill is most vigorous while hiking. On the trails he seems like a sportsman. He lumbers at the right speed and has good shoulders and legs. Hiking is something he has done on three continents. His stamina can match that of his wife. He is like Freud holding forth in the Caucasus. He has great respect for Freud: his perseverance, his relentless rethinking of clinical parameters.

Hiking suits the clinician in Bill. It is a tradition. Each year they take the ferry to the north shore and climb to the plateau on the mountain. The firm path gives way to mud and then to snow. On the plateau there is a small pond in spring, but in winter it is frozen over and white. There are five of them in the photograph: Bill, Rachel and three friends. The other couple is more at ease and the fifth, somebody's brother, is smiling broadly. The seriousness of Bill and Rachel dominates the picture, focuses the joy of the winter expanse.

For Bill, travelling the highway is also a sport. He prefers to have Rachel drive when they set off together. He is most distractible if he is not alone in the vehicle. If he forgets a rule of the road, they will all fly away.

In the 1930s he considers going to Spain as a medic. It suits his temperament. But he knows his limits: he would be blown up in an instant and he has three girls to think about. Instead he stays in the west and edits his Dnieper journal. The spirit of 1905 is infused with the spirit of the Spanish Civil War, honed on the fairways of Shaughnessy and on the beach at Kitsilano.

His real talent is that he can watch others and extend their reach. Before his first grandchild can crawl, Bill gives him a stick to fetch a ball stuck under the couch. It is a moment of imprinting that skips a generation.

Later he leaves his wooden clubs to be discovered in a suburban basement behind the detritus of the boom years. With the rusted clubs you could no longer hit a ball; you could only pick the clubs up and swing them back and forth to reach back in history.

What did they play in the Russian Pale? Nothing.

ANOTHER SABBATH STORY

Bill and the three girls are sitting around the sabbath table. Rachel comes in carrying the roast beef and Yorkshire pudding. She has cooked for the sabbath but is still wearing her tennis whites. His heart leaps when she is like this: mannish, strong, almost radiant. Cooking for him seems like an act of free will to her, but when he dies she will never cook like this again. She will never drive a car. She will not golf, hit a tennis ball or dream of climbing mountains.

Tonight the children are irritating. The eldest is coarse and sullen; she has been teased at school. Sarcasm from the youngest is incomprehensible to him. He takes his middle daughter on his lap. She is serious and confused, like her mother. She will do anything for someone she loves and she loves only him. He sends her for his slippers and she goes willingly, which saddens him.

He has a habit of introducing stories as ordinary circumstances. Perhaps this means they are not ordinary. Perhaps it means that there are tricks in them to listen to. Perhaps it means that this life, the ordinary life, should be questioned. He has other sayings, many of which are confusing. His favourite: Sometimes the safest place to be is among your enemies.

The children clatter about. Rachel thinks Bill's sayings are from Maimonides. Is he preparing for a synagogue address? she wonders.

Bill is thinking about how he survived.

On the first day of the pogrom he roamed with the peasants and was almost killed three times. The town was big enough for that, big enough for him to fit in and not be recognized. He mussed up his blond-brown hair, left straw from the barn sticking out of his clothes, and went looking for food. He imitated their walks and their half-smiles. He averted his eyes naturally and spoke from the side of his mouth.

He often thinks of his journal. Thinking of the events and thinking of his journal have become the same memory. At fifteen, reunited with his mother and with straw still sticking out of his hair, he began his journal. She encouraged him from the start: a note here, a note there. On the transatlantic crossing he wrote out the first narrative, remembering her, in Yiddish. In medical school he did more work: filled in the detail and translated the memoir into English as if justifying to himself why his life had taken this unexpected turn. He would further revise his notes in the 1930s, in middle age, after *Kristallnacht*, when he saw what could have been his own weatherbeaten memories plastered across the local papers.

The memoir troubles him over the years. It is the focus of his trouble. Not so much the trauma but its unfinished form. He returns to the journal repeatedly. In the end it fails to convey the power the events had on him.

Day one, three events, followed by purposeless wandering.

The banality, the arbitrary flatness, troubles him. He puts the journal away, noting the general displeasure that accompanies the retelling. What interests him—what he is good at—is blending in with his enemies, at being invisible. He is good at being safe.

He files the notes away in his bookcase next to Friedlander's Maimonides. They are easy to find there. He often reads Maimonides but he does not get anywhere with it. He is perplexed, that is all. If there was no purpose to the deaths in his town there was no purpose to his survival. In the meantime he has his patients and his family. Life moves on. Sometimes he can't tell if he is still among his enemies, despite being in a new world.

In the end he will give the story to his children. Perhaps they will do something with it. This is a despairing and hopeful thought all wrapped up in one.

As the children climb on him and drink his wine and pull his moustache and push his glasses off-centre, he knows that Rachel and the children will see the wrong things. The misunderstanding will take on new forms. They will idealize his past and exaggerate his greatness. They will be immune to his stilted English, his repetitive stammering, the lack of cohesion in his paragraphing, the absence of moral purpose. It is his only story, but he has made a life of it; that much they will understand. Eventually he moves the notes away from the *Guide* and in with his journal ramblings and case material, his thoughts on antibiotics, his newspaper clippings and his one or two medical publications, where his few words will be safely absorbed into his new life.

When Bill rereads his notes he is astounded at the death of his friend, the seventeen-year-old who worked in the pottery store with him. His name is not mentioned—he cannot remember his name. He cannot remember if the store was in the Dnieper town or Odessa. One minute they are running and the next he is down. He cannot remember the shot. The shooting provides the background noise of the pogrom, a manifestation of constant fear. There are no separate shots, only the pervasive noise and dread. And then his friend is down. He falls without warning. It is an accident, as if the boy falls due to a natural disaster.

And Bill runs on. He does not look back.

What he remembers most—what he doesn't tell—is that they were running together as one, holding hands. The image that sustains him is that they were two nameless, faceless boys running from trouble to trouble. Like an anxiety dream that has no end other than waking and knowing you are alive.

He tries to indict the church. The church turns him away and the church protects him. It is the same church. He accosts the weeping face of Jesus the perpetrator; he recoils from the weeping face of Jesus, a lost and hounded jew like himself. The contradictions neutralize themselves, leaving him drained of all words.

His friend falls when they are running. His friend falls and he is still running.

He slips out the window and falls to the ground. He sees another set of feet, legs dangling above him. Legs that are not yet stuck, attached to a body not yet burnt. He runs.

He is almost killed by a coachman who recognizes him from Dniepropetrovsk. What is Bill the jew doing here, away from home, with no papers?

The coachman has a weapon, reaches for it.

Bill freezes. He is too close to run. He is saved by a drunk Cossack who has seen more than enough violence for one day. The Cossack says he has had enough. He belches at the coachman, pushing at his arm, and Bill walks away.

After this Bill knows he cannot die; it has been determined.

He sleeps in a barn and dreams of feathers. It is a dream about the freedom to dream and to sleep.

Then he goes about dressed like his enemies and he is safe.

LAST IMAGE

When he dies it is in the living room of his home, where his three daughters have been married. He does not see the hardwood or the fine furniture; he sees the dirt of his Russian town. He crawls through a small brick opening, kicking his legs. He finds his way to the church. The priest is still there weeping.

He tries to take his own blood pressure but he cannot find his arm. He cannot speak. The blackness is softer and more present, no longer camouflaged by the altruism of the physician. There is a prayer for a moment such as this, a famous prayer, but he cannot remember it. Nor will he say, "If god wants me to die, let him kill me." The coldness of his freedom has eaten him away and left him without words. A question comes to mind: Is the killer the enemy? In the end he loves the tubercle bacillus more than anything. He has faced his opponent in honour.

The plethysmograph that has been dangling from his arm drops to the floor with a smack. The head of the stethoscope swings gently back and forth outside his jacket. The stethoscope, he often liked to explain, is an ear. It catches natural sound and propels it, allowing the waves to strengthen along the length of its tube. That is all. This image closes his life.

POST MORTEM

This scene takes place shortly after Bill's death. Given that there are no photographs some imagination is required.

Three babies in carriages. It is the middle of spring. The crocuses and daffodils have come and gone. Even the tulips are wilting. By noon it will be warm.

The three girls have been pregnant together. Their husbands, contrary to community expectations, are weak men. They hover somewhat timidly. They live in Bill's shadow in the minds of their wives. They will all grow broad in middle age and speak a presumptuous English derived from the beginnings of failed educations.

The family is gathered on the terraced back lawn of Rachel's brother's bungalow. These days her brother Harry is master of the family by default. There are other brothers but they have done things that have taken them away. Rachel has granted her one remaining sibling the titular honour. Harry is so gentle he is saint-like. When the grandchildren are older he will sing them nonsense rhymes he learned at sea, but there is nothing to suggest that side of him today.

The carriages are lined up in a row beneath the stand of poplars that marks the back of the lot. Smokey the dog—old, deaf, blind and lame—is a reminder of Bill. Smokey is eccentric and demented but the girls find him almost regal. Uncle Harry thinks the dog may bite one of the husbands. The newborn children, he knows, are safe.

All three babies are called Bill. The moment is beyond irony. The sun is warm and the flowers are out. The husbands (two Irvings and a Ralph) are still getting along.

In time, each Bill becomes the spitting image of his respective father. Each clings to his mother later in life and, in time, the community breathes a sigh of relief. All three Bills faintly acknowledge the blessing of their name. They consider it a minor honour, a subtle joke or a quiet curse and leave it at that. As children they rarely play together. As adults, a reminder of their lineage generates mild curiosity and an unexplained formal pride.

Some say that their birthright had already been stolen by Uncle Harry's eldest son, the other Bill. He was born at the end of the second war and spent his formative years on Dr William Morosov's knee. Himself a doctor of some distinction, he champions shifting clinics into the communities where they belong, and does some work against the fabled immune deficiencies that plague the late century. It is said that he too has three daughters, but here our comparison must end.

Four:
Dr Z and all the Ends

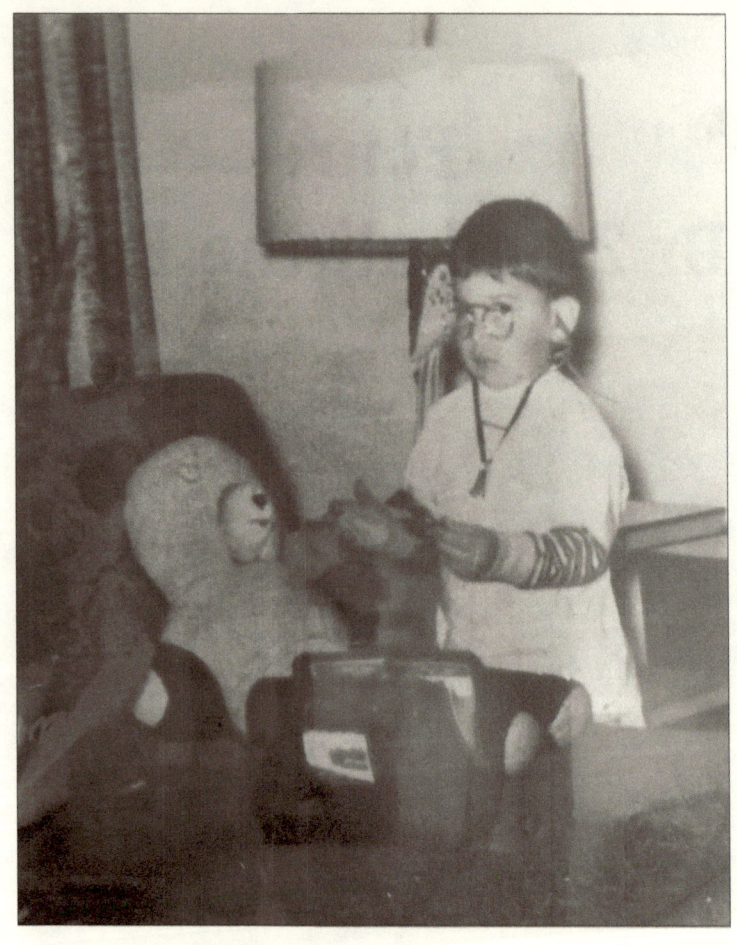

SO MUCH FOR GRANDPA BILL

There is a family photograph of a child with a stethoscope and a teddy bear. The child is not me. Thank goodness there are curves in the universe. I am Dr Z and the child is not me. The story may not be over.

My mother is not speaking to me. She is not angry about my manuscript, only confused and blocked. She likes my synopsis of her father's story but there are problems.

The biggest problem: it is too short.

Our lives are like that, I tell her. They are safe and they are short. I have known this a long time. My life would also take up only a few pages. I stalled on the way out, it would begin. I didn't like the look of the birth canal so I dug in my heels. How many times have you heard such a thing? A hundred? A thousand? Is it such a special beginning? Since then I have been doing some things a little backward. Not so backward that it would fill a whole book.

As you know, I am left-handed and my nose is crooked. There are a lot of people with crooked noses and clumsy hands doing things just a little backward. The world is filled with them.

My middle daughter pointed out my facial disfigurement after dinner recently. "Your nose is crooked," she said. "It is probably cancerous. There is diseased cartilage in there."

On the other hand, my mother used to say I was born old. More than crooked, I am a man with no childhood. On this point I could try to refute her: the Hanukah presents, the treacherous games in the apple tree, my grandmother's morning voice, how I learned to ride a bicycle by crashing up the hill. But she is right. Old and crooked, that's me.

And now what does she get from me? Thirty pages tops.

"It is longer than the draft I started with," I say. "It is longer than your father's account. It is not repetitious."

"And less accurate."

I am stumped. I made up the story so of course it will lack accuracy. But I understand her suffering. She is temporarily silenced by her father's brief appearance in the world. Is that all there was to him?

She begins to research further, unearths octogenarian relatives, papers, events. She wants more. She wants the story to go on.

"That pharmacist," she says. "He had a connection."

She stops. She knows I am right.

"I like the part about Siberia and the pogroms," she says. "I didn't know his brother was like that."

Neither did I but I don't move a muscle.

"Wild and strong," she says. "Him you could write a whole book about."

"Are there really chains in that picture?" she says. "Is that really Isaak's cell in the background?"

"Siberia isn't always a bad place," she says. "Famous violinists are born there and don't starve. It's cold in winter, like where-you-used-to-live. That's all."

I wait.

"Daddy really did walk to the next province to go to medical school. That was real, heroic. I will vouch for it. It was the only sport he did well, walking."

I cannot look at her.

"I'm telling you things I already told you," she says. "I'm telling it again."

I don't say a thing.

"Thirty pages."

She is still not listening.

"The burns in the carpet from that bridge group, that was true. Your grandmother hated that bridge group with a passion."

There is nothing for me to say.

"Your grandmother knew the bridge group would ruin more than her carpet," she contends. This is one of those new tangents that thankfully never materialize into much. Tangents that lead relentlessly to Wolf at the Door, a man who smokes while inside his lover, her right leg straight up and over his shoulder, her back against wood. This is the man who memorized Tolstoi and the bible so he could scoff. A man who knows how to drink and fight. How to impress his will on beast and men. A drunk with an enormous moustache. This is a man I do not know.

"Maybe you are right about him not liking to turn left across traffic, but how do you say that in a story?"

I don't have to tell her what I'm thinking: Be grateful for thirty pages.

"A disaster," she says. "You have made for us a disaster."

I know she is proud of me. I am her son, crooked and hesitant, born an adult.

SOME MORE MESSAGES FOR DR Z

Dear Dr Z,

Now that you have gone, I need a report to be sent to my new doctor. Please forward the necessary documents.

Dear Dr Z,

I have recently lost my job. I am sure you will support my disability claim. Please forward my chart to the following address.

Dear Dr Z,

I have decided to traverse the country to be close to you. I will be at my sister's on the Island by the first of the month. Please leave an appointment time.

Dear Dr Z,

My new therapist passed away suddenly after five sessions. It apparently had nothing to do with me, but I will never be sure. Can you please refer me to someone else?

Dear Dr Z,

What was the name of that book you recommended? I cannot find it in the stores anywhere. If you could send it to me I would be very grateful.

Dear Dr Z,

My mother says you were a great doctor and did a much better job than the guy I am seeing now. Can you please call her and set the record straight?

Dear Dr Z,

I called you yesterday and the line was disconnected twice when your secretary tried to transfer it to your inner office. Please call me back tomorrow after seven my time. I'll be waiting.

Dear Dr Z,

This is your mother calling.

Your secretary told me you were having a rough day and were considering changing careers. May I recommend golf? You always had that wonderful nine-iron lob that dropped the ball three feet from the pin. Your brothers, I am told, are in similar moods. It seems to be a coastal phenomenon. Now for the purpose of this call: I have booked a foursome. I will drive the cart and the three of you can share the passenger seat and my ear; I can only handle one of you talking at any given time. Please don't complain too much. At least you have a real job.

DR Z MISSES MAX TERRIBLY AND RUNS OUT OF GAS

Dr Z is very busy in his new life in the big city on the coast. He is so busy he has slipped from the first person into a less intimate grammatical form. Indeed, he is having a challenging time saying "I." He is stuck in the third person from here on in. At least he is stuck somewhere; he still exists. He cannot afford to live here but he has moved nevertheless and now he has to put his head down and tough it out. The three boys (Dr Z and his two brothers) are on the same footing. They live on faith and find their entertainment cheaply.

Dr Z drives the new highway. In the morning, south; in the evening, north. Smooth and free and against traffic. Ten times a week he swings along the bog-ridden delta, the panoramic ridge, the alluvial plain. Past where his father used to live. He notes the eagles in flight, the herons in mud, the hawks on lampposts. There is an occasional coyote loping along in the bog, even deer. He tunes out and the car drives as if by itself. He wakes up as he is gearing down around the cloverleaf exits. He drinks coffee from a travel mug, shifts gears, speaks on the phone, all in a slow rhythm, passing the necessary articles from hand to hand. He gets entangled in his greatcoat. His hat skims the inside of the roof, bounces off the passenger seat and onto the gritty passenger-side mat. He feels the most at home here, in his vehicle. Driving is his time alone. He is safe until he pulls to a stop at either end.

It is a rainy day and Dr Z suspects he will run out of gas. He is not convinced because it has never happened before.

The yellow light of empty is piercing the perennial gloom of morning, beaming straight into his right (migrainous) eye. As usual, it is raining. Uphill the needle swings to the left of empty. On the way down, it overcorrects halfway to a quarter-tank.

He exits and follows a sign that indicates food, lodging and gas. He turns right and traverses the entire delta to its end. No luck. He turns right and continues until he hits the river. He retraces his slippery steps and follows the heavy rush-hour traffic. Where there is traffic, there will be gas. Finally he is correct; he cannot be wrong forever. But his bladder is about to burst and the detour has been unnecessary.

Eventually he is back to the sign that indicates food, lodging, services. He sees his error. He has food and a telephone in the car as well as an Executive Deluxe Automobile Association Membership Card but still he feels vulnerable. He would vow to pray daily but knows it is a sin to vow something that is a quotidian requirement. He thinks, Can I write my memoirs while driving? Compose a tune? Rehearse a prelude? Talk to my mother? Could I learn a page of Talmud or memorize a soliloquy? Most of the time he turns off the radio and lets his mind wander. The weather is self-evident, the traffic report is always wrong and he refuses to listen to three instalments of the same news.

Here he is, in his car.

This is Dr Z before he picks up his messages and sorts his charts and says hello to any number of people and stops to chat with any number of clinicians about inpatients and outpatients he may or may not remember, who may or may not be ill or who have deteriorated or attempted suicide or gone off their medicine or been arrested by the local police under the Mental Health Act or been dropped off in the emergency department by concerned or disconcerted relatives.

This is Dr Z before he hits the ward and talks to the nurses about what may or may not be encoded in their progress notes; before he talks to the first-year resident about differential diagnosis and investigations or to the chief resident about the same topic except more finely focused; before the ward administrator accosts him about bed management or the bed manager about ward administration; before he crosses paths with the ward social worker looking for beds in the community or the community social worker looking for beds on the ward.

This is the way he is before he sees his first colleague, who performs electro-convulsive therapy despite the impending end of the millennium, and talks to him about meditation, commuting and beginnings; before he meets his second colleague, who shares an interest in language and distance running and talks to him about balancing the professional and the personal; or runs into his third colleague, who is a true expert in the diseases that exist (for Dr Z, diseases are hypotheses that rear their ugly heads in too many ways to be of much comfort) and has to tolerate that inexorable feeling of preferring to go off to coffee with someone you like and who is not like you at all but instead you have to work; before he will see his fourth colleague and marvel at her speed and grace and her ability to always be in motion (he himself seems to be forever mired somewhere between here and there, like an anxiety dream); before he will speak to his secretary about dyslexia and diets and the myriad of things that will never get done today or perhaps ever.

This is the way he is before he instantly becomes the master of short snappers, getting in and out of conversations without missing a beat. It is a matter of synaptic survival—you can hold your breath only so long.

But, it must be said, he will falter. His fourth colleague may wish to redecorate the waiting room. His third colleague may push the wrong files into his box and his second colleague may require a third opinion on a fourth patient who is refusing to see Dr Z's first colleague regarding that life-saving and barbaric procedure, ECT. Before he realizes there are an infinite number of items he has forgotten, before he remembers his secretary will bail him out and his boss will bail him out, before he remembers to turn on the beeper he carries after more than a decade of normal life without it but doesn't seem to mind this time around, before his second coffee (drunk standing up while dictating), before he makes daily lists and throws out yesterday's unnecessary messages and piles yesterday's questionably necessary messages next to his phone and boots up his computer and checks that his outpatient files are in the right order (sometimes they are piled down-up instead of up-down), and ensures yesterday's billing is discharged and finds yesterday's unanswered collegial messages that have been blown about by the fan that he turns on to ensure that no itinerant pneumococci have followed him 2800 miles across the Great Lakes and the Prairies to the new coastal land to haunt him in his new closeted consulting room.

This is the way he is before he starts to work. It is the way he is deep down when he is working, also. Even when frenetically busy he is certain this can nevertheless be seen in him: the way he floats in transition, his inarticulate self, the part his old patients used to call Dr Z.

Dear Dr Z,

I know you are gone but I must speak. Please listen. You're all I've got.

I am thinking of leaving my boyfriend. He seems to be a nice guy but he has a serious problem he won't talk about. He does a lot of things without telling me.

I might try to talk but what good would it do?

I should try to talk to him about it, that's a pretty good idea.

I will probably yell at him about it, I won't be able to hold back.

I will try to talk to him about it again; maybe I'd better not give up.

To hell with him. I can do fine on my own.

Dr Z. I was thinking through the above possibilities one evening in the bath. It was a "Eureka" moment, if you know what I mean. I saw that the single rule of the game went something like this: choose where you want to go.

To review, first I tell you the introductory scenario, then I choose one of the options above. You, the anonymous narrator, must comment and away we go.

Now, Dr Z, think of me as the sum of everyone you have ever seen in the clinic. Here goes.

As you may remember, I spent many mornings putting the house in order. I did the washing and the cleaning. I was pretty tired. I was still tidying up when the phone rang. It was my boyfriend and he wanted to come over.

My mind was suddenly in a whirl. I thought of giving up, moving on. I thought of walking in front of a bus. I thought of calling you and making an appointment but I couldn't remember what province you were in. I thought of moving on and starting a new life but then what would you think of me?

Anyway, I decided I would never speak with him again, that's it, never.

Time for a cigarette, I thought. It's okay, really, for him to come over—it's his house too.

Well, maybe it's okay for him to come home, I was almost finished cleaning.

Right, it's okay for him to come home as long as it's to clear out his things.

Let him come home, I'm tired, ready for a truce.

Maybe it was my fault. I knew it was going to happen.

Maybe I should let him have it. If only he could help clean once in a while, why did I have to pick up all the slack?

He might clean if I asked him, so I didn't have to tire myself out so.

I told him I was tired from all the work and he didn't say a thing. Let's meet for lunch, I said.

I worked all morning to keep the pain away and now he wants to come over, so let him.

Dr Z, are you still listening?

You know there are many options for me. Where else did we all learn how to choose? This is what I have learned: no matter what you choose, go to the next scenario. The set of options you get depends on what you chose before. Mark your answer on the virtual self-answer sheet and stop holding your breath.

As you yourself used to say, Dr Z, this is your life.

Or, don't worry, there is always a chance to make up lost ground, to get back to where you might have been before.

And there is always a chance to get behind and mess up so don't get too cocky.

The Virtual Dr Z gives you a visual representation of yourself. This Virtual Dr Z shapes you into a football stretched out along the x and y axes. Proceed from stage to stage. First you go and then you rest.

Sometimes you go back and do it again.

Sometimes that helps, sometimes it doesn't.

Sometimes it seems to help and only seems to set you back.

Sometimes it doesn't and you move forward despite your lack of momentum.

You plot your own scores from the Virtual Dr Z's answers and use the code you are learning to translate them into the location coordinates on the score sheet. You colour in the dots and the computer screen smiles at you. The self is a brightly coloured neon billboard twirling neatly on itself, visible from all sides.

Well, to bring you up to date with the clinical facts, I had another argument with my boyfriend and he moved in with a friend of a friend. It's been a week since we have spoken. I am itching to talk but I find myself sitting in the kitchen with my feet up. The phone is in my hand and I am dialling his number.

Men. If only he would do a little housework.

If only he hadn't married his mother.

Lots of people marry their mothers and have to live with it, but that doesn't let him off the hook.

Okay, maybe he's hurting.

Maybe I said something I shouldn't have. He's still got to learn what he didn't learn before, how to stand on his own two feet.

Perhaps my yelling reminds him of all that. I raise my voice and he's in a major funk. I will apologize and he will come home.

I will stay in my pyjamas and he will be crawling to me on his hands and knees.

When I am strong he will miss me.

Dr Z, I have a job for you. If you can put up with my letter you can put up with anything. So take my statements and put them in order. Then give them a rank from one to thirteen. You can choose any number you want but I like thirteen. You will have to simplify language and intent. Then give each statement a value. How well do I engage my lover? Am I on track? Do I defend myself ably? Am I running away? Will I be able to take it, whatever he does in return? There is more than one variable here. You know how many, how to tell them apart. There will be a next column; there is always a next column. It will be where to go after I was where I was before that.

Did I tell you that after my boyfriend left I thought a lot about his good points? He is good with my daughter. He is rational, but does he really care?

I am still sitting in the kitchen thinking about my mother. I used to love her but now I am not so sure. She must have been a saint to put up with my father.

And my father, was he really so bad?

I am thinking of getting a job. There are many ways I can try to do this. I will spend the morning staring at the phone.

What I really want is to go back to school. It is a scary thought.

In the middle of everything my sister shows up. Can you believe it, after all these years? She comes through the door, sits down and will not leave. A ton of feeling floats up to the surface and cracks the corners of my mouth.

Now that my sister is here I would like her to get more serious, for her to be a support. I would like to tell her what I really think. I would like to say, "Look, your timing is off. I am not up to a visit," but I cannot. I make no eye contact and tell her to leave.

No, I just think it, simple as that.

I am angry, to hell with my sister. I tell her I am not in a great mood; things haven't been good lately and I want to be left alone. I tell her I am depressed, I start to cry. There is an insincere wrinkle around the edges of my mouth. It is then that I ask her to leave.

I am not in a great mood and she seems to understand. She has been through similar stuff. When it is time to leave, behold, we hug. We sit quietly for a while. I do not say a thing and neither does she.

Somehow my sister gets the message and leaves. When I don't say anything she wonders what is wrong.

She doesn't leave.

She will be back soon.

Later it is the same when my boyfriend comes to visit. I give him the cold shoulder and he gets up. He walks around, he sits back down. He scratches his head, he reaches for a cigarette. He is about to say something. I am not ready to make up what he is about to say. He puts out the cigarette. He sits down. For now he will stay.

The above possibilities jump into my head. I must have done some of them, thought some of them, all of them. I wrote them down for you.

The story is as relentless as life in your office.

It goes around itself for as long as you can take it.

You can turn it off and go to sleep for a while but only for a while.

You can drift up and you can drift down but you always have to come back.

You, Dr Z, you can make it into a game and sell it. I myself lack the patience and the skills but you will become famous and then you can happily retire. Please take time off and write that book, about how the healing brain twangs along your infamous axes. You know what you are doing. I have been listening for years.

Here are a few rules for the player.

Set your baseline and be consistent.

Push yourself but be forgiving.

Don't go back too much, just often enough to learn.

Cheating is okay, more or less.

Imagine yourself as having done the right thing, whether you did or not.

Plot the answers on the three-dimensional grid.

Try to crack the code but don't try too hard.

In the end you will crack it in your sleep. When this happens you will wonder what all the fuss was about.

And where will it end?

Will each scenario be grafted onto its predecessor?

Will events deteriorate?

Will my boyfriend's daughter show up smelling of alcohol?

Will her boyfriend's shirt be ripped?

Will one of the sexy teenagers want the keys to the car?

When my little girl spills her milk will I reach for her face with my red nails?

Will I lose control at a party and throw alcohol in my own boyfriend's face for the wrong reason?

Is there ever a right reason?

In the end will someone betray me?

Will I be on sick leave?

Will I see a doctor, a counsellor, take medicine, fulfil my diagnosis?

This is a summary of our counselling since you have gone: the house now belongs to me and the car belongs to him. Child support is likely to be an issue but we both hesitate to bring it up. How much is he willing to help? I don't ask and he doesn't offer. And how much is up to me? Before anyone can answer, our daughter is whiny and clingy. My boyfriend says, "Let's toughen up with our little girl." And I say, "Let's be more attentive to her needs." In the session she stays close to my lap but pesters her father for the crayons and glue. There will be a decision soon. There is less noise and one day he moves back in. When I cook dinner he is around for the cleanup. We invited his mother over, my mother, my father. There are jokes to relieve the tension.

One day we miss a session with the counsellor and do not reschedule.

Now, the wedding. Everyone is here except for you. My stepdaughter is not that drunk. My daughter is not that clingy; she gets to carry the ring. My father is softer than usual, my mother is proud. The only one crying is me and that is only on the outside.

All in all I have forgotten what is bothering me.

If you market the Virtual Dr Z, call it Psychotherapy in a Box. It is more intelligent than the real Dr Z and more properly constrained. I suggest you include some video clips or a narrator for readers with tired eyes. And don't make me too attractive. It will be enough to have me holding onto the phone.

There is an expert or two on these matters in your neck of the woods. A couple who live on an island with a treacherous stairwell dangling down to the surf. And a lovely professor in that university up the hill where it rains more than anywhere else on earth. You could get a job there, I am told. The bulk of the student body is depressed and the rest, I am sure, are even more worthy of your services.

DR Z, WHERE ARE YOU?

Dr Z is gone, ensconced in the third person and not likely to ever return.

Dr Z is on call and far away. As anyone might expect by now, he is about to pull in at the curb at home when the beeper goes off.

He puts something in the oven and registers the evening homework. Someone needs a bath. Someone is learning a chromatic scale. Someone is on the phone too long. Someone cannot be reached. Someone is playing solitaire on the computer. Someone did not unload the dishes or walk the dog. Someone will not answer his questions.

He does the dishes, dry-mops dog hair, sings along with the chromatic scale—that scale picked out note by note when all relative intervals are forgotten.

Eventually he answers the page. He knows he has to go back. He is more weary than tired. As usual, it is raining. When it is not raining it has recently stopped. If it has not recently stopped it is about to start. The rain has a presence. It is inside him. He looks at the rain as if he is looking at his insides. Is it any wonder he is grainy and bleary-eyed?

On the way back in he has the usual thoughts. That his life is piling up its sweet repetitions, that he is using up too much gas.

Tonight he will sleep in the on-call room and think of Max. He will be awakened for an unnecessary order and think, What would Max do? What would Max say? The light over the parking lot outside his window will invade his dreams. Locating will rouse him at five-twenty-five to move his vehicle. The reason will not be readily apparent. He will have forgotten his toothpaste. He will shower without a towel. He will go to the ICU with his friend the internist. There is a woman in there in a delirium. When isn't there a woman in there in a delirium? His friend will say, Not everybody in the ICU goes snaky. Indeed he is right. Some do not go snaky and some do. His friend lives nearby; he will sleep in his own bed. At five-thirty Dr Z will go somewhere for breakfast. It will be light by twenty past seven. His mind will be abuzz for an hour or two until he is interrupted by routine.

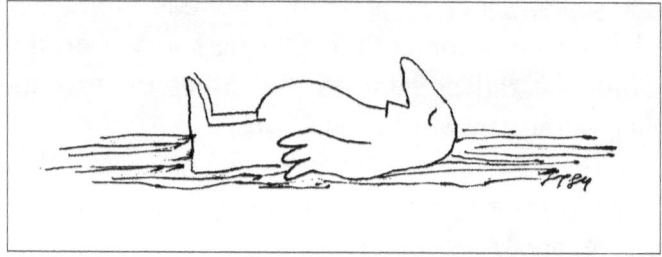

He will not sleep in the on-call room again. Instead, he will float back and forth all night and hover above his own bed. He will reminisce with himself in the vehicle as it floats along the highway. He will review his options, hitting balls or playing geriatric soccer. He will try a mood stabilizer for a while. If indeed he has a mood to stabilize. His brain is like an electrical field. The accuracy in that image is enough for him. He will neutralize the electrical field. He will foster that moment before action, when he is waiting. He will feel before he acts. The mood stabilizer will be like a piece of god sent down to instil him with detached resolve. His mood will go to sleep and settle in his gut. He will go off the mood stabilizer and experience a resurgence of the vital force. Such is the course of his life, forever forward, looping along the past.

Sometimes random thoughts come to him.

He will forget how to ski.

He will learn the Hebrew word for leopard from a two-year-old.

He will joust with an imaginary friend who is writing a book about attention deficit. The book will be erroneous, redundant. The author will merge with his friend the activist who lives in Japan. Sayonara, Dr Z.

He will not work out or drink coffee or take a holiday. He will be happy where he is.

He will shop for clothes in a foreign country where the likelihood of being observed by a patient is somewhat diminished.

He will do push-ups in the hospital washroom with the fan on to muffle sound.

He will translate the Book of Genesis. He will be the first to get it right. It will be done correctly, with the force of an axe.

He will see too many patients; he will learn to set boundaries.

He will do more consultations; he will do less.

There will be too much work; there will not be enough.

He will straighten his charts.

He will do more push-ups and sprint the stairs.

He will steal a soda from the ward and listen to nursing woes. They are ordinary woes and will become his sooner or later.

He will lose the need to correct. He will finally become a good listener.

He will love to instruct. He will become a good parent.

He will often be incorrect. He will have developed false humility.

He will perform bad therapy but at least it will be therapy.

He will be on-call far away from home, asleep in the on-call room. He will make objects personal: scratchy cold linen, dry hospital air.

His favourite driving dream: he finds a small lot on the west side and rebuilds the house he lost 2800 miles away. The balance of light must be preserved. The rain must fall away from the roof. It must be a white barn trimmed in Glen Green, with a semicircular garden out front. It will be the same only transformed. The study will have a screened door to the garden, the dining room a small alcove, the salon a nook for reading magazines. His middle daughter's room will be bigger; his eldest daughter will go into the renovated attic; the master suite will be more contained. The kitchen will have the right light for Italian yellow. The foundation will sit two feet higher above the ground, where it belongs. There will be no driveway out front and the yard will be small. A wooden trellis. A chain link fence. A majestic maple in front, planted fifty years ago. The requisite neighbours, animals, bugs.

The scene always ends the same way, with an image of his wife with her hand firmly clasping the sign. SOLD BY OWNER. She is smiling broadly, happy to have been there, happy to leave.

Such a colossal liar he could be at times, to himself, to others. He has not seen his wife in a week. More than likely he will turn on the radio, listen to the traffic report and the news three times. He will call the ward on his cell, bringing reality crashing down upon himself.

Commuting has its down side. He thinks too much and realizes that he has rejected moral relativism. Soon he will read too much and stop sleeping. He will become his own patient. He will pine for the days when he took himself for granted. He will multiply himself and install his virtual remains in a box, for all to see and scatter to the wind. He will transform his speech into a virtual voice and clone himself over the Internet. He will form a company to market himself and be known as the Virtual Self (physician, retired). He will install himself as the perfect reflection, on disk.

He wakes up on the highway, gearing down. The rain has lifted but the wind is coming in off the shallow bay. He can see the whitecaps reflecting dirty evening light out of the corner of his eye. The pattern of water out there is alive beyond all reasonable expectation.

He plugs in the cell and calls the emergency line. There is a patient there more ill than himself. Someone who doesn't know where to draw the line, at least not tonight. There is a little blood but not too much. The police are waiting, just in case, and so is the family. For them it is a routine; they have been here many times before. Blood and urine have been collected and sent off to the lab. Medication has been given. A venous line has been inserted. The patient is warm, in a double hospital gown, waiting, ready to go off to sleep. Perhaps already asleep. Perhaps wanting something from him. The patient will have to stay. The real Dr Z will write the last orders on the left side of the form. "Admit, watch closely, no street clothes for now, eschew the secure room, a sedative if necessary, repeat once under duress, sweet dreams and see you in the morning."

DR Z ENDS

In the end Dr Z runs out of gas. There could be a lot more to tell, but he has told enough. He no longer knows where he ends and his patients begin. He has taken them in and then spewed them out along with his friend Max and his grandfather Bill. He will take responsibility for all of them.

He resists the desire to provide a summary but there are problems. Should he end somewhere in the middle, allowing a sentence—any sentence—to trail off into nothing? Should he reconcile with his women? Finish the biography of all the Bills? Remarry his wife, vacation in Hawaii, buy a house?

His youngest daughter, the channel-surfer who eats ice cream for breakfast, is playing the right hand of Bach's first two-part invention. He will not call out the sharp that goes with the recalcitrant F. He will not offer to play the other hand, as in a duet. He is distracted by her notes. She is, in fact, practicing, not merely playing. She is listening to the notes and he is listening to her listen to the notes and not getting his work done. She becomes frustrated and hisses in mock hysteria through her teeth. She smacks the keys lightly and cajoles the dog. If this were to progress any further she would yell into her pillow to let off steam.

In a moment the tension will dissipate and she will be back at work. She grabs onto his right shoulder and moans. She opens *The Basement Book*, a self-help how-to renovation manual that happens to be on the couch.

"Dad, let's finish our basement," she says, for no reason whatsoever. It is not our basement, she knows, and it already has walls and a floor. She is stalling. Her right leg is crossed over and she is sitting bolt upright. Then she slams the book down on the couch and says, "I am never going back to that instrument," but her tone is not convincing.

"Do you remember... " she says, her voice trailing to nothing. She is holding a picture book about a man who cannot manage to complete his wife's household tasks and finishes his days upended in the chimney, a cow on the roof, the baby unattended, his wife vindicated. Then she is holding a book about a man with one boot and a woman on roller skates and a man who enters his own painting. A small pile forms under her feet and soon she is reciting out loud. She remembers something from somewhere deep in her brain. Like Grandpa Bill's Talmud, forgotten at birth when the angel imprinted his upper lip and said, "Shshsh."

Dr Z can no longer pay any attention to his own sentences and paragraphs. He is listening to his third daughter. "The first Chinese brother swallowed the sea." She might as well have said, "I am Joseph your brother. Is my father still alive?" Tears jump into his eyes and he can listen to nothing else. "On the morning of the execution... " he hears once, twice, three times. He gives up on his paragraph—it will go where it wants to go, completing itself somewhere. "It must be that you are innocent... " The story he is listening to is over but the paragraph is not.

The paragraph will not end itself. It is a stubborn paragraph. It knows that it is designed to close the chapter, the book. It cannot remember much of anything. It has shifted into the present. The phone is ringing. The beeper has gone off. Max will be in town soon for the launching of Dr Z's brother's film, *Planting Dad*, Dr Z's dad. Dr Z's brother got to him first.

A CLOSING IMAGE

Where the story comes from.

In the picture there is a toddler with an open face. There is a stethoscope around his neck and he is imploring the camera with astonishing depth. The stethoscope is planted on the chest of the teddy. Dr Z can make out the furniture in the background. The picture—enlarged, faded, damaged—hangs on the living room wall above old vinyl records and books from school.

The toddling physician is not Dr Z; it is Dr Z's middle brother.

As for the golf picture next to it, the five-year-old with the perfect takeaway, stance slightly open, the weight transfer and ball positioning natural and perfect, that is Dr Z.